Elizabeth Cameron
Copyright 2011 by Elizabeth Cameron

PROLOGUE
THURSDAY OCTOBER 26, 3:00 P.M.

Margaret Rutherford knew as she sat calmly and quietly in his office, that she was going to die. She'd known that for some time. What she didn't know was when. And on this final visit, it was this one remaining detail in an otherwise finely executed plan, that she was going to have determined.

To Dr. Ian McTaggart it was always THAT question, first before any others, that provoked the same uncomfortable response in him. Visible perhaps by a frown that tightened the premature lines around the cobalt blue eyes and encouraged them to shift like a pendulum from his folded hands to his patient's face. After seventeen years it was not a difficult question. His "sentences" of years, months or even hours were unusually precise. But then his specialty offered him ample opportunity to cultivate this skill.

No, what really disturbed him with this case, over and above his role as executioner, was this woman. There was something something unnatural about her. Not that he'd expected tears, denials, or even the brittle veneer of bravado. From her first symptoms she seemed to have evaluated the statistics, considered her options and projected the probable outcome. There was no hint of pretense, even in her appearance. Dressed in what had been, perhaps still was, her Sunday best, she wore a dowdy brown tweed suit, oxford shoes and placed tidily on her lap were gloves and a leather purse, shabby with their years of service. Not even the cream blouse seemed to soften the contours of the face or the mouse colored hair streaked with gray in its utilitarian rigidity. Both appeared lifeless almost wax like, even more pronounced by the shadow of deteriorating health. When she spoke, her voice had a crust like day old bread that made each word sound dry and course.

"Well doctor, let's have the news." The words implied a cold air of efficiency which McTaggart responded to with an equal economy of words. Void of the carefully worded phrases, the veiled probabilities, the "news" was frank, almost brutal, but it was brief.

"I must remind you that surgery..."

"It's out of the question. I've told you."

"Then I'd like to schedule you for further chemotherapy..."

"I don't think that will be necessary doctor. If there were to be a remission with the treatments I've already had, we know it would have happened by now." She was stating a fact, neither expecting nor wanting a contradiction from McTaggart. He gave her none.

"I have responsibilities that must be attended to, doctor. I would appreciate knowing just exactly what I may expect."

It was an oblique question. He glanced down at her file which gave him her extensive medical history, but offered pitifully little in the way of a personal profile. Fifty-four years of age, widowed, no children or family, employed as a Chief supervisor, Island View Hospital. The one and only time he'd seen the place, it had left him with a feeling that it offered little more than custodial care for the hopelessly insane. Maybe that's what accounted for her peculiar detachment to any kind of emotional expression. For a moment McTaggart hesitated, assessing how close to the truth he dare come, just how deep her emotional immunity was.

He compromised only slightly. It was spoken tactfully but explicitly. Other patients would have recoiled in denials and disbelief at what they would ultimately endure. She remained unflinching, passive, unmoved.

"So that's it. And what time do I have left?"

"Three months...with medication for pain, of course. Beyond that, deterioration will require brief hospitalization, a week maybe ten days." He stopped. There could be little speculation left even for the most unimaginative mind.

"Very well doctor. Thank you for your time." She stood abruptly and extended her hand to him across the desk. He had expected it to be cold, even moist.they nearly always were. It was warm, with strong fingers like a peasant's hand. But the handshake was a mere formality, like an ingrained habit, a descendent of a Victorian upbringing. He scrawled out the prescription, came around the desk and handed it to her.

"Meperidine, I expect." It was more of a thought she'd spoken out loud rather than a question. Confirmation was irrelevant. She took the small sheet of paper with obvious distaste, turned and left the office. It had all been concluded. She had dismissed him with no reference to further appointments. He suspected he would not see her again.

McTaggart returned to his desk, scrawled the few abbreviated notes, closed the file, then slowly walked over to the rain streaked windows and stood staring out into the bleak wetness of late afternoon. It was some time before he became aware of an unusual chill in the air, made even more pronounced as the fading light of the wintry afternoon washed the office with a ghostly gray. Yet he remained by the window, a dark, featureless profile while a vague oppressiveness stirred somewhere in the recesses of his mind. Unconsciously, he found his mind had begun to recall the horrors he'd witnessed at Island View Hospital those many years ago. For Dr. Ian McTaggart it was a distinctly strange and disturbing mood.

* * *

THURSDAY, OCTOBER 26, 4:30 P.M.

Across the city on West Eighth Avenue, Dr. Christopher Choo reviewed the medical history of Susan Chambers with a similar uneasy feeling. His concern, though, focused on the prognosis rather than his patient. Obstetrics was a specialty with considerably better odds than McTaggart's field. Even better in fact if one were fortunate enough to be a patient of Dr. Choo, particularly if complications existed or were anticipated. It was, in fact, complications factors that had shifted only slightly away from the normal and were as yet undefined that were now giving cause to his uneasiness.

At twenty-two, Susan Chambers bore only a trace of the wide-eyed prettiness of her youth. It was all that remained after running away from home at 14, living homeless on the streets, drugs, alcohol and, ultimately, prostitution. The abuse had left her aged beyond her years, her body worn and battered, her mind confused and unfocused and very much alone. The waiting room held neither a husband nor family, nor even a friend. Set in the gaunt damp face, her eyes searched for relief from the pain, her mouth tightened in a grimace scarcely concealing exhaustion. She was now approaching her nineteenth hour of labor.

"I'm convinced it must be a girl, Susan," Dr. Choo teased. "Women have no understanding of time."

She spoke with effort. "You said...mid November. It's...it's still only..." she had to think hard…"October."

"That's not anything to be overly concerned about. You're doing just fine, Susan. Miss Ross here will keep me informed when November arrives and you decide to have your baby." Miss Ross, who was approaching the bedside, wrinkled her nose in mock disapproval as Dr. Choo gave her his small oriental bow and a mischievous grin, and left.

She was twenty-one days premature for a prima gravida. She'd dilated to only three centimeters with no change in the last two hours. And she was rapidly nearing the verge of exhaustion.

A small knot of apprehension stayed in the back of Dr. Choo's mind as he made his rounds, extending gentle reassurances and tending to the details of the care and treatment of those who had preceded Susan Chambers. Downstairs in the cafeteria, he selected the most recognizable and edible of the day's sacrificial offerings, ate the few mouthfuls worth eating, then headed back toward the elevators.

The alarm went at precisely two minutes to eight, when the fetal heart monitoring system which had been in position since the beginning of Susan Chamber's labor, began a sudden and erratic pattern.

In less than sixty seconds the medical holding pattern of the hospital began to move in response.

The anesthesiologist and the pediatrician, alerted by Choo some hours ago, responded to their page and began to scrub along with Choo.

Susan Chambers was quietly but quickly moved to Theater "B". The blood pressure cuff was placed on one arm, the other arm strapped to the arm board and the I.V. connected.

Less than nine minutes had passed. Susan Chambers had reached a level of unconsciousness that was acceptable to the anesthesiologist.

He gave a slight nod to Choo.

Choo, poised and ready with the first of several instruments to be used, made the long vertical incision down the exposed belly. Only a few brief words were exchanged, barely audible above the rhythmic beeping of the electrocardiograph and the mechanical breathing of the monitoring and life support systems. The muscles of the lower abdominal wall were separated, the peritoneum was opened. The uterus was revealed. The last incision was now carefully made, six inches long.

As Choo ruptured the amniotic sac, the fluid which had cushioned the baby spilled out, mingling with blood and covered his gloved hands as Choo reached into the uterus for the baby.

"Oh Jesus...Christ!" It came from Walker, the anesthesiologist as he stared at the infant held upside down above the abdominal cavity. For the moment Choo remained silent, then sudden realization and anger thundered across his face.

"Oh Mother of Mary!" Nurse Kathleen O'Reilly, who had been preparing to administer the silver nitrate drops, stopped in her tracks, her horror filled eyes not quite comprehending what she saw.

Choo was the first to speak. "Get McGibbons up here and call Chase and Markham." Somewhere behind him a nurse moved in response. The shock for a moment had held them in suspension. Very slowly they resumed the routine, silent now, each performing his function, each averting his eyes from anything beyond his territory, while in each of their minds they tried to accept what instinctively was unacceptable.

By two a.m. five specialists had been summoned, had examined the infant and reviewed the tests and X-rays. The decision had been unanimous. Now only McGibbons, hospital chief, remained with Choo in the consultation room on the surgical floor.

"Sorry Chris, not a damn thing we can do other than spare our nursing staff here. I think we'd better make the transfer now." He glanced up at the clock. "There shouldn't be a problem getting an ambulance at this hour. I'll make the call directly to the Chief Supervisor. Perhaps you can get O'Reilly to get the infant ready."

Twenty minutes later, Choo himself stood by the ambulance doors as the small bassinet, discreetly blanketed, was placed inside and secured. There was no incubator, no oxygen, no attending medical personnel.

Nothing.

No one.

If the driver questioned such an unusual procedure, he remained silent. Some things perhaps were best left unknown.

Choo spoke quietly. "The hospital has been notified. They're expecting you." There was nothing else to be said. Nothing else that could be said. He watched the ambulance slowly pull away from the service entrance and slip into the night. Long after it had gone, he stood staring into the rainy emptiness, remembering the tiny infant only hours old, sentenced and committed to the only journey it would ever make.

* * *

FRIDAY OCTOBER 27, 6:00 P.M.

Friday night was the best night. Even Seymour knew that. His short spaniel tail wagged as his eyes in their near blindness followed the movements of his master shuffling from the cupboard to the hot plate. The spaghetti and meatballs were steaming and the Italian sausage and bread sat in a small basket beside the solitary place setting, marked by the jelly glass filled with a local wine of recent and dubious ancestry.

As always, Joe Romano served up the meal, selecting the English Dalton china plate for himself and the Irish Belleek for a smaller but identical serving.

There was no need for an announcement. With the slowness of his fifteen years, the dog approached his plate, which had been placed as it always was in front of the ice box and, with an expectant look at his master, began his meal.

For what dietary deficiencies the meal may have had, it appeared not to have evidenced itself in either the man or dog. Rather, age appeared to slow their movements, and stiffen their bones. True for the man, a small belly had been acquired but at fifty-eight years of age his stature though short was well muscled, and strong. The sea green work shirt and pants, though clean and mended, had molded themselves to the familiar shape of the stooped shoulders, the barrel chest and the heavy forearms and legs. In his occupation they had served him well.

The meal was eaten in silent enjoyment and while the dog napped, Joe carefully washed and dried the dishes and put them away.

By seven o'clock, as always on a Friday night, they would begin their route. It would include the industrial parks with their banks of warehouses that fringed the city, the small manufacturers littered along parts of the Trans Canada Highway and the docks on the south side of the inner harbor. For all the economics of such industry, Joe neither knew nor cared. What they discarded, what to them had served its purpose was to find its place in the usual refuse containers, positioned for the disposal trucks was merely garbage.

Garbage had made Joe Romano a wealthy man.

Ironically it had changed his lifestyle little. The occasional inconsistency such as the small Kilim prayer rug worth three thousand dollars, he used in front of the kitchen sink. And the Irish Belleek would appear as often as the Melmac on the red and white checkered oilcloth. The dog biscuits were stored in an eighteenth century silver tureen that sat on the aging black and white TV set. But his other assets were more traditionally distributed amongst a sizeable savings account, bonds and a few of the more respectable stocks. There could hardly be found better testimony to the accumulation of dollars from even the most humble profession than that practiced by Joe Romano.

Very simply, Joe was a scavenger.

First they headed out across the Second Narrows Bridge, turning left on Hastings Street to the Barnett Highway, going as far as Coquitlam. Then they looped back towards the city on the Lougheed Highway as far as Main Street. By midnight it brought them to the Terminal Pier. The back of the aging pickup was now heaped with an assortment of boxes, a barrel, scrap iron, hardware, wire, cans and plywood all of which, over a period of months, would be turned into cash.

It had begun to rain a fine mist that, combined with the dampness of the sea air, lay like an oily film. Through the haze the three disposal units appeared gray in the distant cast of the sodium vapor lights that illuminated the docks. Joe checked the first with the flashlight and moved to the second. These were always unpredictable. The transient nature of ships and men, of freight and cargo and the often shady world of the cargo handlers caused the most unlikely objects to be found.

He'd already taken some steel cable, wire rope, a small winch, a battery and, not surprisingly, a slightly damaged case of canned herring. It was as he approached the third and last container that two small, furtive shadows slipped from the bin and scurried into the night. Joe frowned slightly. Rats were by no means unfamiliar to him, but here it was unusual. They'd come to eat and now whatever it was would be contaminated. The flashlight picked up their trail. A large cardboard box marked with the name of a vegetable oil had been chewed in several places. The faint trace of oil having saturated the cardboard had been the invitation. Joe pushed it aside, expecting it to collapse. It didn't. The box had been resealed with tape. Whatever was inside was of a different content than its original. What weighed about ten pounds should have weighed considerably more. Even the still faintly discernible lettering read twenty kilos. It was not often Joe took anything on spec. But on some occasions it had paid off. Maybe this would too.

By the time they got home, the cardboard box, now buried under an assortment of fishnet and wire rope had been all but forgotten.

Seymour had remained in the front seat and dozed; the nights when he'd chased the alley cats and bounded along at Joe's heels were gone. But there was still hot chocolate in a large mug for Joe, and because it was Friday night, a big dish of spumoni ice cream for each of them.

As always, Joe worked late into the night sorting his spoils; bundling, packaging, assembling, cleaning, dismantling. He'd almost finished when he remembered the cardboard box. He made the trip once again to the pickup, returned and placed it gently on the kitchen table. He was curious now. He cut the tape and folded back the cardboard flaps. He slowly removed several layers of newspapers, folding each sheet as he went.

The smell was vaguely unpleasant and he became just a little apprehensive. Whatever it was, it lay wrapped in sheeting, which had stood little defense against the gnawing teeth of the rats. The once white cotton was stained and dark. Joe carefully lifted the bundle from the box, unwrapped it and peered closer. Suddenly his eyes grew wide in horror and disbelief. His legs gave under his weight and he collapsed on the kitchen chair. Sounds came between gasps as his chest heaved and his hands trembled violently. Sweat glistened on his wrinkled brow. It was many moments before he gradually overcame the shock. When he had, though his hands still trembled, he carefully returned the contents to the box, resealed it with new tape, He drove a long time and some distance. When he found the right place he took the shovel he kept in the back and dug a hole. Carefully he laid the cardboard box in the hole and draped some plastic sheeting over it. He replaced the soil, kneeling in the rain to smooth the last layer of sod in place.

He was doing what someone else should have done God rest their soul. Surely, as He looked down at an old Italian man kneeling by a grave in a field in the middle of the night repeating the Lord's Prayer, He would forgive.

SUNDAY NOVEMBER 19th.

The eyes, glazed with a bloody mucous, stared blankly upwards at me from the bottom of the pail. The mouth gaped open in a shark like grin, exposing razor sharp teeth. Most of the other mouths however were frozen shut, resisting the wire I was attempting to bore through their heads while they slithered in my grasp, the teeth of those with open jaws more than once piercing my fingers. As I knelt at the very end of the dock, the cold damp sea air had already crept through my sweater, chilled my face and ears and turned my hands numb and stiff making the job even more difficult.

I was thinking some very unkind thoughts about the salmon head I was retrieving from the bottom of the trap for a third try when I heard a voice over my shoulder.

"You almost look like you know what you're doing."

The voice had come so unexpectedly I jumped, and then winced as I felt the rusty wire mesh of the trap rake my exposed arm. I turned awkwardly to look up at the tall figure that had obviously been leaning over my shoulder. Then I rose stiffly to face him, my initial fright giving way to a mixture of relief and annoyance.

"You startled me! I didn't know you were standing there!"

"Sorry. I was just curious to find out who was winning. I don't often see a good looking woman conducting her own personal war with a bucket of fish heads on the end of the dock in the middle of the night. Catch many?"

I ignored his subtle flattery assuming he must be new here and hadn't observed my daily ritual of setting my crab trap. Probably a new owner of any one of the three hundred or so pleasure craft here at the Lynnwood Marina that mysteriously lost their appeal as the summer faded into a long, dreary winter. He looked the part: faded jeans and deck shoes, dark green turtleneck under the fluorescent orange of a well used floater jacket. Dark brown hair that extended to a wiry beard out of which a pipe appeared to make its home. Very clear blue eyes, a keen hawk like face chiseled by some forty odd years of what must have been a rugged life. Handsome, about the same way precast concrete is over steel.

"Crabs? Usually. I'd say it's a pretty typical late afternoon for November in Vancouver it just looks like midnight. And yes. I do this quite frequently since I live here and as for the "war", I usually win. Most of the time." It was poor timing. I glanced down at my arm to find the long ugly welts had begun to bleed into a half dozen rivers.

"Oh, oh." He took hold of my wrist and turned to inspect the scratches more carefully.

"Assault and battery with a crab trap. The least I can do is help repair the damage. I'm right over there."

He nodded in the direction of the last slip on M float.

"But I live only..."

"I know you do, but two hands are better than one. C'mon. Gangrene will set in at any moment and your whole arm will fall off." He led me carefully around the crab trap and the pail of fish heads back several yards along the dock before he turned onto the float that paralleled the harbor.

"You're so reassuring! I'd hate to know what you'd tell a five year old with a scraped knee! "

"Why? Have you got one?"

"A scraped knee or a five year old?"

"Either."

"Just gangrene and a geriatric cat. Is this it?" I was looking at an old but seemingly well built yacht somewhere around sixty feet in length.

"It is and we're in luck. It's still floating too." He led me along the dock, up onto the deck, and slid the door open. As I stepped over the sill I felt the delicious warmth of the wheelhouse, an unexpected pleasure in a lady of her vintage. Most boats at this time of year wore a perpetual mildewy chill. He cleared the built-in seats of a jumble of wire and tools and beckoned me to sit.

"Welcome aboard. Try not to kill yourself tripping over all this junk. Be right back." He ducked his head with a practiced move as he disappeared down a nearly vertical set of stairs which I assumed must lead to the galley.

She'd been a great lady in her day and although no longer in her prime, she was well fitted out, appeared comfortable and at least looked like she had every intention of going to sea. Or having been. It was hard to tell. The wheelhouse was liberally equipped with radios, radar, a depth sounder, compass and charts while the floor was an obstacle course of power tools, wrenches, reels of wire and paint cans.

He reappeared with a bottle and two glasses in one hand and the first aid kit in the other. He put them on the built-in table in front of me, turned on the brass lamp that swayed gently above it, tossed his jacket over the back of the captain's chair and settled himself across from me.

"The name by the way is Paul Montgomery and the "vessel", he stressed it with mock importance, is the Snow Goose." He was working as he talked. He poured two glasses of brandy and placed one in front of me.

"Cheers! Drink up. Won't do much for you but it will help me endure your screams of agony." He took a quick mouthful, then reached across for my arm and the first aid kit.

"Mia Daniels." I took a small sip and felt the rich mellow bite of the brandy slip down my throat.

"Mia?"

"Mia Natasha Daniels, if you want the whole name. During her "confinement" as my mother preferred to call it, she spent her time reading historical romance novels."

"And you have a brother called Ivan the Invincible presently living in Russia and in someplace with a name requiring half the alphabet and an interpreter to pronounce?" He didn't glance up but the lines round his mouth crinkled into the hint of a grin.

I laughed. "Sorry, no brothers or sisters. But you can understand why I prefer Mia."

"Your father?"

"American. He's travels the world on business. Mother's in England. My gaze wandered about the cabin and then back to him. "The Snow Goose looks quite comfortable. Have you had her long?"

"About three weeks." He talked while he swabbed my arm with cotton balls soaked in an antiseptic. "Her original owner was responsible for maintaining the woodwork and navigation equipment and kept her in good shape for many years. About ten years ago he sold her to a guy who was in love with boating more than the boat itself. Boats like this one take a lot of maintenance, which she hasn't had. The engines need to be overhauled and she has to be scraped and painted along with a lot of work to be done inside as well. And you?" He glanced up briefly with a semi curious expression. "What made you decide to become a water rat? You look more the type for a carefree West End condo than a houseboat."

"Floating home," I corrected, with a smile. "Thanks if that was meant to be a compliment. It's the Floating Home Association's attempt to get us to upgrade our image by referring to our "floating homes" instead of our "houseboats." Sounds more impressive to the politicians who we're up against for moorage rights.

I condensed my answer. "I love the water and I was able to have her built for a fraction of the cost of the waterfront views in the British Properties or Point Gray Waterfront. As for rats – the hairy kind - they were my only nasty surprise. At the rate I was feeding my cat he should have looked like a Christmas turkey with whiskers. Until I discovered I was feeding more than him. He gets fed inside now instead of on the deck." I took another sip.

"Any regrets?" he asked.

"No regrets but I learned some things the hard way about living on the water. I do my grocery shopping now according to the tide table. That became apparent when a week's groceries went overboard while I tried to carry them down that ramp which at low tide practically becomes a ladder. But then I'm sure that applies to you on a boat as well. Do you live aboard?"

"Ship not boat, if we're going to be precise about a vessel over fifty feet. But that makes me sound like the captain of the Queen Elizabeth, so I use the word boat too. For the winter, yes. There's so much work to be done inside, I might just as well. I'll remember though not to carry down my TV dinners at low tide." He rolled the sleeve of my sweater down gently over the gauze that he'd taped lightly in place.

"Providing you give it some air and don't get it infected it should heal quite nicely. If you do this regularly I hope you've had a tetanus shot?"

"Yes, but thanks for the first aid. I'm afraid my own first aid kit amounts to remedies for fur balls and fleas." I swallowed the last of the brandy I'd been sipping and eased out of the seat. "If I'm ever going to have crab for dinner one of these nights, I must get that trap down."

"The least I can do is help. It's called preventive medicine." He gave me a quick grin and retrieved the jacket he'd shed and we climbed back outside to the dock.

The afternoon had slipped its fingers into the sleek satin glove of night.

Lights teased and flirted in their watery reflections like a princess before a mirror, caught in a hundred vain decisions. Across the harbor a weary freighter waited patiently to be loaded with timber for a port halfway round the world. A tug moved steadily west to meet its waiting barge in the dead of the night like a pair of clandestine lovers.

We had reached the end of the dock and stood for a moment looking out over the water.

"I envy you your view of the harbor" I said. Are you going to retain that particular slip for the Snow Goose?"

"I have to because of her length. She's fifty-four feet. I agree, the view of the harbor and the city on nights like this is spectacular."

They were meek now. Their mouths obediently opened as Paul wired the heads in place, closed the trap and gently lowered it over the side and down till it reached bottom.

We walked back along the dock and shivering now with the cold, I went ahead, stepped up onto the deck of my houseboat, slid the glass door open to the kitchen and turned on one of the under counter fluorescents. The kitchen came alive with color. Enamel pots and gaily colored dishes lined the open cedar shelves. Art prints and posters took over where utensils left off, while giant ferns and spider plants reigned over it all from their lofty positions under the angled skylights of the ceiling. Paul put the plastic bag with the remaining fish heads in the sink, put the pail outside on the deck, turned and surveyed the kitchen with obvious admiration.

"If you can't even fry an egg nobody would ever guess. I bet you can perform miracles with a can of mushroom soup."

I was aware of more bait than what at the moment was lying in the kitchen sink.

"I don't know about miracles but I'm at least as good as Swanson's TV dinners. If you'd like to consider that an invitation...maybe next Sunday? It's the least I can do to thank you for saving my arm from amputation."

He looked pleased with himself. "Excellent. Sunday nights are usually peanut butter and jelly sandwich nights. You won't have to bat an eyelash to surpass that!"

"Peanut butter and jelly you say?" I gave him a wide-eyed look. "You must give me the recipe some time."

He chuckled as he moved to the door. "Next Sunday then. Time?"

"Around seven?"

"Seven it is. Good night Mia." He stepped out into the night and quickly faded into the shadows.

For a moment I stood staring down at the bait in the sink, aware of a common denominator we shared.

Interesting man. And I enjoyed cooking. It would be a pleasant evening. But I wasn't that naive, despite his subtle flattery not to recognize that this encounter had been entirely premeditated. The first aid treatment had been the only incident unplanned. Why, I had no idea. Just a suspicion. One more to add to those I'd started to acquire in the last couple of weeks.

MONDAY NOVEMBER 20th.

It must have been like dying. To be taken inside those cold gray walls, never knowing if you'd see fresh air or sunshine again. Even the ivy which stretched its long bony fingers across the face of the building seemed lifelessly fused to the damp stone facade. Row upon row of narrow windows, each wearing their iron veil, cast their shadows downwards like the suspicious, wary eyes of an ancient face. As if seeking isolation, the building reared itself on a bluff facing north and looked down on the cold green waters of Burrard Inlet and the small spit of land from which it had erroneously taken its name. Island View Hospital. The letters had been chiseled into a tombstone of granite, under the logo that testified to it being a government rather than a privately owned institution. It seemed ironic that such mental health facilities reflected so little to do with life.

If there had been even the merest attempt at either comfort or convenience, the visitors' waiting room had failed to achieve it. Shabby vinyl mismatched furniture lined the walls of a room perhaps twenty by thirty feet, while the greenish cast of the overhead fluorescent lighting exposed the cracked and peeling paint of the ceiling and the worn linoleum that had seen too much wax and even more wear. Two tired pictures hung by exposed wire, someone's feeble attempt at the usual cliché of flowers in a vase, probably done by some patient a long time ago. It was at least comforting to think that his degree of insanity relieved him of the creative responsibility for his work. They were awful. If this pitiful attempt at cheer was the best they could do for relatives and friends, I had little doubt as to what kind of hell hole lay beyond. In fact I was wondering about a lot of other depressing details such as why on my first day on the job as a volunteer if my own mental health wasn't questionable, when the chatter of high heels in the corridor emerged through the door.

They weren't really high. In fact they were little more than the most modest of classic brown leather pumps that seemed to match the rest of the simple prim appearance.

"And you must be Miss Daniels. How very nice to meet you. I'm dreadfully sorry to have kept you waiting committee meeting you know and they do go on about things. Come with me and we'll go to my office ... here let me take your coat. Miserable weather isn't it? Would you like a cup of coffee?"

I nodded in reply. It seemed simpler than trying to interject between the smiles and the extended greeting.

The neatly organized and not unpleasant bundle that was Ruth Wainwright had extended to her office. It was reflected in all the carefully arranged paraphernalia on her desk, the books displayed in the well used bookcase, and an equally old rug (I suspected she had supplied it) which covered the floor. She offered me one of the two chairs in front of what served as a coffee table and then saying something about being only a moment, left me alone, to return in a few minutes with a tray that contained the coffee cups, a plate of assorted English biscuits, and napkins, grouped on a matching cloth.

I guessed her to be in her late fifties. She had rather plain features and brown hair which looked like she had worn it in the same style most of her life. Her voice was gentle, her smile sincere. She smoothed the skirt of a beige wool suit beneath her as she settled in her chair behind her desk.

"When Dr. Mannering called me about the program I was most impressed though he told me very little about it. You must find it very challenging." She smiled and continued. "Have you covered all the hospitals and will you be involved in other aspects of the program?"

"Well," I took a deep breath and began, "S.P.A.C.E. Special Programs in Assistance, Counseling and Education is designed to assist patients in intermediate and extended care facilities. The goal is to provide them with the educational skills that will assist them in either returning to the community and finding employment or helping them bridge the gap in their own education because of their illness or accident. The program is being introduced here in British Columbia by the provincial government. It's been very successful in Ontario and Saskatchewan. Yvonne Yuen who is the director of the program has covered all the major hospitals and institutions here in the Lower Mainland. Island View is the last, and" I hesitated, "the only psychiatric facility large enough to be included in the program. Miss Yuen has tried to find candidates who are eligible and who would benefit from the program from each of the other institutions. Though my work with the program ends when the C.E.A's the Candidate Evaluation Assessments are completed, I'm hoping we'll be fortunate in finding a candidate here." I'd tried to sound more confident than I was. From what little I'd seen of this place I had a feeling that they would consider a medieval rack innovative.

Miss Wainright very delicately stirred her coffee with a demitasse spoon and took a small sip. "Well. I'll be more than pleased to help in any way I can. My position as community services coordinator involves a great deal of public relations.

I'm afraid that while medical science has made enormous progress in treating the mentally challenged, the public still has a distorted image of them. There is a great deal of resistance to placing patients back out in the community, and even greater resistance to this institution being here at all." She looked decidedly discouraged.

"But hasn't it been here for years?"

"Oh yes! Island View was built in 1932 when there was nothing but forests and fields for miles around. But as the community developed, people managed to forget that it has always been here. With the new wing at the University Hospital we now take only the chronically ill or designated patients, as they're called those who need maintenance rather than those undergoing therapeutic treatment."

Puzzled, I replied, "Not having a medical background, I'm not sure I understand."

She smiled and dabbed at the corners of her mouth with the napkin after nibbling the corner of a biscuit. "You needn't worry. The greatest change in the treatment of those who are mentally ill has come about by drug therapy the use of drugs to stimulate and re align responses. Today's patients are hospitalized for days and weeks as compared to years. Advances in this kind of treatment have been developed as little as ten years ago. The objective is to place them back in society as soon as possible so they can learn to cope in a normal environment." Her expression now became solemn. "Institutions like this one, I'm afraid, are not very normal environments. Here everything is either done for the patient or the patient follows a routine that almost never changes. Some patients who have been institutionalized for many years can never be placed outside. The world has changed so much for them and is so different, they simply couldn't cope. Our geriatric ward, in fact, houses close to eighty percent of our patients. The remaining twenty percent are the patients who are being maintained here. We used to be terribly overcrowded and under staffed. Now with so many fewer patients the nursing patient ratio has become almost ten to one. I feel it helps in a way to make up for the lack of facilities." She smiled sweetly as she got up from her chair and replaced her napkin and coffee cup back on the tray. "If you've finished your coffee, I'd like to show you the facilities."

"Fine," I hoped I sounded more enthusiastic than I was. I passed her my empty cup and saucer as she stood ready to return the tray when a white moustache poked itself around the edge of the door. She gave me a quick wink before she turned to greet it.

"Good morning, George!" How are you today? I see you've had a busy morning."

"George" had emerged now at the door, an elderly small white haired man with twinkly blue eyes above the moustache that curled up at both ends to give him a perpetual smile. The wet rubber boots, jacket, suspendered trousers and a battered all weather hat seemed quite appropriate for what I assumed was custodial work around the grounds. Several magnificent red tulips bent their heads coyly as he extended them to Mrs. Wainwright.

"Here you are m'am ... first of the season. Thought you'd like them for your desk." He eyed me inquisitively.

"Why thank you, George! I think these are even bigger than last year's. Oh, I'd like you to meet Miss Daniels. She'll be working here with us for awhile. Mr. George Abernathy, Miss Daniels."

He doffed his hat and gave a little bow. "I'm pleased to meet you Miss. Do you like flowers?"

"Yes indeed."

"Well I can't promise nothin' but I'll see what I can do. I got to be goin' now." He turned toward the door and gave me another little bob. "Nice meetin' you." The moustache "twitched" in a smile and he disappeared.

I was impressed. Maybe there were touches of some of the nice things in life here after all.

The tulips in their pear shapes promised a spectacle of vitality. "Obviously your facilities include quite a greenhouse!"

She looked puzzled for a moment. "A greenhouse..." then laughed. "No, we don't have a greenhouse. You see Mr. Abernathy doesn't work here, he's a patient ... been here for years. But he was and is a gardener. In fact, as I understand it, he was one of England's finest. Actually worked for the Royal Gardens at Buckingham Palace. He'd been working for the Civil Defense when London was bombed. It must have been quite awful, the noise and destruction and death for such a very young. quiet, peace loving man. He was never quite the same. Very forgetful, confused. A sister had lived in Canada, - Langley - actually, for many years and she looked after him till she passed away. Then he came here." She now lowered her voice with the hushed whispers of a conspiracy.

"He hadn't been here very long when we got a complaint from the kitchen staff that things were missing. It seemed that Mr. Abernathy was ... pinching things."

"What kind of things?"

"Onions, potatoes ... and eggs."

"Eggs?"

"Yes. In those days we got farm eggs that arrived in grape baskets. He would take a basket or two and plant the eggs. You see, he was pretending they were bulbs. So we took some petty cash, bought some bulbs and put them in the egg baskets.

Now..." and as she made the statement it all seemed so logical, "Mrs. Woolsey who is the dietitian and does the ordering, simply puts in a standing order for bulbs for the local nursery every so often when she's ordering other things."

"But it's October! Isn't that when most people plant bulbs? For the spring?"

She gave a small sigh. "Yes it is. Mr. Abernathy does get confused about the seasons but he seems to have marvelous success in spite of that. He's found all the sheltered nooks and crannies about the grounds and the warm air vents around the buildings and things seem to thrive no matter what the season is." She started to give a school girl giggle, then immediately hushed it behind her hand. "When tulips and crocuses and daffodils began popping up all over the place, our staff gardener got quite upset. But Mr. Abernathy was a patient and gardening was the only thing that seems to `keep him sane', as they say," (here she smiled graciously) "so we had to compromise. Mr. Bartholomew eventually left and Mr. Abernathy has been our gardener ever since."

Like a child's story with a happy ending, she concluded the tale as though it was all very sensible. I began to think if it had involved monsters and devils and fairy godmothers, she would have been just as convincing. But then it had made perfect sense to me too so I wasn't going to question that any further.

I should have guessed, of course, that the monsters and devils were there somewhere.

* * *

By lunch time I had seen the lounge, the occupational therapy rooms, and the craft room and had met several staff members, most of whom appeared to express little interest or concern in the program, over and above a few polite questions and perfunctory smiles.

Lunch was a small buffet of breads and cold cuts, fruits, cake and coffee served in a small dining room off to one side of the cafeteria. A small dark haired woman called Vera joined us with another younger woman, Nancy something. Several times the conversation slipped into familiar ground: recipes, Vera's teenage daughter, the price of groceries, so I gathered lunching together for them was quite common. There was never any mention of either patients or facilities, or any work related topic. They could have been assembly line workers for General Motors.

At two I was to meet Dr. Woodcroft, senior staff psychiatrist and his associate Dr. Caine. I was going to have to work closely with them so I made sure I was there and waiting.

At precisely two o'clock I was ushered into his private sanctum. Dr. Woodcroft rose from behind his desk, a small stout man in his early sixties, his white coat starched and crisp which, as I soon learned, seemed to personify his personality.

"Miss Daniels..." it was a cold, limp handshake, "welcome to Island View. I understand you've been given a tour of our facilities. Are you impressed?" A half smile barely disguised the condescension in his voice.

I returned an equally obtuse smile. "I'm sure facilities are never as extensive as one would like."

He ignored my answer. "Of course our patients, for the most part, are long-term, chronic care cases. I don't see that we can really offer you a candidate. However, since you've asked to meet a cross section of them, Dr. Caine will be taking you through the wards."

As if on cue Dr. Caine stuck his head round the door.

"Ah yes, there you are. I'd like you to meet Miss Daniels. Dr. Phillip Caine." This time the handshake was warm and firm, the voice younger and friendlier. Caine was the antithesis of Woodcroft. Tall, casually dressed to the point of being almost sloppy, he wore his white coat unbuttoned, no doubt to accommodate both his slouch and his garb. He lounged against the door jamb, his hands stuffed in the pockets of a pair of beige corduroy pants that in turn were trying to hang onto the tail end of a cotton turtleneck. He also wore a mixed expression of boredom and curiosity. "If you've purchased your tickets, the tour will begin in five minutes."

It was the kind of remark Woodcroft disapproved of.

"It was a pleasure meeting you, MissDaniels." I was offered the same weak handshake.

"I'm sure Dr. Caine will be able to answer any questions you may have." He returned his attention to his desk. Clearly, I had been dismissed.

I waited till we were well along the hallway before I turned to Dr. Caine and with candor said, "I have the distinct feeling Dr. Woodcroft doesn't expect to see me again. Or want to."

"Don't take it personally. If you'd worked as long as he has with some of these head cases, you'd probably be just as cynical. He's not very impressed with anything that's new or different."

I must have looked surprised because he stopped suddenly and his gray eyes settled on mine through a haze of impatience that now seemed to suggest a challenge.

"Frankly, neither am I. I'm not going to waste your time or mine doing a Phillip Caine presentation of sugar and spice and everything's nice. Wainwright does that. You, your program and all the government bureaucrats may have very noble intentions about enriching the lives of some of these patients but if you want the truth about what this place and the patients are really like, that I'll give you and you can judge for yourself. Okay?"

"Okay."

We continued down the hall and he went on casually, "This place is the bottom of the barrel. We get the dregs. We get what everybody else has finished with, botched, can't handle or doesn't want to. Sure we treat them, we just don't cure them. Because "A" they're too far gone don't look so dubious we're not miracle workers, "B" neurologically, they're irreparably damaged ... Humpty Dumpties, or "C" we can't guarantee they won't revert." We'd reached the elevator; he pressed the button and then lounged against the wall, hands in pockets as if prepared for a long wait.

"Take a suicide for instance. If we release a patient after treatment and he has a relapse and knocks himself off ... so what? We may get our wrists slapped but that's just about it. But if we let some nice guy out and he tries to hijack an airplane or blows up a school bus, then we get the riot act." The elevator door yawned open and I followed him inside. "Better safe than sorry, see, so they whittle away their lives here and everybody's happy." The elevator whined its way slowly to the second floor and when the doors opened I followed him as he turned left and strolled down the corridor. Two orderlies passed us and a few moments later a nurse. They moved at almost the same leisurely pace. It seemed all very static, very dreamlike ... like a custodial service, not a hospital.

He turned through a doorway that led to a small office and storage area. Glass windows looked out to a large, shabbily furnished room where tables and chairs occupied the center and old-fashioned vinyl sofas and chairs fringed the perimeter. Faded curtains hung wearily at the windows vainly trying to shut out the dreary afternoon.

"For starters, let's take this pair." He nodded in the direction of one of the sofas. "See those two over there?"

They were maybe thirty feet away on the farthest side of the room. A young man sat with his head resting on the back of the sofa, his eyes and mouth open, canted toward the ceiling. Beside him, his head bent down to a book, sat a much older, smaller man, a hardened but wiry figure ... his lips moving slowly and with difficulty over the words.

"See the old guy? That's Tom Whittaker. One of the old-time prospectors from up near Whitehorse. He gets sent down here to us each fall, spends the winter here and gets out in the spring. He may look like a typical patient for a place like this but he's every bit as sane as you or me."

"You're saying he's a fake?" I was astounded.

"You bet!" Caine grinned. "Every system has its loopholes and Tom conveniently makes use of one of them. See, when the weather's good, Tom lives by prospecting. He's got a horse, a bedroll, a pick and a shovel and enough hardtack and beans to keep him alive. Been doin' it for years. That's all he's ever had except for a couple of times he's hit pay dirt. But come winter ... forty and fifty below, he has to hole up ... so he does it here at the taxpayers' expense. About September he takes a room in a boarding house and begins to see "ghosts". He also begins to make a public nuisance of himself. Minor things; he puts the farmer's chickens in the feed store, corsets on the sow, or lets a few field mice loose during Sunday service. When they can't take his pranks any more or when he gets close to embarrassing some righteous and indignant citizen, they get him certified and ship him down here for the winter. Here he gets three square meals a day and a bed what more does he need? Come spring when the weather warms up, he gets discharged."

I was incredulous. "But how can he get away with it?"

Caine shrugged. "Simple. The system works on repetition. Once the pattern has been established it's not likely to be questioned. Maybe the original doctor who certified him way up there in the sticks really did believe old Tom was bonkers. No doubt he can be convincing, but then he spends his winters boning up on what's new in mind games. In fact what's under that book cover of cowboys and Indians is probably this month's issue of my psychiatric journal that disappeared a day or so ago from my desk. But he'll wade through it and in a few days it will arrive back."

"But surely he can't masquerade here ... in a hospital!"

"Oh he's pretty good. He pretends to slip up every now and again when he drops a word like "syndrome" in among the gophers and grizzly bears and the "ghosts". But he has his pride. That's just to remind me of his "unique condition" in case I forget the rules of his game."

The young man beside him continued to stare vacantly up at the ceiling.

"And his friend...?"

"Ted Polanski. Brain damaged. He was the victim of a gang of hoodlums who decided one night for entertainment they'd take somebody into an alley and kick his head in. Along with internal injuries, two broken arms and a dozen fractured ribs, they made a good job of it. They split his head open. When they got him on the table, the surgeons shoveled his brains back into his head back into his skull but they might just as well have used sawdust. Scramble your brains like that and you got yourself a vegetable. Brain tissue doesn't mend. Coming?"

I continued to stare at this pathetic, mindless young man. "The old man - Tom - seems to be reading to him ...does he know his friend doesn't understand?"

"Oh, sure. Tom adopted Ted. Feeds him, looks after him, takes him for walks ... kind of like having a pet. At any rate, it's safe for Tom. He knows Ted isn't going to be talking to anybody and he knows he's always going to be here every year when Tom comes back." He added then with an equally casual air..."After all, everybody needs somebody!"

It seemed a callous remark. But then perhaps without Caine's experience, I was being too sensitive. At least for the moment I preferred to think that that was what it was.

We moved up another floor and through dormitories that housed four to eight patients in each room, the beds separated only by a curtain. The rooms were empty and with a set of keys Caine unlocked one of them for me to see and then re locked it, explaining that they were kept locked from eight till four forcing the patients to at least "exist" in the lounge, recreation room or the grounds. This floor had a small solarium and, except for the yellow painted walls and the few prints scotch taped in place, both faded with age, it was equally as dreary as the rest of the building.

Occupying the solarium, a misshapen, frail figure slumped in a wheelchair positioned in front of a black and white TV the picture quality so poor that it offered only unending unrecognizable images.

"Hello Mary, how are you today?" Caine addressed the woman from a distance as we approached behind the chair. Long, untidy brown hair spilled down around her face, which I was horrified to see was that of a young woman perhaps twenty-five. Her body looked like that of a woman in her seventies. Her eyes roved along the walls and passed Caine with no acknowledgment or recognition, her lips whispering gibberish. She was obviously in some other place. He stroked her hand briefly. "Remember to tell Mrs. Peters you're to come and see me next week. Okay?" Her lips continued without change.

We moved out of ear shot into the corridor.

"Mary Sneider, nice kid ... from a broken family, into a broken life, now into a broken mind."

I waited for him to continue.

"A mother who drank, a father who abused her. She gets in with the wrong crowd. They party it up. Four of them get into a car and it ends up at the bottom of the Fraser Canyon. Three of the kids died in the crash. She was the unfortunate one. She lived.

"You mean to say she's going to be like that for the rest of her life?" I was staggered.

"Yep! Severe head trauma. As I've said, brain cells don't regenerate. She's barely got enough left to be classified as your average garden variety vegetable."

He moved off down the corridor and I took a last look at Mary Sneider. Oblivious to who, what or where she was, the slumped, thin figure in the wheelchair seemed hardly different from the colorless box in front of her receiving its electrical impulses and sending out its senseless static pattern.

We entered a small workshop, set up with basic woodworking tools and equipment. Two men sat at the opposite ends of a long table, one man making long even strokes with a sandpaper block over a piece of wood, the other appearing absorbed in some detail with another piece of wood.

"Ivor Staniskis," Caine spoke in a lowered voice and glanced in the direction of the man engrossed in his whittling. "Steel worker, here because of an industrial accident. He was working on a bridge when one of the girders collapsed and he fell two hundred and twenty-five feet ... and lived."

I could hear the man's deep, rich voice as he sang in what must have been his native tongue. I couldn't understand the words but I was captivated by the rhythm and quality of his voice. Caine had moved to a shelf a few feet away and returned.

"This is his work." Exquisitely detailed in wood was a horse and wagon with a mother and father and two children seated in the wagon. I gently touched the wagon wheels and they turned easily under my fingers. The traces were as delicate as toothpicks and ended in the carefully carved hands of the father. It must have taken great skill and infinite patience.

"Incredible isn't it?" said Caine. "He can do this kind of work with his hands, sings like something out of an opera and after eleven years here still has to be led by hand to the john!"

It seemed so unfair and so sad. I wanted to ask Caine if the man remembered his early childhood in his homeland which I guessed to be Poland.

His songs and the obvious joy of a simple family life depicted in his wood carvings suggested such a wholesome, happy life. If he at least remembered... I didn't ask. I remained silent and simply followed Caine out of the workshop. Maybe it was better not to know.

The fourth floor was little different from the others except that it had no workshops or lounges. We passed doors marked laundry, maintenance, washrooms and supplies. Caine stopped outside an unmarked door, and took his keys to unlock it.

"No tour is complete without a look at one of our padded cells." He mocked a bow and beckoned me to enter.

It couldn't have been bigger than eight by twelve with perhaps a fifteen foot ceiling. A solitary light bulb cast a pattern of eerie shadows down the padded walls and across a high narrow window was an iron curtain of steel bars. Except for a narrow mattress on the floor and a single blanket folded at the foot of it, the room was empty. Even the floor was covered in the same heavily padded canvas as the walls. On tip toes I could scarcely see out the window. It was terrifying. I wondered how long even a sane person would remain unaltered, kept in such a prison.

"In polite circles," Caine pointed out, his voice edged with mockery, "these are known as containment rooms. Each floor has one has to have one. A patient who suddenly gets out of control has to be locked up, for their own sake and for the sake of the other patients. They're not kept here long, seldom over twenty-four hours nowadays since we can sedate them, but isolation is still the best treatment for some..."

It happened then. A piercing, animal like scream penetrated from somewhere, riveting me back against the window where I stood. The scream turned to a long, low pitiful cry that died as suddenly as it had started.

Even Caine had been affected. His expression hardened as he shook his head, glancing up to the floor above where the scream must have originated.

"C'mon." He put an arm on my shoulder and steered me toward the door. My knees felt weak and I knew my hands were trembling. I buried them in my jacket pockets and hoped he wouldn't notice how much I'd been shaken. Whoever or whatever had screamed must have done so from the pit of a hell I could not even begin to imagine.

We took the elevator back down to the first floor in silence. Caine's flippant air seemed dampened. He led me back to the cafeteria, found us a small table in the now deserted room and a minute or so later, returned with two cups of coffee.

It gave me a few moments to collect my wits. "The patients on the fifth floor..." I began. I wasn't really sure how to phrase it. I was both curious and yet reluctant to know more. The scream was like a knife wound in my mind.

"Yeah." Caine bent his head slightly as he sipped his coffee. For a moment, caught in serious reflection, he seemed older; a shadow of apprehension or concern slipped briefly across his face.

"That's a restricted floor. Patients requiring intensive care and/or those who are criminally or violently insane demand high security measures. The fifth floor is off limits to visitors for that reason."

"Were you politely suggesting I'm a visitor?" I teased.

"Well, if you are, we could stand to have more like you." He seemed to have returned to his more typical manner, which I wasn't surprised to find included some pretty basic male banter. He'd done quite a thorough job assessing me during the afternoon. I hadn't entirely missed his glances.

"Thank you, but I'm really not a visitor. I may not like what I see on the fifth floor but I have been given the responsibility of seeing a good cross section of patients."

He gave me a long, steady gaze, as though assessing my motives. Maybe I was a new kind of thrill seeker getting turned on in this vicarious and unorthodox way.

"You're not going to find any patient up there a likely candidate that I can guarantee!"

I met his cool, gray eyes and replied evenly. "Most patients I see aren't likely candidates." I doubt my answer had any influence. He seemed to have reached a decision. He lowered his gaze and took a gulp of coffee.

"Well, if you insist. I'll have to make the arrangements with Woodcroft and Mrs. Rutherford. She's the floor supervisor.

Normally we have very severe restrictions on that floor. Personally, I don't think it's a good idea. They're not exactly candidates for kindergarten."

I ignored his last remark. Either he was tolerating me and the S.P.A.C.E. program, which is what I suspected, or he'd thrown out the remark to test my reaction.

"Those cases make a Greek tragedy look like a picnic." His expression took on a more intimate cast as he tried to change both the subject and the mood of a moment ago. "Do you ski?"

"No, why?"

"You must do something with those nice long legs to be in such great shape. Swim?"

"What, and get all wet?"

"Come on. You must do something ... even just for exercise." The male instincts had surfaced.

This time I'd assessed his motives, but that hadn't been difficult. His gaze hadn't stopped with my eyes.

"Oh I do." I took my last sip of coffee and slipped the strap of my shoulder bag over my arm as I stood.

"What?"

"Work. Bye and thanks. See you tomorrow." I gave him a cheeky smile and left him to chew on a different kind of proposition than the one he'd been anticipating.

I left by the front doors, following the narrow sidewalk that wrapped itself around the building and would lead me back to the parking lot. It had started to rain and I flung my coat over my shoulders and tucked my head down into my collar for the short distance to the car. I was just turning towards the lot when I heard him.

"Miss ... Miss ..."

His jacket and pants were the same chameleon like gray of the stone walls. Except for the white of the moustache I would never have seen him. Mr. Abernathy was standing in the shadows of the building, insistently beckoning me with a bouquet of enormous red tulips. He glanced quickly over his shoulder as I approached and thrust the bouquet into my hand.

"Watch her..." he whispered. His eyes darted furtively beyond me searching the grounds. It was obvious he neither wanted to be seen nor overheard.

"Watch who?" I didn't understand what he was telling me. "Mrs. Wainwright?"

"No, no!" He leaned closer and his blue eyes were intense, fearful. He strained to make me understand with brief, hushed words.

"You be going to the fifth. You watch her. I know ... I see things. The one on the fifth." He thrust the bouquet into my hands, turned, and hurried away.

I stood in the rain holding the flowers and wondered why I was being warned to watch out for someone I had yet to meet.

Particularly by a little old man who'd been a mental hospital patient for years and who grew tulips in November.

TUESDAY NOVEMBER 21st.

By one o'clock the next afternoon, Phillip, as I had been asked to call him not Dr. Caine was ready, reluctantly, to take me up to the fifth floor. His usual seemingly flippant manner had been replaced by one that was remote and serious. My own frame of mind was a strange brew of tension and anxiety. Yesterday's introduction to Island View had been decidedly depressing and today promised to be even more so. Mr. Abernathy's "warning", though I had made a brave attempt at dismissing it, had not remained dormant, only adding to my increasing apprehensions. He had been so earnest almost desperate to warn me about "her" that I found myself wondering just what to believe.

Either way, I was likely to soon find out.

The elevator doors opened to reveal the sign RESTRICTED ADMITTANCE AUTHORIZED PERSONNEL ONLY prominently displayed before doors similar to those throughout the rest of the hospital. These however, had heavy wire mesh in the glass windows and iron bars over top. Phillip selected a key from a ring of several he carried with him and unlocked the door, standing to one side as he motioned me to enter. I heard him lock it again behind us.

We were directly in front of the semi glass partitioned nursing station in front of which Mrs. Rutherford stood. She had been expecting us.

"Good afternoon, doctor." It was a civil but cool tone.

"Hello, Mrs. Rutherford. This is Miss Daniels of the S.P.A.C.E. program."

"Yes of course. How do you do?"

"Mrs. Rutherford." I smiled and extended my hand and found hers as cold as her greeting. Her thin lips hadn't a trace of warmth and her pale eyes, set deep in the hardened face appraised me like a microscope monitoring all that entered her domain. Her weight over some fifty odd years had been distributed to give her a solid, heavy build, though she was neither tall nor large framed. Her white coat covered most of a dark gray gabardine dress only a shade lighter than her black oxford shoes. There wasn't a hint of make up on the colorless cardboard face nor of jewelry of any kind except a watch; apparently indulgences she considered quite unnecessary.

"I can assure you, Miss Daniels, the patients on this floor are quite unsuitable for your purposes. I believe Dr. Caine has already made that very clear to you?" There was no pretense in either her words or her tone.

I tried to keep my own tone of voice conversational and pleasant. "The most important part of my job is seeing patients and their circumstances. Since the program is just being introduced here in British Columbia, we don't want to preclude hospitals, institutions or other health care facilities that might have patients who at some time in the future might benefit from the availability of the program. Selecting and assessing candidates for the program is a secondary phase."

Phillip sensed the building conflict and intervened.

"We won't be long, Mrs. Rutherford. May I have the records?" For a moment she hesitated, and then appeared to reconsider.

"We've had to restrain the Drysdale girl. Otherwise you'll find the patients as well as can be expected." She turned to a four drawer filing cabinet at the back of the nursing station and removed several manila folders, some seeming to have the thickness of a book. She handed them to Phillip and with relief I watched her return to the station. I wasn't looking forward to her presence any more than I'm sure she welcomed mine. I sighed as the tension eased now that we were moving down the corridor and out of her earshot.

"Lovely lady," I growled. Do you get all your staff from Auschwitz?"

He cracked a grin. "Oh, before we had Godzilla but we had to let him go. Hospital policy. They frown on floor supervisors hurling the patients to their death from the roof of the building."

We reached the first of the patients' doors and he hesitated, quickly glancing at the number above the door, then leaned back against the door jamb and selected one file which he placed on top of the others.

"All right. First patient. Julia Fairchild. Played the London stage, and theatres in Europe. Was one of Hollywood's hopefuls." He slipped an old eight by ten photo out of the file and handed it to me. Despite the crimped hair and the rather outlandish dress she was wearing, the photo showed she had been an extremely beautiful woman. Large eyes coyly looked up from an exquisitely shaped face, partly hidden by a feather boa.

Phillip leaned over my shoulder and tapped the feather boa with the end of his pencil.

"It was probably that thing that did most of the damage. Something happened nobody really knows but at the peak of her career she left Hollywood became a recluse,built herself a mansion on an island up near the Queen Charlottes where she lived with a butler and a maid. She would dine by candlelight alone each night, dressed in her most elegant clothes, music in the background and champagne at her fingertips." Phillip took a deep breath. "Anyway there was a fire, probably just a candle that caught part of her clothing. If she cried out for help, the staff never knew. They lived in a separate building. She was badly burned from the waist up. The fire burned itself out. They found her still sitting at the dining room table in the morning ... by some miracle still alive."

"Ready?" He put a hand on the door knob. I nodded and felt the clamminess on the palms of my hands at what I was going to see.

I saw nothing.

The north light coming in the window silhouetted the slumped shape of a figure seated in a chair. It was only as I followed Phillip out from behind the figure that I began to see the horror of what fire can do to human flesh.

"Hello Julia. Do you remember me? I'm Dr. Caine. I've brought someone to meet you." He reached for her hand which lay coiled in her lap. It was like a skeleton. Thin waxy skin barely stretched over the bones that had been turned into claws.

She made no sound.

Her mouth was no more than a gaping hole breath coming and going in shallow, raspy gasps. The skin was stretched over the face like a hideous white mask, no flesh any longer to provide shape or contour. Small, lizard like eyes moved only once under half closed lids that years ago had been delicately feathered with long curving lashes. There were no lashes. No hair. The skin, mutilated and scarred, covered the skull, the neck and mercifully disappeared from sight into the collar of a pale yellow nightdress.

She neither spoke nor moved.

Except for the smallest trace of life, she could have been a mummy, exhumed from a grave of some forgotten civilization. Phillip replaced the hand carefully in her lap, straightened and moved to the door, taking me by the elbow.

"If they ever decide to remake the Bride of Frankenstein, she'd be a natural!"

I wasn't at all sure my voice wouldn't reflect the revulsion and pity that alternated in my mind.

"How ... how long has she been here?"

"Since the accident. She was hospitalized for a couple of years while they tried to reconstruct something like a face for her. It was pretty hopeless. She was then moved here. Let's see..." He flipped through several pages. "Twenty-six years."

He moved down the hall to the next room and I followed, still numb from what I'd seen. This time he neither waited for me nor bothered to knock.

She was sitting huddled on a straight chair, the stooped shoulders moving forwards and backwards, the shabby blue chenille dressing gown barely disguising the frail, aged body. The straggly white hair hung from the bent head, half hiding a face shriveled with age. From her mouth a thin trickle of saliva crept down her chin to the dressing gown as she continued to sing a lullaby, words almost unrecognizable, the voice dry and cracked.

There was little doubt that the tattered gray blanket she held tightly with gnarled, arthritic hands was a substitute for the infant she was intent on rocking to sleep. Phillip made no effort to speak to her. Instead he spoke to me.

"Mrs. Henrietta Farley. Born in Ellisbrook, Saskatchewan, 1927. Been institutionalized since 1952."

I watched this haggard, old woman endlessly rocking her "child" like some pathetic charade and listened to her voice scratching out the tuneless sounds. Yet I imagined her as a young mother with her child as I felt sure she must have been. I wondered what must have happened to her over fifty years ago.

"Phillip ... why? That blanket is a baby to her. Did she lose her own baby?"

"You might say that." His voice sounded too casual. "She had six children the youngest was the baby, three months. They were deserted by her husband just after the baby was born, during one of the worst winters of those depression years. Fifty and sixty below and I suppose they had little food. Those were lean hard years for a lot of people. They all died." His jaw tightened and he paused for a moment. "She took an axe one night and hacked them to death. The baby was dismembered." He gave a light shrug to his shoulders, turned and headed out of the room. Evidently there was little else to say.

As I left the room, the cracked, hollow voice faded away. Out of sight, I could imagine the tenderness and love of a mother and infant. I wanted to believe that this was what she was remembering.

That, and nothing more.

He tapped lightly on the next door and entered the room. How I wished for a moment's reprieve! A moment to somehow find acceptance of what I had seen and what I knew could never be changed. But, reluctantly, I followed and steeled myself for yet another horror.

I was looking at an angel. My gaze fell downward to the tilted head of a half child, half woman. Though part of her face was hidden by long strands of sand colored hair, she couldn't have been more than twenty. Her features were delicately carved in a soft ivory complexion and her blue eyes stared sightlessly off into another world. Her head tilted to one side seemed to suggest a not unnatural pose, as though she was waiting, listening for something.

She was in a straight jacket.

The heavy canvas sleeves crossed her body and I could see they had been securely tied behind her back. She had been placed in a wheelchair and, as much a prisoner as she was physically, so was her mind, behind the bars of insanity.

"Jennifer, Jennifer can you hear me? Are you feeling better today?" Phillip squatted down on his haunches in front of her and looked up at her face. He pulled the wispy strands of hair gently back from her eyes. There was no response. Her eyes remained sightlessly fixed beyond him great blue pools neither seeing nor recognizing, her face now framed by the soft pale hair that fell back behind her shoulders. Somewhat sadly, Phillip straightened, walked the step or two to the edge of the narrow hospital bed and sat, with his elbows resting on his knees, his hands cupped like fists locked one inside the other. I seated myself in a small straight-backed chair near the window that, aside from the small night stand, the bed and the wheelchair, comprised all of the furnishings in the room.

"Jennifer Drysdale, eighteen years old." He flipped the folder open but only glanced at the contents. "She's spent most of her life here. That scream we heard yesterday was Jennifer."

I was shocked. I could still hear the anguished, almost inhuman cry, in my mind and it seemed impossible it could have come from her. She seemed almost too frail, and somehow, with those gentle features and large expressionless eyes, too detached. I wondered what horrors had so suddenly possessed her mind to cause her such anguish.

"Why ... is she here?"

He took a deep sigh as if it were a long, sad story he would rather not begin. "She was born in Kimberley, a backwoods, very rural area ... to a Bokarite family. You know about the Bokarites?"

I nodded. "A little. I believe they're a religious sect, not unlike the Shakers or Amish... keep to themselves and don't believe in using such modern things as medicine, machinery and the like?"

"Yeah, they also believe when someone does something wrong, they're a bad seed. Not exactly possessed by the devil but just about. They have a very rigid code of behavior. They farm and raise crops exactly the way their ancestors have done for centuries... without tractors or insecticides. They live in a commune and the women and children may wear only black and their heads must be covered at all times. The women do all the domestic work, they eat only after the men, and all meals are eaten in strict silence. Prayers are spoken by the elders before and after each meal."

"Sounds like you could choke on a cherry stone and be hanged for it!"

Phillip gave me a quick grin. "Just about! Prayer and eighteen hours a day of labor, floggings even for the most minor infraction, and hangings for "sins" we'd probably rate as misdemeanors."

"That's barbaric! Surely they can't get away with hanging their own people without a trial, a judge and a jury?"

He shrugged. "They have their own system of justice, as they have everything else. They're self sufficient, keep entirely to themselves. Folks just tolerate them... what they do is their business. I don't think anyone really cares as long as they keep to themselves."

I was looking at Jennifer, trying to imagine her as a child, dressed in black. I wondered if she had ever been allowed to laugh and play.

He must have read my thoughts. "I can't believe it's much of a life for a child but then they don't know anything else. No radio, TV or books except those few used to teach the children and then only how to read and write and most of them live their entire lives without going any farther than their wheat fields."

And Jennifer?" As Phillip had described their lifestyle I couldn't imagine how or why she had come to be institutionalized.

"We don't know all the details you can understand why. What we do know comes from a farmer's wife motherly old soul who was involved in the last incident."

"Incident?"

"There were three, according to the farmer's wife, a Mrs....." He turned to the records beside him on the bed and shifted through several pages before he caught the name he was after. "Agnes. Agnes Millard... Jennifer had always been a problem. About the age of two she started bouts of whimpering and crying and as she got older they got worse, ending in fits of thrashing and screaming. Even in a young child they don't tolerate that kind of behavior so she was first whipped and then sent to her bed.

Shortly after she'd had one of these fits, she was found near a stream. One of the other children about her age had drowned. About a year later one of the elders was killed by a pitch fork while tending the livestock in the barn. She was found in the hayloft.

Several months later a fire broke out in one of the barns and it went up like a tinder box. It was August and one of the driest summers they'd had in years. It spread to several other nearby buildings and some of the women and children perished.

The fire broke out at night and was therefore visible for miles around. The townsfolk came in droves to help them put it out. Probably one of the only times they'd offered help and the only time it was ever accepted. The men came with buckets and shovels and the women came with food and blankets. That's how Agnes Millard became involved.

One of the Bokarites had found Jennifer in her nightdress with a lantern exactly where they believed the fire had started. They had tied her to a chair while they fought the blaze and the Millard woman found her there in one of the storerooms where she'd gone in search of bedding an hour or so after the fired had started. Jennifer had been burned but even worse were the scars on her body where she had been beaten and whipped numerous times. Maybe the Millard woman suspected they were going to do something even more dreadful to her or maybe she did what probably anyone would do. I suspect it was a bit of both.

She wrapped the child in blankets, loaded her in the back of the wagon and took her back to her home. There was so much commotion, no one noticed. Of course the next day one of the elders arrived at the Millard farmhouse to take her back. Instead, Mrs. Millard wrapped up one of their freshly slaughtered pigs all neatly sewn in blankets and sacks ready for burial. She must have been pretty convincing tears and all at how she'd tried to save the child, nursing her through the night. That's when the elder called Jennifer's "death" a blessing and gave the Millard woman an insight into what they had been through with the child.

But she'd had seven of her own and as she explained to Doc Williams..."ain't nothin' wrong with a child that love and vittles won't cure!" I guess she ought to know. Her own kids were as big and strong as they come. Anyway she kept the child in the root cellar, hoping the Bokarites wouldn't unwrap "the body" and meanwhile got Doc Williams involved in the whole thing as an accomplice. Between the doctor and Agnes Millard woman they nursed her back to health physically that is, but that's as far as they could go. She was catatonic, like this, ever since the night of the fire. Maybe in time if the Millard woman could have kept her which I'm sure she would have done it if wasn't for the fact her ruse would have been discovered sooner or later, and there's no way the Bokarites ever let one of their kind get away she might have recovered on her own. It's doubtful but as it turned out Doc Williams finally had to place her. She was seven years old when she arrived here."

It had been a long and tragic story and I felt deeply saddened by it. I sensed Phillip felt the same way. It was the first time I had seen him affected by it all and one of the few times I'd seen him shed his usual casual detachment he seemed to protect himself with, like armor.

"Have you any idea what the cause of her condition was?"

"Nope. Kids don't thrash and scream for no reason. We did all the checks for the most probable causes. Brain tumor, epilepsy, nerve damage and diseases like Scarlet Fever and Rubella. Neurologically and physically, there's simply nothing wrong with her. It could have been a reaction to something like migraine hell even a toothache! There's all kinds of things we have no way of tracing."

"But then if she's always like this, why is she being restrained?"

"She isn't always. She had a seizure a fit yesterday. Remember the scream? She becomes very violent so for her own protection we keep her restrained for twenty four hours afterwards."

"So suddenly! How..."

"Neurologically, electrical stimuli are received by the brain about the same way electricity travels from a transmitter to a receiver. But every now and then something overloads the circuits, all the wires get crossed and the receiver or the brain goes out of control and the circuits blow." He added more casually, "I'm a psychiatrist, not an electrician, but that's about it."

"Phillip, you said something overloads the circuits. What kind of thing does that?"

"Stimuli. It varies with each person and their reaction. With some people it might be a chemical imbalance maybe drug related, or an allergic reaction, even a particular sight, sound or smell can be all it takes."

"And with her?"

"We don't know. We've tried to determine what triggers them, but so far no luck."

"Does she have them very often?"

"No..." but he looked puzzled for a moment and leafed through the pages of her file. "Come to think of it, they could be happening more often. She had one... let's see… the most recent was Oct. 27th. then yesterday. She used to average maybe three four a year. I'll have to remember to mention that to Woodcroft."

He stood suddenly and closed the file abruptly. "This is enough psychiatry for one day." He glanced at his watch. "I want to get away by four and it's after three now. How about a coffee before I have to get back to my desk?"

I was surprised at how late it was and how suddenly spent I felt. "Great idea providing we can continue another day. Are there many more patients?"

"Not many. If you're willing to incur the wrath of Rutherford again." He grinned and stretched his back muscles. "Be right back. Let me get these records filed and I'll tell her we'll have to come back next week." He quickly shuffled them back in order and disappeared.

Now alone, my gaze returned to the girl who had sat motionless, staring into space all the time we had been there. If anything, her head had tilted downward, and the silvery strands of hair had fallen back over her face. On impulse, or perhaps because I had seen Phillip do the same thing, I reached over and gently pulled the strands of hair away from her face.

It happened.

My hand stopped in mid motion as I caught the movement of her eyes. I watched them pull away from their dream like gaze and travel ever so slowly a winding path of vision to meet my own. She was focusing as intently and clearly as I was. Like a young fawn's, her eyes were large, soft pools. Clear, steady, sane.

"Jennifer," my voice trembled. Suddenly I was struck with an overpowering sense of perception, of acute awareness buried in the depths of her intense watchful eyes. "Jennifer?"

Her lips parted, the movement ever so slight, at perhaps an attempt to speak. But it was too remote from the sound and meaning of even a single word.

I could hear Phillip's footsteps as he came back into the room. "I've told her we'll come back next week because," he teased, "you're wild about the place!"

"Phillip..."

He looked at me puzzled.

I'd taken my eyes from her face for only an instant. "Yes?"

Like shutters drawn across her mind, her eyes had returned to their former position unfocused, empty, staring, her head tilted to one side, her hair fallen across her face. She looked exactly like a rejected rag doll tossed aside by a bored child, a lifeless toy no one loved or wanted.

"Nothing."

FRIDAY NOVEMBER 24th.

The windshield wipers could only protest against the blurred images of headlights and tail lights as the rush hour traffic tangled itself in a Friday night exodus. What few pedestrians there were made vain attempts to avoid the muddy spray tossed up by the wheels of passing cars.

Kids in their ski jackets retracted their hands into their sleeves and their heads under hoods like turtles and trudged home.

I wanted to get home too. I was weary, and a vague headache lingered low down in the back of my head. Everything I'd seen and heard during the week seemed to tug at my mind for attention. Tired as I was, the thoughts refused to leave and instead stayed and sulked. It was a bleak and depressing mood.

I stopped at a Safeway supermarket to buy some groceries and by the time I pulled into the marina parking lot the rain was beating down in a renewed frenzy and bouncing in anger off the pavement. Leaning over the open trunk door, I separated those items that needed to be refrigerated, carried them and what little else I could manage down the ramp and deposited the now soaked grocery bags on the kitchen counter. Between a tiny pantry and the refrigerator, I stowed everything away and then made myself a martini which I carried upstairs, got a small but vigorous fire going in the fireplace, and felt the bite of the martini ease down my throat as I huddled near the spreading warmth of the fire. A pile of wool heaped on the floor near the loom parted and Humphrey emerged. He stretched, yawned, freshened his face with a licked paw and approached for a petting. Once he'd dispensed with the niceties, he positioned himself at the top of the stairs expectantly waiting for me to move, while he anticipated which of nine flavors he would condescend to dine on. I stretched and yawned too and pondered the time – now after eight - and the seemingly enormous effort it would take to go back downstairs and feed us compared to falling into my bed that was less than five feet away.

    I don't think Humphrey liked my choice one bit.

* * *

I woke up warm, refreshed and ravenous. Through floor to ceiling windows I could see that morning heralded one of those rare, gloriously sunny winter days. The water was a mirror of a thousand broken pieces stirred by the brisk breeze and the gulls climbed and arced calling and crying in their eternal search of the sea.

Humphrey on the other hand was only concerned with his belly, principally the lack of what was in it. He was sitting on my pillow; his two large, copper eyes looking down at me, his whiskers vibrating from a very wheezy purr all intended to bore through my brain. It was aided by a pussy willow paw that every now and then poked me in the head.

"Hungry old man? Me too." I gave a final stretch, climbed out of bed and donned a tatty but favorite old sweater, a pair of cords, socks and a very comfortable but decidedly decadent pair of slippers. To Humphrey that was definitely encouraging. The tail was raised like a mast and he whisked down the stairs to take up the final position in front of his food dish.

Twenty minutes later we both had polished off the last traces of breakfast, he of cat chow chicken flavored, I of toast crumbs downed with a Spanish omelet and the second mug of coffee, which I now sipped as I strolled out onto the deck.

The roar of a small outboard started and Rob waved and shouted a greeting that drowned before I caught it as he headed out of the marina to the harbor.

It was a firewood finding expedition which the eternally penniless art student was forced to feed to the black bellied stove, his only source of heat in the barely floating, rather derelict house beside mine. It turned my thoughts to more domestic things. A mutual trade off firewood for food, which somehow Rob and I had arrived at, each of us convinced we had the better part of the deal. Sure enough, three hours later I heard the outboard approaching. I had just stepped onto my deck from setting the crab pot and saw him cut the engine and guide the small boat up alongside my deck. It was low in the water and stacked high with driftwood, boards, bark and tailings.

"You got yourself quite a catch! That should keep you toasty warm for a week or two!" I watched him climb gingerly out of the boat, one side dipping dangerously close to the waterline under his weight.

"Yeah! These high tides we've had for the last few days made it pretty easy picking." It was a statement that seemed in conflict with his appearance. Despite his height, which was probably close to six feet, he was a string bean. An anorexic would have appeared robust in comparison, yet he appeared utterly competent and self sufficient with every manual task which is part of the life of living on a floating home. He wore an old Indian toque over a mass of dark curly hair but his cheeks, nose and the tips of his ears were blanched with cold. He blew into his hands and rubbed them together. They were stiff and red, having been in and out of the water as he'd salvaged the wet wood from the shores.

"Hey, how about lunch?" It was an offer I knew he wasn't likely to refuse.

"Sounds good! Let me get some of this wood upstairs for you and give it a chance to dry out first, though."

A half hour later Rob shed a couple of sweaters and a jacket and sat down to onion soup, and a toasted clubhouse sandwich, washed down with two beers.

In some ways it was like watching a starving dog gulp down his first food in days, except that Rob did it with great restraint coupled always with profuse compliments. There seemed to be artistry in his soul as well. I was always amazed at the delicacy of the fine brush work and the minutest details of his paintings. I watched his long fingers clean the wire rimmed glasses that always seemed to slip down to the ridge of his nose and they moved with as much care as I imagined he handled a paint brush.

But shortly he was gone. He had his wood to cut and stack and his chores to be done and I had mine.

I vacuumed, dusted, and as I had so many times in the past two weeks, stopped in front of three glass shelves lined with the dozen or so small ethnic dolls I'd brought back from Asia. They were exactly as I'd positioned them... this time. Two weeks ago, they hadn't been. They'd been... adjusted. It was after all, a houseboat. It moved with the wash of a tug, the wind, the tide. And things inside could move, topple over, fall down. They had. Until I had managed to arrange them in a devious fashion whereby they propped themselves in place and stayed there. The dolls had been moved, I knew, I could tell. Even the dusty disturbed imprints on the glass shelf said so. A desk drawer had been searched. A fine film of bath powder had told me that even the bathroom had been investigated. And then there had been a rash of wrong numbers. Nothing had been stolen. Nothing damaged.

Why?

That's what nagged at me till I once again pushed it back in a pigeon hole, grabbed my jacket and went out to retrieve the crab pot. What I had tried to contain in that pigeon hole was the only disturbing element to a day that was clear, bright and much too brief.

As if yesterday's brilliance had been Mother Nature's mistake, Sunday arrived sullen and brooding. It didn't rain, it just threatened to. A gray sky descended and stayed put. It somehow managed to contaminate my mood. I had succeeded for the best part of the weekend to forget some of the things I'd seen in the first two days of the past week at Island View. The remaining part of the week I'd be left on my own. But now I felt those images waking and stirring in the back of my mind.

Paul Montgomery was due at seven for dinner. I'd caught myself more than once during the week looking forward to seeing him again, despite my preoccupation. I'd even half hoped I might have run into him on the dock but his comings and goings and mine had not coincided. Perhaps it was just as well. I made up my mind not to be dragged down by the oppressive thoughts of what the week had been and the coming week would bring but to enjoy the evening. And Paul Montgomery.

By late afternoon, the dinner preparation complete and the house in order, I began the luxury of self indulgence. I lit the fire, ran a bath, put on some music and slipped into a heaven of bath oils and bubbles.

An hour later I had preened and pampered myself, perfected my hair and make up and had rejected a half dozen wardrobe choices before deciding on long sleeved wheat colored velour ensemble. As loungewear goes, it was soft and clinging, comfortable and casual and seemed appropriate both for my mood and the evening.

Paul appeared to think so too. Promptly at seven the door knocker sounded and he arrived, giving me a long admiring look as he shed his jacket and I took it from him.

"I'm impressed! You don't look a bit like a crab fisherman, though even in hip waders and rain gear I'd say you'd be a knockout."

I'd hung up his jacket and came back to stand before him. His eyes hadn't quite finished exploring the contours of what I had on. Provocatively I put my hands on my hips and looked at him with attempted seriousness. "That's something we'll never know, will we? I have no intention of owning either one. As for what I'm wearing, forgive me for wanting to keep warm but I find sequins and gold lame chilly at this time of year." Then I smiled up at him. "I have the fire going upstairs, would you like a drink before dinner?"

"Please. Whatever you're having."

"Vodka martini?"

"Excellent."

I carried the tray with the chilled shaker and glasses upstairs and found Paul standing by my loom where it occupied the corner by the windows.

"You have more talent than in just catching crab. You must need papers to run this thing."

"I thought so when I first got it, but that was years ago. Weaving takes as much patience as it does technical skill." He accepted the glass I held out for him and settled down on the floor cushions before the fire.

For a big man he moved with ease and grace. He extracted his pipe querying my acceptance by a gesture only and in a moment had it alight and his drink in hand. His attention went back to the loom. "Does that have anything to do with the kind of work you do?"

"Only by default. My degree is in architecture and interior design but I developed an interest in textile art along the way." I would have been content to leave it at that, not wanting to indulge in a monologue about myself but it begged for an explanation. "My field is corporate design - specifically hotels. I work for the Kaiser Corporation – perhaps you've heard of it?"

"Yes I have, as a matter of fact. They build those exotic resort hotels in off the beaten trail locations around the world, right?"

"Right," I agreed I'm a field designer. That simply means I go to the site and do the preliminary workups."

"Does that mean next week you could be off to Mombasa or Marrakech?

"I laughed. "Sorry both those locations are too mundane for the Kaiser Corporation. No, it's a barely inhabited island in the Marianas. Too small even to be noticeable on a map. And no, not week. Next April."

"And until then…"

"Until then I get to do some of the finishing details on the houseboat the builders left for me. And I get to do a dear friend a favor. In a mental hospital."

"If you don't mind my asking, how many dear friends do you have in mental hospitals?"

I laughed. "One too many, if this last week is any indication." My dear friend is Yvonne Yuen and she's not in a mental hospital she's in Australia on her honeymoon. And I, good Samaritan that I am, allowed myself to get talked into being her temporary replacement. She is the director of the S.P.A.C.E. Program Special Programs in Assistance, Counseling and Education being introduced to intermediate and extended care patients." I sipped my martini and rearranged the olive.

"Is the purpose of the program then to supplement their education or to retrain them?"

"Supplement mostly but it depends on the individual. Twenty thousand children had to be hospitalized last year in Canada alone anywhere from overnight to a year or more. In Boston where the program was first introduced, in the long term cases, there was a substantial improvement in those children who had been involved in supplemental education. They exhibited fewer chronic symptoms, their general health improved, hospital staff found them to be more co operative, and they adapted more quickly to their home and school life when they were released. Kids at a young age are really eager to learn but if they become misfits in the educational factory they seldom if ever can make up for it and it often follows them through their entire life. But hospitals are hospitals not schools. Now, because of computers, video tapes and the educational channels on TV, we can bring highly specialized education to the individual, and right to a hospital bed if necessary, using nothing more than a cassette recorder or a television set."

"Then the program only involves children?"

"No, when the program was first introduced it was confined to children but now it's been expanded to include adults. Yvonne interviews those patients who have been or will be hospitalized for an extended stay and administer a C.E.A. a Candidate Evaluation Assessment, which helps determine the specific educational or technical training most appropriate

"Sounds like she's done them all."

"Not quite. She left the last one for me." I hesitated. "Island View."

"But that's the provincial mental institution isn't it? Are you likely to find anyone there eligible?"

"In theory if their impairment is not overly severe, the program can benefit those with mental challenges as well as those with physical ones. And we won't really know till we try. But that part hasn't been easy!"

"Problems?"

"Not exactly. Just some very weird things." The memory of Mr. Abernathy's strange warning came back to haunt me. It was something however that at the moment I was reluctant to mention. I continued, "And some very tragic cases."

"Like?"

"Oh..." I munched my olive and then continued. "Like this old prospector who gets sent down from up North every winter and gets released every spring. Evidently he's as sane as they come!"

Paul tossed his head back and laughed. "So he found a way to beat the system! Good for him! Don't think I'd enjoy it though. And...?"

"There's a little old man who used to be a gardener in England. He still is a gardener, except that he's a bit confused; plants things all at the wrong time of the year and he gets them to grow!"

Paul chuckled. "Maybe he's not as confused as everybody thinks."

"Perhaps not." Again I remembered the strange, huddled figure in the shadow of the building and his words of warning. I had mulled them over so many times. It had been a sobering thought which my face must have reflected.

Paul became serious.

"You mentioned some tragic cases..."

His response dragged my attention away from the words of warning that again had lingered in my mind.

"What? Oh sorry. Yes, the worst are on the fifth floor. They keep them confined to it. I had to go through a lot of red tape to even be allowed up there. Mrs. Rutherford she's the floor supervisor wasn't exactly thrilled with me or my presence. I get the impression that she runs it by herself and doesn't want anything to do with the rest of the place, or even the staff. Maybe I'm being a bit hard on her; her patients are pretty pathetic victims."

"Victims?"

"Of themselves or of circumstances. There's one poor soul a burn case I won't even describe her to you." But I shuddered at the thought. "She had been an actress. I saw a picture of her. Paul, she was absolutely beautiful!"

He winced. "Burns can be very mutilating."

"Another poor woman sits and rocks an imaginary baby hour after hour and sings to it. She axed her own children to death!"

"I don't suppose it's much consolation to you but I'm sure it's much more difficult for you than it is for them. Many of them must live in their own worlds with little awareness of what's around them."

My thoughts turned to Jennifer. Those clear, lucid eyes as she had looked so directly at me. I had said nothing to Phillip. I now said nothing to Paul.

"I'd like to believe that." It seemed the conversation had brought about a strange aura of gloom and despair that threatened to haunt the mood of the evening. I stood up. "Enough of this monologue. Excuse me a minute while I check our dinner. Then I'd like to hear about you and the Snow Goose." A few minutes later I was back upstairs with a tray of fresh crab cocktails, lemon wedges, crackers and the martini pitcher. He nodded his approval at the crab cocktails as he stoked the fire and refilled our glasses.

"I see that risking life and limb paid dividends. How is your arm by the way?"

"Oh much better. And yesterday's catch didn't even require a Band-Aid." I pulled up my sleeve to expose what was now little more than a few faint scratch lines. "Now tell me about the Snow Goose. Have you been working on her this week?"

Between bites he answered. "On and off. Mostly tinkering with a couple of old engines. Too dull and boring to even talk about. And that's all that's new, other than to report" his eyes took on a glint of amusement as he took a sip from his glass, "she's still afloat."

I let a few moments lapse before I responded. I'd begun to feel the alcohol ease the remnants of the gloom that had been present moments ago. The fire had settled down to munch away on fresh firewood, and Johnny Mathis mingled with the sounds of the wind whining in the night. Paul too, appeared comfortable, relaxed. He was obviously strong and well built, even under the fishermen's knit sweater, the muscles in his arms and shoulders moved in response as he turned to rest his glass on the hearth. Yet at the same time it was a kind of contained strength, like a jungle cat, resting but eternally wary. This made me want to know more... not about the Snow Goose but about him.

Very simply I asked "and you?"

"Would you like the true life story of Paul Montgomery or the condensed version in twenty-five words or less?" The amusement remained in his eyes.

I teased back. "I'll start with the condensed version. After all, I might be bored to tears."

"That's guaranteed!" Then he continued more seriously. "I'm a marine biologist which means I've spent a lot of time on and under the water studying for most people, some pretty dull things mostly for the government. You've heard about the oil rigs in the Beaufort Sea?"

I nodded and he went on.

"A lot of research is involved in projects like that. I've spent the last two years at a research station on Kodiak Island. Very cold, very dark and not very exciting, let me tell you. So I decided to thaw out for awhile and work on the Snow Goose, which will probably take me till spring to finish."

"And then will you go back up north?"

"I don't know. The cold gets to you after awhile. It seems to get into your bones. I'll make that decision when the time comes." A buzzer sounded in the kitchen downstairs. "Gee," he grinned, "you really were serious about the condensed version. I didn't realize I was being timed!"

I laughed. "You weren't but the dinner was. I think we can eat now."

I had debated what to serve this man I hardly knew and in the end had reverted to what I considered a safe and acceptable choice. Prime rib of beef, baked potatoes, gravy, broccoli and peas and Yorkshire pudding which had risen high and light. Paul retrieved a bottle of red wine which evidently he'd left to keep cool outside on the deck and with our plates filled we sat at the dining room table, just beyond the living room, the candlelight bowing and swaying and we ate with appetite and pleasure.

"Surely you don't keep that lithe lean figure of yours by eating like this every night." His gaze had more than once discreetly traveled beyond the expression I had been wearing.

"You're right, but that's only because I don't often have the time to cook or eat. I love to do both but it seems I miss so many meals that I've come to think of a granola bar as a dinner." I dredged a piece of Yorkshire pudding in gravy and savored the flavor. Then nibbled away at my vegetables.

I was enjoying Paul. This great bearded man with dark eyes and a haunted face. He seemed to have gentleness beneath his strength, a dry humor beneath a rather stern facade and a tolerance towards life which I suspected had been acquired through some solitary and hard years. It seemed like a long time ago that I had enjoyed someone like this. But then my own years had been solitary too. I'm not sure whether by choice or fate.

He had obviously enjoyed his dinner, and I was beginning to believe his peanut butter and jelly sandwich joke, except that, even more, I suspected him to be competent in more things than he let be known.

We took large wedges of strawberry cheesecake, coffee and a bottle of Tia Maria back upstairs, settled back down before the bright orange embers of the fire and enjoyed the remaining evening with easy and relaxed conversation. Humphrey, who till this point had remained in his cave of wool, came forward, sniffed Paul's hand and a good portion of his sweater. His inspection complete, he rolled over, stuck all four feet in the air, and began his usual, wheezy purr, signifying that he would like some attention.

"He's huge! Does he always sound like that? His ball bearings need oiling!"

I had to laugh at Paul's dismay. "He didn't always sound like that. Since I moved down here he's fallen in so many times I think his purr machine has rusted out!"

"Fallen overboard? I thought cats were far too agile for that kind of thing."

"Me too. I think he's on the twenty-sixth of his nine lives."

"It's a wonder he could ever stay afloat. He's nothing more than a ton of gray fur... it must be six inches long!"

"Not quite that long and he really only weighs seventeen pounds. And he's blue not gray."

"Blue is he?"

"P.B.'s are blue. The riff raff are gray."

"P.B.'s?"

"Purebreds."

"Well, purebred or not his purr machine needs an overhaul. I have two old diesel relics in the Goose that don't make as much noise as he does!" He glanced at his watch. "And ... I suppose if I'm ever to get them working the way they should I'd better get going. Six o'clock comes pretty early."

Downstairs again, I got his jacket from the closet when he suddenly seemed to remember something.

"By the way, I have something for you I thought you might like to have. I don't know where you could put it but if you're going to live on the water I guess you could do with a nautical touch or two." He returned from the deck with something wrapped in several layers of newspaper. I cleared some counter space for him as he unwrapped it.

I was ecstatic! Even under the layers of grime I could see the dull brass of a porthole. Even the glass encrusted with barnacles was intact and the latch, though stiff, I could move.

"Oh Paul! How wonderful! I've wanted one for ages. But they're so expensive..."

"I guess. All cleaned and polished sitting in an antique shop. I picked this up from a wreck up along the coast when I was diving up there a few years ago."

"But can't you use it on the Snow Goose?"

"No, she has four and they're all intact. Have you any place you can use it?"

"Oh yes! The front door! I've always thought one would be ideal there."

"I don't suppose you have a jig saw?"

I looked crestfallen.

"Well, it will take you awhile to get it cleaned up. Next week end, maybe Sunday, if you'd like I'll cut the opening for you. It will have to be bolted into place and I think I have some brass ones that will probably fit."

"Oh Paul that would be marvelous! That's very kind of you and that's an extremely generous gift. Thank you so much!"

"Thank you for a most enjoyable evening." He slipped into his jacket and then turned and approached me. He reached down, brushed my hair aside and kissed my forehead. Then in the next moment he headed for the door giving the porthole a backward glance. "I don't envy you that job! Thanks for a wonderful evening. See you next Sunday."

"Good night Paul."

For a few moments I stood and savored the memory of the brief kiss, the touch of his lips and the final sounds of the music and the wind and the night. Then, though pleasantly tired, I collected the dinner dishes and tidied the kitchen. Upstairs in the bathroom, I gave my hair a bedtime brush, and cleaned my teeth. Beneath the porcelain vase on the counter that held Mr. Abernathy's tulips, the once bright crimson petals now lay pale and lifeless. The flowers had lived for just one week.

The next day as I was to find out, so had Mr. Abernathy.

MONDAY NOVEMBER 27th.

Whether they liked it or not I was back on their doorstep. I would have much preferred to have seen the last of the place but for what little time I would have to spend here, I convinced myself I would tolerate it in the best spirit possible.

It was a simple errand. They had found a small unused storeroom I could use as a temporary office, together with a desk and a chair that were both threatening to fall apart. But according to Mrs. Wainwright, there was also an assortment of miscellaneous furniture down in the basement.

"I'm sure my dear," she cooed, "we can find you a better chair than that." She handed me a flashlight from a cupboard near the entry and we walked down to the end of the hall to the door that led to the basement steps. She was at the top of the stairs when she was summoned back to her office by a telephone call.

There was barely enough light from the dusty yellow light bulbs to make out the old mattresses, filing cabinets and cupboards that filled a large area that disappeared into darkness. Beyond that, the bulbs had burned out or there weren't any; I had to strain to distinguish the shapes stacked one on top of another. There were crates and boxes and cardboard files with file folders their exposed edges yellowed with age and thick with dust.

It was the files that enticed me to poke my way deeper into the maze. If they were patients' records which I began to think by their number they must be they could prove interesting reading. Beneath my natural curiosity was a sense of...something wrong about this place – something I couldn't identify. I pulled one file out and opened it to find several pages written in longhand. The pen nib had been very fine and the style ornate. Even with the flashlight focused I could barely read a single word. I did catch a date nineteen forty-two and for a moment lost interest, as that would have been too long ago, I thought, to involve those same patients today. Most would be dead by now.

Maybe there were more recent files. Judging by the thickness of the ones Phillip had referred to, they couldn't store them forever upstairs. Maybe after a few years they moved inactive files down here.

Suddenly, as I moved in the direction of a faint pool of daylight, my eyes were caught by an awkward dark shape sprawled on the floor against the far wall. Pale rays of daylight seeped through the small barred and dirt encrusted window enough light that I could see the two protrusions sticking out at awkward angles were legs. Alarmed, I moved slowly closer. Then, from a few feet away, I recognized the thatch of white hair, the moustache and the blue eyes that stared blankly up to the cobwebbed ceiling. I stood absolutely still and waited for a voice... a movement... and then cautiously crept forward, avoiding the shattered flower pots I could now make out littering the floor.

"Mr. Aber..."

Whatever that subtle difference is between life and death became apparent. For several moments I stood staring down at him, my heart pounding and my hands trembling, while my mind tried to grope with the threads of some reasonable explanation. From somewhere in the distance I heard drops of water echoing, which only seemed to intensify the dank, gloomy atmosphere. An icy chill shuddered up through my body. The drops of water seemed to grow nearer. Then a cold hand clutched my arm.

I wheeled around.

"Mrs. Wainwright!"

Her eyes were fixed on the motionless bundle against the wall.

"Oh my dear... oh dear me! Mr. Abernathy what are you..." Realization abbreviated her question. "Oh that poor man! Whatever could have happened...?"

The realization that she was about to faint cleared my mind. I steadied her with my arm and directed her back along the narrow pathway to the stairs.

"She continued talking as if to ward off reality."Perhaps he had a heart attack, yes; it was very likely a heart attack. We'd better call Dr. Caine, though I don't think there's anything he can do for him now. Poor Mr. Abernathy. I was so awfully fond of him. He was such a gentleman... with his daffodils and tulips... and the roses...." She was moving very slowly along the dimly lit passage till she reached the stairs. Phillip had apparently just arrived and was struggling with the sleeve of his starched white jacket as he met us outside of Mrs. Wainwright's office. By the looks on our faces he knew we had had some sort of shock. I blurted out quickly what we had found in response to his few brief questions. Mrs. Wainwright, though, remained unnaturally silent. I thought I saw some glimmer of warning shoot from his eyes to hers, but it may only have been a silent command to spare him her babblings. We sat her at her desk and made our way back to the basement door as I filled him in on the few details I had.

In the basement, we picked our way back through the maze, single file, to the area by the window. Phillip knelt over the body and in the dim light I could see his movements as he removed a stethoscope from a medical bag he had grabbed on our way. It must have confirmed his death. A moment later, he stood and removed the stethoscope without any hesitation.

"Looks like the old geezer had a stroke. Too bad but not surprising in a man of his age."

"Are you sure? I mean..." I stopped short. There was no blood, no odor, other than the dank musty smell of the place, no look of pain or terror in his face. Instead a look almost of surprise. Cause of death then, stroke. Short, sweet and simple. Was it really that easy to determine the cause of death or was it being used for my benefit? My mind went back to Mr. Abernathy's words of warning to me. How much of a coincidence was it that only a week later he should suffer a stroke? A stroke that a doctor diagnosed and dismissed in only a few seconds as the cause of death. "It's just that...I always thought of strokes as...being serious but not necessarily fatal." I let my words detour around my thoughts.

"Call this one serious then if you'd prefer. Either way, it's not going to change the outcome."

I glanced down at the body of Mr. Abernathy, dressed in his gum boots and weatherproof pants, a warm flannel shirt pale under the bright red suspenders, as if life had just been snatched from them too. A lonely place to die but perhaps fitting for him. It was apparent that to him this tiny basement corner had been most of his world. Cracked clay pots teetered on the window sill reaching for the cold gray light. Beside the upturned stacks of flower pots, several opened sacks leaned against the wall, containing whatever one puts in soil for fertilizer, and his few simple tools a small trowel, shovel, pruning shears lay carefully beside the shards of the broken clay pots. Amongst several assorted bottles, one lay on its side; a dark, wet stain beneath it.

It was twenty minutes later when I suddenly "remembered" the chair I'd intended to get from the basement. It took some mild persuasion to discourage Mrs. Wainwright from having one of the maintenance men bring it up. And it took me only a minute or two to do what I wanted to do in the basement before arriving back upstairs with the chair. In the pocket of my jacket an innocent aspirin bottle now held a wad of soaked Kleenex, wet with whatever the contents of the bottle had been that I had seen opened and spilled beside his body.

I spent the next several hours shuffling papers and hoping Phillip would stop by. Finding Mr. Abernathy's body had been both shocking and disturbing to me and my mind seemed to dwell on every detail of the discovery. Still, I had the rest of the 5th floor to see, something I was determined to do, maybe as a matter of pride and maybe to get it over and done with. But still lurking in the back of my mind, also, was Mr. Abernathy's warning. What had he meant by those few brief words? What was there about the fifth floor that I should have to be warned about? A sudden chill crept across my mind. Who had he meant when he said "her"? I had assumed he had meant Mrs. Rutherford. Was it someone else? Jennifer perhaps? Another patient? Even another staff member I hadn't yet encountered? Why the warning in the first place? More unanswered questions. And now Mr. Abernathy was dead. Was I being overly suspicious or did it seem an odd coincidence of circumstances? The thought of leaving this place once and for all was beginning to have decided appeal. But I would have to be patient. I was being treated with courtesy and tolerance, but without either rank or privileges. Yet the time on my hands only seemed to encourage my suspicions and arouse even more disturbing thoughts.

    Why though, when I did return to thinking with a degree of common sense, did I persist in sensing something about this place that was decidedly evil?

WEDNESDAY NOVEMBER 29th.

The death of Mr. Abernathy had left me both depressed and disturbed. Yes, I had been the one to discover his body, a shock in itself. And haunting his memory was still the warning he had given me. I had tried to convince myself that I'd had only two brief encounters with the man and he was after all a patient in a mental hospital and he was elderly – certainly well into his eighties. Perhaps he suffered from paranoia, perhaps he believed he was being persecuted. Perhaps. I was going in circles. Meanwhile I smiled and nodded and pretended just like everyone else that nothing had occurred.

Two days later, my pretense and my patience were wearing thin. I had shuffled papers in that dreary little room till I couldn't stand it any longer, and twice only glimpsed Phillip as he'd passed by the open door. Once he waved and the second time he'd started to come in when he was paged. I'd waited for him to return but he didn't and at 4:00 I gave up and went home.

Thursday morning I decided to take the bull by the horns. He was sitting at his desk just after he'd come in and I concentrated on sounding casual but determined.

"Hi! Gotta minute? I'd like to finish the fifth floor and be done with it. Do you think you could arrange the time either today or tomorrow?"

"Oh yeah, that's right." He glanced up and frowned. "All right, I'll see what I can do. Probably tomorrow I'll have to make the arrangements."

I felt annoyance creep into my mind. What arrangements? It was hardly a state visit. What was I interrupting? Unlike the routine of therapy sessions and recreational activity the rest of the patients were programmed to, as far as I could tell the patients on the fifth floor were gotten up in the morning, dressed, fed three times during the day, then put to bed and that was it.

But at least he'd agreed, however reluctantly, to take me up once more, so I begrudgingly contented myself with that. I'm sure that the suggestion that I would then conclude my study would be the passkey, at least to Mrs. Rutherford.

It worked. Friday, shortly after lunch, we were back once more behind the locked doors.

"Good afternoon doctor." It was a cold, barely civil greeting. Mrs. Rutherford stood waiting for us, defiance in both her stance and her voice.

It had been a week since I had first met her and yet I was struck by a distinct change in her. She seemed somehow more brittle than before, her eyes cold and piercing and the bony angles of her features more pronounced. Maybe her attitude had occupied my attention before, certainly that hadn't changed. If anything, there was now only a thin veneer scarcely covering the obvious hostility in her manner and voice. Again Mr. Abernathy's words echoed in my mind.

She chose to ignore me entirely. I approached her and made my voice sound as soothing as possible.

"Thank you for your patience, Mrs. Rutherford. I'm sure we won't be very long."

"The patients on this floor can be of no interest to you. You've been told that before." She spewed the words out like venom, her eyes cold, direct, hateful. It seemed for a moment incredible that a woman in her position should be so rude and resentful.

I glanced down. Her right hand gripped the counter edge. The knuckles were white with tension.

Phillip must have been embarrassed.

"If we could have the files ah we can get started."

For an awkward moment as I returned my glance to her face, she remained still. The lines round her eyes seemed more pronounced the skin strangely wax like and colorless, the graying hair dry and thin. Then she turned abruptly to the filing cabinet and slowly withdrew several file folders and handed them to Phillip while she returned her cold stare to me.

It was Phillip's turn to break the tension as we moved down the corridor.

He put his arm round my shoulder and whispered, "I think she's really becoming quite fond of you probably wants to invite you to tea!"

I hissed back, "Served with ground glass! She absolutely hates me! Why?"

"This is her territory, has been for years. She lives here, works here; this is probably all she has to live for. I suppose she considers you a threat you're young, pretty, bright, full of all kinds of new ideas and she doesn't want any part of them. Changes are threats to most people, and she doesn't see any reason to tolerate any kind of change after all these years."

"How many years?"

"God knows! They probably built her the same time as they built this place back in the Dark Ages. I dunno. Thirty forty years? Woodcroft mentioned once that she'd emigrated from

England where apparently she'd been a nurse in a psychiatric unit of one of the veteran's hospitals in England. Probably good practice. I imagine she had to deal with some pretty severe cases."

"You say she lives here?"

"Yeah." He turned and nodded his head in the opposite direction. "Down the end of the hall see that door? They had a staph staphylococcus epidemic back in nineteen eighty-two. It hit a lot of the hospitals pretty hard at a time when nursing staff was very hard to get. What staff they had were working twenty-four hour shifts, sacking out on cots in the corridors. She had the whole floor to handle practically by herself. There were probably three times the number of patients there are now. That space used to be a dormitory so she stayed on and made it her quarters. Not unusual they used to provide housing for almost all the staff in those days since this place used to be pretty much out in the sticks."

"But she must get some kind of help or relief?"

"Oh yeah. During the day the aides and orderlies do all the work feeding, bathing, etc. Midnight to 8:00 and weekends there's a relief supervisor who comes in a Mrs. ah Shirk Shirkosky something like that. Really doesn't do anything I suppose but there has to be someone on duty twenty-four hours a day. Besides, units like this are required to maintain twenty-four hour security checks."

"What's she like?"

"Shirkosky? About as lovable as Rutherford!" He grinned as I made a face. "Seriously, I dunno. I've only met her once. She's a big Ukrainian woman, reads romance novels and sips coffee laced with Scotch all night long. At least that was what she was doing the one and only night I ever saw her."

"Isn't drinking on duty usually frowned upon? Most places you'd get fired!"

"This isn't most places! We don't exactly have people beating at our door wanting to work up here. In fact, to get anybody to stay any longer than six months in places like this is rare. This isn't exactly a Teddy Bears' Picnic."

"I gather that."

"You ain't seen the worst yet! Ready?" He'd been standing outside a door, his hand resting on the door knob. I gritted my teeth and nodded. Whatever horror I was going to be confronted with was going to be presented without introduction.

I was surprised at seeing a man I assumed to be a native North West Coast Indian. He wore his white hair in a long braid down his back. His weathered brown skin was creased and cracked like a desert, darkened with long years of wind and cold ingrained in his native Indian heritage. He held a small box in his trembling hands, mumbling either about it or to it, the words quite meaningless.

"Your typical lunatic." Phillip stood in the doorway, his hands deep in his pockets. "Or if you like, the third stage of syphilis. Leave syphilis untreated for twenty years and it eventually invades the brain. A few cc's of penicillin even ten years ago, and he would have been enjoying his grandchildren now instead of being locked up here."

He slung an arm round my shoulder and spoke in mock seriousness.

"The moral of that story, luv, is to be pretty picky about who you sleep with." He steered me out the door. I grimaced at his remark.

"But surely syphilis never reaches such advanced stages anymore?"

"Wanna bet? It's now considered to have reached epidemic level among teenagers, many of whom will never receive treatment and who will infect their unborn children, unknowingly. Hell, half the asylums throughout the world, up till even this century, were filled with victims of one kind of venereal disease or another!"

I must have looked shocked.

"Hey, the medicine man isn't the twentieth century miracle worker a lot of people think he is. Nine tenths of what's out there we know nothing about, and the tenth we treat we don't prevent it, we don't cure it, we treat it."

I wondered what short, sweet appraisal he'd give his own field.

"And psychiatry?"

Witch doctors, with their black spells and magic and potions, their charts and evil spirits." He hadn't had to give it a moment's thought.

"It would seem by that you have a rather low opinion of your profession."

Just an honest one. When you strip away the theories and philosophies and the medical jargon we know bugger all about the brain."

"That must be depressing."

"Around here it is caretaking this vegetable factory. Don't look so appalled. Have you seen anyone up here who isn't?" I wanted to say yes, the Drysdale girl, but I bit my tongue. He shrugged with a sense of finality.

"See, they've all been through the mill – lobotomies, electro shock, drug therapy, insulin. Anything that was worth a shot has been tried. Nothing worked. They go on living because physiologically the body will damn well do as it pleases with or without most parts of a brain. And the laws stand behind the organ called the heart not the brain. As long as it functions, the taxpayers pay the forty-nine thousand per person per year to see they get put in their jammies and go to beddy byes each night."

He put an arm on my shoulder and led me out of the room. I hadn't been as shocked at his cynicism so much as surprised that he would display it so flagrantly in front of me. He was undoubtedly bright, with a promising future and I couldn't think of him as having any intention of making this place his career. Why then the vendetta? What in fact was he doing in a place that he had himself called nothing more than a vegetable factory? What possible sense of challenge or accomplishment would he find here that would keep him on staff? I drew the only conclusion I could.

In his peculiar style he was telling me I was wasting my time here at Island View. Here particularly on the fifth floor. If they hadn't been able to find the key to unlock these broken minds, I with my Florence Nightingale bag of toys and trinkets was wasting their time, even adding insult to injury, since surely these patients had to be termed their professional failures. It was a humiliating thought.

How many patients were there left? Surely not many. I suddenly wanted to get it over with and leave. Rutherford had been right. I had no business up here.

"Hey." He cupped a hand under my chin and I was forced to look up. "I'm sorry to lay it all out on you, but you didn't look the type to be sold the "oh Mr. so-in-so "is making steady improvement" routine that everybody else buys. I may not be the whole answer to schizoids and psychos but I'm deadly on the tennis court and I make the best damn banana daiquiri you ever tasted!"

I had to laugh. The tension, at least for the moment, had gone.

"I'll remember that! Who's next?"

"Oh, just a couple of your average garden variety psychopaths."

We tapped lightly on the next door we'd reached and a deep voice muttered from behind, "Yeah?"

It was a slightly larger room than the others, and with the two male patients in it I could see why. One lay stretched out on his bed, fully dressed except for his shoes, his head cradled in his folded arms. He had reddish hair and freckles in a face that, with his eyes closed and feathered with long dark lashes, was angelic. A trace of a smile curved at his lips. Whether he was actually sleeping or not we were not to know.

"Hello Benny."

"Hi doc." Benny sat at a small table that faced the window. He was preoccupied with balsa wood and wire which he, in a crude attempt, was fashioning into a replica of a sailing vessel, the old and faded drawing he was using as a guide taped to the window above him. He was a large hulking man, the muscles in his massive shoulders and neck only beginning to soften with age. I'd guess him to be fifty or so. He wore a dark green shirt and pants which I'd come to know as the institution garb for patients. His graying hair had thinned, revealing traces of scars that ran across his forehead and back across his head.

"This a new ship?"

"No."

"Did you finish the last one you were building?"

"No."

"How's Ted?"

"Okay."

"And how are you?"

"Okay."

"Good luck with your ship."

"Yeah."

We were back outside and headed slowly down the corridor before Phillip made any comment.

"The red haired fellow lying on the bed? Decided in the middle of the high school prom to have his own celebration. He drove two of his classmates and their dates out near Burnaby Mountain and blew their heads off with his father's shotgun. Five years later, after presumably being cured, he beat an old man and wife senseless. They had refused to hand over their car keys when they caught him attempting to break into it. The husband died of his injuries and Ted was up on another murder rap. This time he got sent here for keeps. After all, what institution is complete without at least one serial killer!"

He'd looked so innocent lying on the bed. I should have guessed that there was an ugly, dark side.

"And Benny?"

"Benny's history goes back to the early 50s. He was a trucker driving rigs up from California to Alaska. He'd come up to the interior of the province and decided he'd spend some time there. He met some gal that worked in the one and only saloon in town and they had a hot and heavy affair, until they found her one morning nude and very dead in a cheap motel just outside of town, with a stocking round her neck. She'd suffocated, but not by the stocking. They found semen in her throat. Benny had left town. Seven years later Benny was charged with murder in the death of a housewife who had been found raped and murdered down in Georgia but he slipped through their hands before he could be brought to trial. For a while he seemed to lie low. Then two teenage girls were last seen in his company at a truck stop in Florida. Their bodies were discovered four days later. They had both been raped, then strangled. There was also evidence of necrophilism.

"There was a statewide manhunt and he was picked up, charged and sentenced for first degree murder. He'd served nine years when, in a prison riot, he escaped custody. He was picked up twenty-three days later. The body of a ten year old girl was found a short distance from where he'd been holed up. She'd been raped and strangled.

"If you know anything about prison law and sex offenders, his life wasn't worth a nickel. They only managed to keep him alive because he'd been segregated from the rest. This time he'd gotten a 'not guilty by reason of insanity.' He was going to spend the rest of his life locked up in some kind of institution. But because he'd been so elusive, nobody was prepared to accept him. He had, after all, gotten away from the police twice and even escaped from prison once. A lobotomy was the only answer."

"But I thought that they found they didn't work?"

"They did. But that was back in the late '50's. And in Benny's case, I'm not so sure they really cared. They were never going to be able to release him but they wanted him manageable. He is. He eats, dresses himself and even does a number of odd jobs round here. This floor is his life."

"But doesn't he remember what his life was like before? Doesn't he think about tomorrow?"

"Nope! You need more brain matter for that than what they left him with!"

"And you said psychiatrists were witch doctors that's diabolical enough to make me believe it!"

"Oh, don't condemn them all. A few have been hacking up brains for the good of mankind. Others have been doing the same thing, except with a few more ah casualties. When the masses said "no" to death and the death penalty was abolished, that left the only alternative. They get to spend the rest of their lives in an institution. For the criminally insane, the only choice is a psychiatric ward.

"Not guilty by reason of insanity is the only verdict any smart lawyer knows he's got half a hope with. As for his client this place is a picnic compared to a Federal pen. The hospital board frowns on the blackjacks and rubber hoses so patients are, 'altered' to make them a little more "manageable."

"C'mon one more to go." He pulled himself away from the wall where he'd been lounging and started off down the hall, while I tried to digest this alternative to death that I had never had to consider.

His cynicism had become contagious. "You've saved the best for last?"

He chuckled. "You might say that if not the best, at least the most interesting!"

Each patient's room had had a locked door, a number and a small wired observation window. We turned off the main hall at the extreme end. Two heavy fire doors stopped us abruptly. There was an old fire exit sign and in each of the doors two observation windows had been cut, under which a heavy iron bar with a padlock rested across the doors. I could barely make out more iron bars on the other side, in addition to the wired glass. I watched Phillip take a small key, which he inserted in a metal plate in the wall by the door.

By way of explanation he said, "We have an alarm system on this door. Forget to turn the bloody thing off before you open those doors and you'd think we were having an air raid."

From the same key ring he now chose another to unlock the padlock. He released the iron bar and the doors gave way to a small chamber beyond. Fluorescent light washed the gray green walls and I picked up the configuration of what must be another kind of alarm, set into the wall.

Another metal plated door occupied the opposite wall, and I could see what must have been sliding panels, probably used for observation. All were closed.

Phillip had closed the doors behind us and moved over to a panel of light switches.

"Okay. I'm going to turn the white lights out and then in a second I'll turn the red lights on. It will take your eyes a few moments to adjust, then I'll open the observation windows."

"Okay." I felt my palms, cold and clammy, and my body stiffen. Blackness closed in. My arm groped out in Phillip's direction but he wasn't there.

The darkness was absolute there was no light whatsoever. A faint smell of disinfectant mingled with the pungent smell of urine and body odor. There was no sound at all the silence and the blackness seemed to press down on me like a weight, and I struggled to remain calm.

Phillip moved somewhere in the darkness and the room took on an eerie red glow. He brushed past me as he slid one of the observation windows open and I sensed, rather than saw, a red light come to life somewhere behind the windows.

I saw nothing. I moved cautiously closer to the window, my fingers against the glass as my eyes tried to see in the dimness. Slowly they focused on what I now assumed was a concrete floor with the remains of what I was beginning to make out to be the carcass of an animal. Blackness stained the floor and pale points protruded from the flesh, I gradually made out to be bone. Then my breath caught in my throat as a great, hulking creature lumbered out of the darkness towards me.

"My God!" I reeled backwards, against Phillip, who stood behind me. Only inches away from me on the other side of the glass was an ape like face. Flared nostrils twitched in an animal like way as the wide, flat face moved even closer. Coarse black hair hung from the cheekbones and jowls and small dark eyes held my stare like deadly steel needles. From some deep, dark hell a sound emerged inhuman, unreal a soft, low growl that seemed to move from some deep and primitive jungle.

"Easy, easy!" Phillip held me tightly as my legs threatened to give way and my breath came in gasps.

I was paralyzed with horror by what I saw and my mind groped in disbelief. It was inhuman. Surely to God...this couldn't be.

It moved toward the carcass a great shaggy body massive in size and stooped as it lumbered the few steps. A great hair covered arm swept forward and grasped with long, claw like fingers into the flesh and effortlessly dragged it a few feet where it crouched against the wall. The fingers dug deep and then moved to its mouth, dripping and bloody. It began to eat.

Phillip slid the observation window closed and switched on the light.

I was aghast. In the sudden harshness of the white light my face must have registered absolute disbelief. "That animal...," I began.

"'The Animal,' as we affectionately call him, is Samuel Louis Johnson, entirely human and not Bigfoot, a Sasquatch or the Missing Link. God, you're white as a sheet let's get out of here and I'll see if I can get you something to drink." He duplicated the same procedure with the locks and I stepped, weak and trembling, through the doors that he closed and padlocked, and reset the alarm system. Along the hall, two straight-backed chairs and a small table passed for a lounge and Phillip sat me down in one of them while he headed off in the direction of an orderly pushing a wheeled cart at the far end of the hall.

Slowly the immediate shock began to wear off and a small degree of resentment set in. I'd been horrified at what I had seen and I wasn't sure if I was more angry with myself at my reaction or at Phillip who hadn't bothered to forewarn me.

He returned with a metal tray with cups of coffee and two shot glasses. He put the tray down and handed me a glass.

"Here, drink it. Brandy I dare say it's not Napoleon, but it's brandy."

I knew that brandy was often given to patients to reduce the after taste of medicine in most hospitals at one time and I was very grateful as I tasted the biting warmth of it that this place retained the practice. It was at least one small gesture of humanity.

Gradually my composure returned. "Tell me about Samuel Johnson."

Phillip leaned back casually in the chair and took a couple of gulps of the steaming coffee. "If you remember your history of the Yukon gold rush, you'll know thousands headed north to make their fortunes, from as far away as even Mexico and Panama. A few made fortunes, but only a few. Most gave up and left, died trying, or lingered on, eking out a living one way or another.

"Well, Samuel Johnson was born to one such family that remained there – generation after generation on a small homestead outside of a town called Quitat. Unfortunately, he was born black. The Negroid color was very pronounced in him while the family was much lighter skinned and was probably accepted as being of Indian extraction. He was also born severely retarded and physically deformed.

"Fear, superstition, whatever, they did what they concluded was the only thing they could do. He acted like an animal so they treated him like one. His old man built a pit beneath the floorboards of the barn and that's where they kept him. They fed him raw game which they threw down to him, and I suppose between the animals and the hay the temperature never dropped low enough to kill him. But one winter it killed the old man and his wife the cold, and tuberculosis was pretty common in those years and he broke out. He must have stayed around the place for some time. Several of the horses had been slaughtered and there was evidence of cannibalism.

"Then he disappeared into the mountains and when a couple of the ranchers discovered the pit along with everything else, they formed a hunting pack to capture him. That wasn't difficult because he could only move at night. But it was some guy who figured he could make a fortune if he used him as a sideshow feature that brought him to the attention of the authorities.

"Believe me, he's been examined by half the doctors in the world. He's nothing more than a human being retarded, deformed, hostile and a victim of an inhuman circumstance."

"The red lights?"

"His eyes are weak and very light sensitive partly because he was raised in total darkness they haven't acquired even slight tolerance to white light. Red light reduces the pain and keeps him calm."

"It was eating."

"Horse meat. You and I might prefer our filets from prime beef but nutritionally there's little difference. He is after all, a big man close to three hundred and fifty pounds. It takes more than bird seed to feed him."

"And his hair it was so long, all over his body?"

"That's not an unusual occurrence. Most people who have that problem can be treated with hormones to either stop or reduce the growth."

"He just lives there... in the dark? Day after day... Does he ever get out for exercise?"

"Don't they all just live day after day? Yeah, he gets some exercise, but not too frequently. See, he's not only a big man but also very dangerous. You noticed the security systems. He's got incredible strength one blow from one of those arms would probably kill a man. He has to first be sedated so he becomes docile, and that's not easy to do. Then he's shackled with chains and taken out into the grounds. It takes about four guys and about two hours. And, of course, it has to be at night. Not only because of his eyes but because if any of the patients saw him they'd probably drop completely over the edge."

"But if he's human can he not be tamed and civilized?"

"If he had the mentality, sure but he hasn't. He's already reached the end of what he's got. He's safe, he's fed, he's warm, and that's as much as we can do."

"That's as much as they do for animals in a zoo!"

Phillip mocked surprise. "What did you think this floor was? A bed and breakfast? We tell 'em to take two aspirins and go home? Don't be naive this is a human waste disposal a dumping ground for human rejects that have time to put in before they get to the pearly gates. They're finished mentally, emotionally, intellectually, physically. All they have to look forward to is dying. And most of them, if they had their brains, would have wished for that years ago."

For a moment I was silent. I had been shocked, sickened, most of all saddened. "I'm sorry. I didn't mean to sound critical."

Phillip seemed to return to a more compassionate posture. "That's all right. It's not your fault. Society is full of people who worship screen stars and football players. We spend more on pet food than some countries spend on food for themselves.

Hell, your average commercial puts us all in a three bedroom rancher with two darling kids, while the wife damp mops her life away and they live happily ever after. Easy to forget about society's dropouts, and places like this and the countless others just like it."

This place had been horrible enough I couldn't bear to hear about any more "just like it." Slowly I drank the last mouthful of coffee and replaced the cup on the tray while I fought to come to terms with what I knew I had to accept. My shoulder bag offered up a compact and lipstick and when I had gone through the brief ritual of composing myself I turned to Phillip, hopefully looking refreshed and composed. Though my mind still wallowed in the shock and misery of seeing and hearing about Samuel Johnson, determinedly I now focused on another 'human reject'.

"Do you mind?" I tried to sound casual. "I thought I'd take a quick look at the Drysdale girl do you remember her room number?"

"Yeah 507." He nodded his head in the direction of her room. "Go ahead. I'll take this back."

It was as much as I could hope for a couple of minutes but it was better than nothing. As Phillip went off down the hall, I pushed open the door.

She was gazing directly at me as I entered almost as though she had been expecting me. We hadn't lowered our voices along the corridor; perhaps she had heard us as we approached.

Her hair had been tied back with a pale blue ribbon; otherwise she was swathed in a green terry bathrobe, like so many of the other patients wore. Without the heavy straightjacket she seemed terribly frail, even in the wheelchair in which she now sat.

"Hello Jennifer. How are you feeling?"

She either ignored my question or preferred not to hear it. Instead, out of the folds of the dressing gown, she extended her hands in which, very tightly held, lay a small blue book.

"Stor... story?" She spoke with considerable effort, the word coming between quick gulps of air.

I took the book a somewhat worse for wear child's book of nursery rhymes. A sudden sense of pity overwhelmed me to think that this frail, lonely young woman had only the capability of enjoying what a preschooler would soon have outgrown. I wondered who had ever read to her up here in this lost and forgotten world.

With only a few moments before Phillip returned and he would no doubt be impatient to leave, I could hardly oblige her. "Jennifer, do you have a favorite story? Perhaps I can come back...."

A shadow crossed her face and her arm groped at something I assumed was behind me. In seconds she had grown tense and small sounds fought their way forward. She was trying to communicate with feeble urgency. There was nothing behind me. I looked down and when I glanced back at her, caught a change of expression. My shoulder bag had been the object of her intention, the book being proffered in her outstretched hand. I moved slowly to put the small book in my bag and her expression calmed immediately. Then I understood. Like a small child with a newfound treasure, a rock, a leaf lovingly given to a parent, her little book was to be a gift. I don't suppose anyone she ever saw was dressed as I was without a uniform, with a handbag if the book was inside it, it would get taken away not casually put back on a shelf to reappear after someone had indulged her wishes.

"Thank you Jennifer." She was very calm now, looking at me like a gentle fawn from the safety of a forest. A faint sheen of perspiration remained on her forehead from the exertion. She looked so fragile and weak that I felt an urge to put my arms around her and comfort her.

Phillip was at the door. "Hi Jennifer feeling better this week?" Her eyes stayed with me, with that same fawnlike expression.

"I have a couple of things to go over with Mrs. Rutherford which will only take a couple of minutes, then we can go." Reluctantly I said my good byes as we left her room. Her gaze remained on me even as the door shut behind me. I don't know what I had gained in seeing her again for those few brief moments and I felt confused and depressed that I would in all likelihood never see her again.

I wished we could have just left. From down the corridor I saw Mrs. Rutherford at the nursing station and I did not want an encounter with her. My emotions were already frayed and the brief if false revival I'd enjoyed from the brandy had now abandoned me.

Thankfully Phillip steered me behind the station that opened to a small room presumably used as a lounge.

"Won't be a minute." He went back out to the desk and, faintly, I heard them talking.

I was in another shabby, dreary room that had, as I guessed by the small television set, been fixed up to accommodate the night supervisor. A hotplate sat on a rickety kitchen table, alongside a jar of instant coffee and cans of soup. A sagging, overstuffed sofa occupied the length of one wall, while a dilapidated table served as a coffee table in front of it. The only small evidence of something with a plan and purpose was the counter and sink with the cabinets above, immediately inside the door. From where I stood, I could see bottles and containers which I assumed to be medications of one sort or another. I was tempted to walk over and look, but I had no desire to eavesdrop on their conversation and less desire to be accused of it by Mrs. Rutherford. Instead, I wandered over by the TV to the windows and looked out.

It was already nearly dark. Night seemed intent on swallowing up these gray wintry days, yet I glanced at my watch to find it barely 4:00. The outside lights had come on and I could look down and see the cement walk that skirted the hospital and the shrubs that huddled near the building. I also recognized the convertible top of my 1965 Mustang amongst several that occupied the `visitors only parking area.' In fact, it was directly below these windows that I had been summoned by Mr. Abernathy exactly one week ago, and almost precisely at this time. Something in my mind tiptoed out of a pigeonhole and slipped into another. I gave chase but it was gone. Only the dust and cobwebs remained, my mental machinery too slow and tired.

I heard movements that suggested they were through their discussion, and this was confirmed by Phillip poking his head into the room. I slipped out from behind the nursing station as Mrs. Rutherford was returning files to the cabinet and so was spared her attention. It was only when we reached the main doors that I, for some reason, turned to glance back.

She was standing perfectly still, her cold eyes directed at me, while her hands on the countertop opened and closed into tight, hard fists. Her mouth had twisted into a hard, thin smile of pure malice. At that precise moment she appeared the personification of sheer evil.

FRIDAY DECEMBER 1st.

The rain slashed into me like invisible razor blades, as I scurried from the car to the marina office to pick up half a week's mail and then along a hundred yards further to the ramp. Exposed to the wind off the harbor now, it drove the rain even more viciously at me, and I cowered into the hood of my raincoat and, chilled and trembling, made my way the same distance again along the dock to my houseboat. She creaked and groaned against her bumpers in the unsettled water, the familiar sounds that on dark wintry nights I'd come to accept as her way of saying welcome home.

Humphrey greeted me at the kitchen door and then took up his position by his food dish. Still shivering, I first nudged the thermostat up a few degrees and exchanged my coat and shoes for a pair of warm slippers and a wooly sweater. Then I poured myself a drink and fed him enough to keep most cats fat and happy for a week. As far as he was concerned, he'd probably starve to death by morning.

Upstairs, I let the bath fill to nearly the top while I lit the fire and fed it to where it glowed contentedly. Then I climbed into the hot, soapy water and sank back in the soothing warmth. I sipped the icy cold martini and watched the flames gently caress the driftwood. I could still hear the wind howl as it threw rain against the windows in frenzied fits as though possessed by a demon to destroy the cocoon that enveloped me.

I lay back in the water for a long time, while my thoughts ambled in and out of the past two weeks at Island View. They lingered on the people I'd met and the patients I'd seen, the small touches of humor almost lost amidst the horror and futility of the place. Yet my reasoning had at some unmarked point in time begun to doubt and to question, and now it lay trapped in a cobweb of suspicions that lurked in the crevices of my mind.

With some reluctance I stepped out of the tub, dried myself off, donned a cozy quilted dressing gown and my slippers, and padded downstairs to prowl the refrigerator. I was in luck if you call cold chicken, salad and a bottle of white wine (cold, naturally), luck. I put it all on a tray, turned out the lights, and retreated back upstairs to the warmth of the fire.

Twenty minutes later, I had finished dinner, checked my email, then climbed into bed. I spent ten minutes trying to absorb myself in a late movie that I concluded was not only bad but quite likely to get even worse. I left the picture on and turned down the volume, in the unlikely event it would all come together, and dug into my shoulder bag for the newspaper and mail I'd picked up on the way home.

There was nothing of particular interest in any of the mail. I sorted the bills and routine correspondence from the junk mail and turned to the newspaper. Government budget cuts, inflation, another Middle East crisis and in the leisure section even a recipe for Soya beans which sounded perfectly awful. I even glanced at the crossword puzzle, when, pondering the name of an Indonesian river fish, that I dozed off. I must have slept quite soundly for the first hour or so. Then the wind increased and the sounds of the house seeped into my unconsciousness. I awoke and lay in the darkness, listening to the rhythmic change in the movement of the fireplace damper, the sweep of the fern against the window, the creak of the downstairs lamp swinging from its bracket. The house increased its moans and groans as it was rocked back and forth in the water by the wind. None of the sounds were loud enough to be disturbing but the movement itself aroused alertness like some early warning system that comes from living on the water. It was an instinct that I had acquired, like most boaters do. Not everybody experiences it Rob, for instance, apparently could sleep through a tidal wave. But I, who had always enjoyed deep and uninterrupted sleep, now like a mother's response to a needy child, seemed to be subconsciously aware of the contrast between the stillness of the house in calm water and its subtle movements in protest to high winds and rough seas.

Still needing sleep, my mind refused it, lingering instead in twilight of scenic wakefulness. It began to play like a cat hunts at night, stalking and pouncing on things both real and imagined. People from the past entered front and center to perform their roles, often ludicrously unrelated to themselves, and irrelevant objects took on great importance as dreams so often depict.

Minutes turned to an hour the charade continued even as the house grew still and the wind called its bluff.

Restless, I sat up and turned on the bedside lamp. Somewhere on the bed the crossword puzzle lay where was it? I fumbled through the newspapers and mail and my fingers felt the hard edge of the book. Jennifer's little blue book. I'd almost forgotten about it lay amongst the scattered papers. It seemed even more dog eared and shabby now. A Child's Book of Fairy Tales was the title. The first pages consisted of big letters and simple illustrations of kittens and houses, smiling suns above pastures of grass and cows in that innocent world of wonder to a child and felt a little guilty at having taken the book. I'd seen no books or toys, games or activities, and I cringed at the thought that they were probably considered unnecessary on the fifth floor.

Mildly curious I slowly began turning the pages. Humpty Dumpty, Jack and Jill until the final one caught my attention.

As any child might do, the page had been scribbled on with wide, inconsistent crayon marks that jerked all over the page green and red and blue and yellow. I could imagine the gentle disapproval of any mother seeing her child scribbling in a story book. Perhaps the countless crossword puzzles and other word games I dabbled with provoked me to reach for a pencil and then down to the floor for a discarded envelope. I was suddenly alert. Slowly I traced each crayoned line in the familiar rhyme. BAA, BAA BLACK SHEEP, HAVE YOU ANY WOOL? And then when I finished, I repeated what I had done, this time, with growing apprehension very slowly, very carefully.

Each colored crayon had either stopped or changed its erratic direction on, around or beside a single letter. I stared at the four of them not believing not wanting to believe that it could be anything more than a coincidence. I stared at them a long time frantically rejecting what I saw, trying to avoid the dreadful significance of what it could mean.

But they were there, staring back at me from the pages of a child's book given to me by someone long ago declared insane the four letters E, P, H, L

H E L P.

SATURDAY DECEMBER 2nd.

I woke up much later than usual, which I guess is the price for being awake most of the night. I donned my favorite slippers, a pair of cords and a ludicrously large wooly red turtleneck. I might not even have bothered with make up but great shadows under my eyes stared back at me over the toothbrush, contrasting harshly against the washed out color of my face. I added some blush and pulled my hair up into a heap on top of my head. It was a long way from great but it was better than looking like something that had washed up on the beach.

I curled up on the sofa with my first cup of coffee and enjoyed the luxury of doing nothing. Even the weather seemed in tune. It was doing nothing. It was still, the water sheet like and the sky gray. It would probably rain it usually did. The West Coast climate had a reputation to maintain. What we got spared in snow and ice and freezing cold we made up for in `precipitation.' It was a term Jack Stamford, the weatherman, always used. I guess it made rain not quite so wet and miserable.

But my conscience got the better of me, or more specifically, the laundry, dishes, the vacuuming and the refrigerator that now looked like Mother Hubbard's cupboard. I'd gotten those chores done and had the bucket of plaster, trowel and sponge out and part of a wall textured - a time consuming project I'd started weeks ago as part of the finishing details to the houseboat - when Paul unexpectedly showed up at the front door. He leaned casually against the wall, the fishermen's knit sweater under the familiar floater jacket emerging to meet his beard. The blue eyes twinkled with amusement.

"Good morning miss. Is the lady of the house in?"

I'd added a speckled work shirt over my sweater and still had the trowel in my hand when I opened the door. I must have looked like a painter on his first and last day on the job. "Thanks a lot!" But I laughed. C'mon in."

"Thanks, but no. I just stopped by to see if you had managed to get the porthole cleaned up. The weather forecast for tomorrow is worse than for today. So, I'm volunteering my porthole installing services this afternoon."

For a moment I'd forgotten it was ready for more work. "You just reminded me. I wanted to give it one more coat of remover before I polish it. It's coming up quite nicely."

"Then how about later this afternoon, if the weather holds?"

"Fine. I've got to do some errands first anyway. How about three?"

"Great, see you later." He turned up the collar of his jacket and waved as he headed off toward his boat.

I finished texturing the last section of the wall, cleaned myself up, made a quick list of groceries I needed to buy and things to do, and headed off along the dock up to the parking lot. By 2:30 I was back in time to add the brass polish to the porthole, put the groceries away and freshen my make-up. I was buffing the porthole when Paul arrived.

He deposited the tools outside on the deck before he came in, and beamed his approval at the porthole. "I'm impressed. When the Snow Goose is ready to have her hull scraped and painted again, I'll know who to call."

"I don't do bottoms, thanks just the same."

He laughed and headed out the door. "Tell me exactly now where you'd like it positioned." We alternately held it in position, Paul first and then me, while he penciled in the markings.

Over the sound of the saw he shouted, "I don't suppose you have any kind of caulking?" I looked blank for a moment and then remembered some half used cardboard containers I hadn't discarded.

"Hang on." A moment later I was back with an almost full tube of caulking.

"Just what we need." He selected one. "Probably just enough left to do the job. Now, a caulking gun?"

I brightened. I remembered the builder using one then frowned. "No."

"Okay. I've got one. If you'll go over to the Goose you'll find it on a shelf by the stairs. Bring a couple of the long handled screwdrivers, too. They'll be there." He turned back and concentrated on the thin, curving line.

I had two routes to his boat that I could use, one of them intended for pretzels, not people. It was the lower dock, an obstacle course of pilings, on which were housed the meter boxes for power and hose connections. It meant leaning out and around the already narrow dock with the cold water waiting for anyone who failed to maneuver the course. The upper dock twenty-five feet above was wide and unencumbered, the narrow ramps leading off on either side down to the slips. A tin shed roof high above that side sheltered the full range of large and luxurious pleasure craft that at this time of year were nearly all in hibernation. The Snow Goose, at the very end of the one hundred foot dock, I reached by the upper dock within a few minutes encouraged by the cold afternoon air that needled its way through my sweater.

I was inside and I'd found the shelf but that's all. There were tools and wire and tubing but nothing even remotely like a caulking gun. Damn... But if he had one, then it had to be somewhere on the boat. I continued down the stairs and found myself in a forward cabin which by the boxes and rolled up sleeping bag I assumed was being used for storage. One of the boxes looked promising. In the dim light I picked my way through more wire and metal, small boxes of screws and nails, but nothing I could begin to think of as approaching either a caulking gun or a screwdriver.

Directly opposite the forward cabin and under the wheelhouse was a door closed by a padlock. Probably more storage I thought, but my fingers hooked through the lock as I maneuvered my way back out into the bottom of the stairwell. To my surprise, the padlock yielded as I pulled down. If it had meant to be locked, it hadn't been. I pushed the door a few inches ajar. Inside was pitch black till I groped and found a light switch.

Two very dark and grimy engines sat connected by dozens of equally dark hoses that led over and under each other. Of course, the engine room! He'd said something about the engines maybe he'd left tools down here. A small bracketed shelf ran across part of the front and side of the hull a good part taken up by black boxes which looked not unlike the batteries in cars. I assumed that's what they were. There was also an assortment of other equipment mostly dials with needles, round compass typefaces and graph type indicators. I couldn't begin to figure out what it was all about.

I still was nowhere. I was about to back out when I saw a toolbox half hidden under some wire. I opened it.

There was a gun.

It was not the kind I'd been looking for. This one was black, heavy, and probably loaded with ammunition. Very gingerly, I picked it up and stared at it for several seconds and then put it back, exactly as I had found it. Guns had always implied a fringe to life I was content to avoid. Whatever his reasons for having one I could only guess. Maybe living aboard a yacht was riskier than I thought. Still I had an uncomfortable feeling of having discovered something I shouldn't have.

I backed out, switched off the light, and replaced the padlock as I had found it, closed but not locked. I climbed the stairs back to the wheelhouse and almost instantly found the caulking gun and the screwdrivers, exactly where he said they'd be. But there were two sets of stairs, the one I had gone down to the forward cabin and the second set leading to the galley, head and aft cabin. He hadn't said which set of stairs. I had the nasty feeling of having snooped into areas that hadn't been called for and I'd been a lot longer than should have been necessary.

By the time I got back he was sanding the edges of the large, gaping hole.

"I thought you must have gone over the side, I was about ready to go and fish you out."

"Nope. Union labor, that's all. I had to have my lunch break it was good peanut butter and jelly sandwiches, and my coffee break. I finished the brandy, then, let's see, time out and then...."

He made a mock attempt to keep a stern voice. "Look, you may have had your lunch but I seemed to have missed mine." And then, just in case I might have ignored the hint, he added "and it better be good! I don't do this kind of highly skilled craftsmanship for nothing! Now if you'll hold it in place...."

"Yes sir," I teased back. A minute later I retreated while he fastened the bolts and was cleaning away some of the opaque waterproofing compound that had squeezed out around the outside edges when the first big splashes of rain began to fall.

I poked my head out of the kitchen like a gopher. "I hope you're serious about lunch – late as it is I just put a twenty pound turkey in the oven." His glance caught my joke. "Steak sandwich and a beer?" I offered.

"Sounds just fine!"

I clattered around the kitchen while he did the last of the work, and when he announced that the job was done, I eagerly stopped to both admire and thank him for the now gleaming porthole residing proudly in place. By the time I had lunch ready, he'd put the tools away and even had the fire going upstairs.

Four thirty Saturday it was already cold, almost dark and the rain was now pelting down.

We were both hungry and the sandwiches were good. Broiled sirloin steak sliced thin and served on hot garlicky French bread. After we had both wolfed them down, Paul leaned back on the floor cushions, with his second beer, appearing quite content.

"Ever considered a career as a chef instead of teaching the sick and disabled to be educated and independent?" His seemingly casual comment I found just a tad offensive. Surely I hadn't sounded like some poor deranged martyr convinced that an educational band aid would make all things better!

"Interesting prospect." I decided to dismiss my initial reaction as oversensitivity on my part. "

"I like my job - my real job that is, and I like people. I just don't like what I'm presently doing or seeing. Or maybe I just don't understand what I'm seeing."

"Such as..."

I hesitated. I was reluctant to delve into the events of the past week. But Paul seemed to have a coolly logical and sensible mind. He was uninvolved, unbiased, and I needed a sounding board, and some input. Maybe the whole thing would make more sense if I talked about it rather than having it rattle around in my head.

"You're sure you really want to listen to this?"

"Bribe me with another beer, and I'll listen to anything." The blue eyes crinkled in a gentle smile and he propped a pillow under his elbow as he settled back against the cushions.

I returned with two more beers and sat down with my back against the hearth.

"Well...," I began with a smile, "I'm not sure if it's the staff or the patients I find disturbing...."

He listened as I expected, quietly, attentively as I related the events, without interruption. I had left only a few details out, for reasons I didn't thoroughly understand, and I stopped with Jennifer's book. I got up and retrieved it from a drawer. I handed it to him. "I'd like you to look at this."

He accepted the book. "It has some significance, I assume." He turned it over and back and then thumbed through it quickly. For a moment I was disappointed; then he started at the beginning and turned the pages very slowly, his eyes scanning the words and illustrations. He stopped at the page scribbled with crayons. I sat very quietly. Then he continued turning the remaining pages and I suddenly felt defeated. He closed the book and handed it back to me. His expression remained unchanged. He spoke very quietly. "Those letters crayoned on spell HELP. Is that the significance?"

I was jubilant. "Yes! Paul, doesn't that seem weird to you?"

"Yes if that is the case."

"What do you mean?"

"Well, there could be a number of explanations. The most obvious could simply be a coincidence. It could have just happened to be those letters."

"But not likely."

"No it could have been planned but I don't suppose even that is unusual. I do know that some mentally disturbed people often think they're being persecuted or imprisoned. I've heard that they drop notes out of windows and do all kinds of things they think will eventually get them released."

"I suppose."

"You believe it was this girl Jennifer?"

"Mmm."

"But you can't be sure she used the crayon?"

"No."

"Perhaps the scribbling of the crayon was already in the book done by someone else years ago. Maybe it was exactly as you thought it was, a gift she wanted to give you nothing more."

"Could be."

"You don't sound convinced."

"Paul, I probably would be under normal circumstances, but there are too many other things that don't add up."

"Such as?"

"Well, Mr. Abernathy for example. He's the gardener I told you about that grows grew things all at the wrong time of the year. He warned me about going up to the fifth floor and about Mrs. Rutherford I'm pretty sure he must have been referring to her and then one week later, he's dead."

"How old was he?"

"In his eighties, maybe older," I said lamely.

"And you say it was a stroke?"

"I was told it probably was a stroke."

"You have a reason to believe it wasn't?"

"I just think it's rather strange that he would have a stroke so suddenly down there in the basement."

"Strokes are usually sudden."

"But they're not always fatal."

"What are you suggesting?"

I took a deep breath. "It was his suspenders."

"His what?"

"His suspenders. When I found him he was sprawled on the floor, his back up against the wall and he had on these bright red suspenders. I didn't think anything of it at first, until I remembered that they were holding up his weatherproof pants."

"Meaning?"

"Why was he down there on a Sunday night wearing weatherproof pants AND gum boots?"

"Maybe he had just come in from outside."

"Then there would have been water stains beneath his body. It poured rain Sunday, remember. That basement was too damp for them to have dried overnight."

"Why do you think it was Sunday night? Could it have been Sunday afternoon or even Saturday? Did you touch him at all to determine the state of rigor mortis?"

"No..." Reluctantly I answered. "I didn't. Somehow, it didn't seem right to disturb him. Besides, he was a patient. Surely a patient can't just disappear for several hours or overnight without somebody becoming concerned as to his whereabouts." I shrugged, the seeds of doubt beginning to grow in my conviction. Maybe he had had a stroke sometime over the week end and nobody knew or cared where he was. Was that possible? Was it also possible that he had become such a fixture around the place that he simply came and went as he pleased and therefore no one was actually responsible for him the way they were for other patients?

"He may not have been eccentric enough to garden in the middle of the night but perhaps he liked to wear his outside gardening clothes insides as well."

"I asked Wainwright about his boots and his jacket. She said that his jacket was always hung upstairs on a hook, and his boots were on the floor. He used to go outside through a door in the basement. They always knew whether he was inside or outside by whether or not his boots and jacket were there."

"Then you're suggesting he died by an unnatural cause." He phrased it discreetly, yet each question was loaded with bait. I was nearing the trap.

I wanted to say yes, damn it, I don't believe somebody conveniently goes down to the basement to have a stroke, when there is little down there of interest except a few pots, some pesticides and tools, particularly just one week after he had tried to warn me about the fifth floor. But I didn't. I bit my tongue.

"If I knew anything about chemistry I could probably prove it."

It was the bait and switch game now. Paul's voice seemed a degree more cautious. "What are you saying?"

"There was a spilled bottle of insecticide beside him. I sopped up some with a Kleenex and put it in an aspirin bottle. Not that that will do any good, unless it was analyzed, but I thought it was strange it should have been opened and spilled."

"It can't be the first time a gardener has knocked over a bottle of insecticide."

"It wouldn't have spilled if it was knocked over, unless the top was off. It was something he would have used outdoors, not indoors."

"Maybe it was hooch. Or rubbing alcohol. Or maybe it was insecticide, and the old boy decided to call it quits."

"You mean suicide? I can't believe that! Why now, after all these years?"

He paused to phrase his next question rather delicately. "Do you think perhaps you're applying your sense of logic to illogical circumstances? It is, after all, a mental institution. People are there because they're neither responsible nor logical."

"That's part of the problem. I've been trying for two weeks to convince myself that's the case. I... I just can't." I persisted. "Even the staff seems weird."

"In what way?"

"Woodcroft, the senior psychiatrist. Probably hasn't had a new thought in thirty years. He's classified them all in their pigeon holes and that's where everyone stays. Mrs. Wainwright is a weak little mouse who keeps herself busy organizing picnics and tea parties and little social outings to help improve `the social barrier' between the patients and the community. She either doesn't know half of what's going on, or doesn't want to know.

"Phillip Caine. Young, clever, probably very competent. But I don't understand why he's there. He fits that place like a square peg in a round hole. He has these cynical little witticisms which he probably thinks are clever. I think he's callous. He divides the rest of his time with wine sorry, daiquiris banana daiquiris, women and probably a bed."

Paul appeared amused. "Not an unenviable pastime. I take it you've been propositioned?"

"I expect to be."

"An offer you can't refuse?"

"Sorry. Too much the playboy for me." But then a thought crossed my mind. Maybe a date with dear Dr. Caine might reveal what he was really like and why he works at Island View.

Could I be that conniving? Maybe. But an evening with Caine, to find that out? I shuddered, and then continued.

"Then there's a Mrs. Rutherford a Margaret Rutherford who has to be the wicked witch of the north."

Why?"

"It's her perfectly lovable personality. Honestly, she's vile. She just reeks with hostility. If I ever turned my back on her she'd probably cut me up for cat food!"

Paul chuckled. "Oh, come now. She can't be all that bad!"

"Paul, she is! She's been there for years, in charge of that fifth floor. In fact, she even lives there."

"From what you've told me about some of the patients, maybe that's to be expected."

"But it even goes beyond that. She's openly so hostile, so protective of that floor, as if I'm going to upset her domain, or find or see something I shouldn't. She barely tolerates Phillip, and I gather he goes up there only when he absolutely has to. The patients on that floor get no visitors, they never go anywhere. They're virtually sealed off, not only from the rest of the hospital but from the rest of the world."

"She may be all those things you describe but even that's normal in some ways. Some people get locked into jobs that, after a number of years, take on undue importance. It becomes the only thing they live for, so it's natural that they would see someone else as a threat to their autonomy."

"That's what Phillip says."

As if he'd picked up my thought waves, Paul became more serious. "Why do I get the feeling you have a knack for finding yourself in, shall we say, unusual situations? Most people wouldn't have volunteered to do what you're doing in the first place."

"Unusual situations seem to have a way of finding me, I guess. I've been told I have a lot of curiosity. And you're right. I'm beginning to regret ever agreeing to do this job, as temporary as it is.

"So now where do you go from here?"

"That's the question. I've two choices. I've seen nearly all the patients out there and I can write up a report saying that there are no likely candidates and then simply fold my tent and steal away forget the place and the people."

"Or..."

"Or stay on some pretense or other. Perhaps do some patient interviews as if they were being considered candidates. At least long enough to find out if Jennifer's crazy or I'm crazy. Paul, if you'd seen her, she's so young and innocent, like an abandoned fawn left in the woods. God, what if just if she's not crazy. She's spent nearly her whole life in there. She'll die there, and no one will ever know."

"That could be a case of professional misjudgment. What you're suggesting happened to Abernathy is something even more serious. That's called `murder'." His eyes met mine with the full impact of that single word.

Despite the now glowing embers of the fire, I suddenly shivered. That one word, spoken so quietly, seemed to spread a cold dark fear through me.

"Would it help put your mind at rest," Paul spoke with sincerity, "if you knew for sure what was in that insecticide bottle?"

"Sure. But how?"

"That's not too difficult. Back in university we had to put in quite a bit of lab time. An old buddy of mine is still there went on into research biochemistry he's now a department head in

Physics York University. I don't imagine it would be too difficult to get him to have the ingredients analyzed."

"Oh Paul, that's fantastic!"

Impulsively, I threw my arms around him and hugged him, then jumped to my feet and returned with my bag and sat cross legged in front of him while I dug into it to retrieve the Aspirin bottle from a zippered compartment.

I was excited. Whatever the results, it was at least a positive move. "How long do you think it would take?"

"Maybe a week or two, I guess. Let's see, they're three hours ahead of us in Toronto," he glanced at his watch. "I'll call him Monday 'round seven, that should probably catch him in his office, and I can send this by air express after I talk to him."

I was jubilant! At least, until Paul's next question. "You know, of course, there's an organization that does this kind of detective work as well?"

"You mean the police."

"Mmm."

"You're thinking I should have gone to the police?"

"Just wondering why you haven't."

"I don't have any proof of anything. I thought there would have been some kind of procedure or inquiry or at least something maybe not the police but at least a medical examination, even to verify his death."

"How do you know there wasn't one?"

"I asked. At least I asked what became of the body."

"And?"

"He was cremated. The very next day. No family left or anything. They have an arrangement with the Memorial Society that takes care of the bodies."

"Body."

"What?"

"Body singular. Put it into the plural of bodies and you're turning the place into a slaughterhouse."

"Oh yeah. Sorry." It was a wicked thought but I couldn't resist. "That's right. The second body will be mine if Rutherford ever sees me again of the fifth floor!"

He gave me a rather reproachful look, then added, "So now what are you going to do, stay or leave?"

"Stay. Well, leave, actually. I've got some reports to be done at Vancouver General and St. Paul's for Yvonne, so I think I'll spend next week doing those. I'll just tell Caine I'll be back just to finish up the paper work. They'll be quite happy with that, if they think they're soon going to see the last of me. Maybe in a week we'll know the results of the analysis."

"OK. Sounds good. You work and I'm going fishing. All very sensible," he teased. "If I catch anything I'll remember what's-his-name. By the way, where is he?"

I reached over and pulled a large batt of raw wool aside. Humphrey was upside down and fast asleep.

"Only if you're in the habit of catching chopped liver, I'm afraid. He's fussy. But I'm not!" It was a rather blatant remark.

"I'll remember that, too." He pulled himself to his feet and looked down at me with a very steady gaze. "Seems I've got quite a lot to remember about you – fish heads, lunatics and a rusty cat!"

I howled at the image. "Not many people know me so well."

"I gather not. And I would like to get to know you even better; because you're definitely shall we say – unorthodox?"

"A ha! Nice way of saying I should be committed."

"No, but speaking of commitments, I have to go." He glanced at his watch. "You realize it's nearly seven o'clock – I've got a lot of work to do on the Goose to get her ready to go and five a.m. comes awfully early."

I wanted to protest. I wanted to say that the evening was still young and that I didn't want him to go. But I didn't. Instead, we headed downstairs and I retrieved his jacket from the closet.

"Thank you Paul. I really didn't mean to bore you with all my problems. And I really do appreciate the porthole. It looks grand."

"You're welcome. I'm glad you like it." Then he turned and brushed my hair from my forehead and planted a brief kiss on it. His hand tilted my face up to look at him. "Take care, huh?" The blue eyes gazed down at me and there was none of the amusement, the gentle teasing hints to his smile I'd come to know. He didn't wait for an answer, if indeed I was capable of giving him one. He looked down at me and then turned to pick up the tools from the corner of the kitchen floor. "I'll be back in touch when I've got some information. Okay?"

I scrambled to organize my thoughts and calm my feelings. "Happy fishing..." It didn't sound convincing. At the moment a week seemed like an eternity. "And thanks Paul. Good night." I watched him for several moments as he headed out into the rainy night towards his boat.

There was a part of me that had definitely been stirred by him. But now, slowly, I felt a calmness return in me, something I had tried moments ago to achieve. Beyond that problem I felt relieved and happy, pleased that I had unloaded my suspicions and now was content to follow through a reasonable course of action.

I collected the dishes and glasses and ran the dishwasher, and then remembered the rest of the groceries in the car. I sighed, reluctantly getting into my own jacket. The lesser of the two evils was to go up and get them now, rather than have to do it in the morning. I slipped into shoes and pulled the hood of my jacket over my head, grabbed the flashlight and my grocery cart and headed up towards the parking lot.

From high above me I saw the bent arthritic figure of Jimmy Nesbitt and heard his cane monotonously tap its way along the dock. As always I thought of the long lonely hours he spent as the marina's night watch man, patrolling the docks in the cold and rain and wind. I had always wondered why he hadn't found himself a job inside a warm comfortable building. But then to each his own, I guess. The thought made me snuggle into my jacket and scurry towards the parking lot.

The few items I left in the trunk of my car were staples that would keep, as I'd filled my grocery cart as full as it would go. I closed the trunk and was about to turn the flashlight off when it picked up on the rectangle of dry space where Paul's car had been parked. I had come to know the steel gray Datsun 280 ZX as I did most of the others if they were live aboards. "Our" parking spots were designated by name and the Snow Goose was freshly painted on the curb stop. He must have just left because the rain had been, and still was persisting. Maybe he'd forgotten something he needed. Or maybe he'd had no intention of going back to the boat. Then I remembered the gun I had uncovered.

My effervescent mood evaporated once more under a cloud of doubt.

FRIDAY DECEMBER 8th.

He was young and frail and dying. By some inexplicable twist of fate, he had survived against incredible odds. His parents, brothers, sisters and most of his village had been killed, and he had been left hungry, sick and abandoned. Days, weeks passed before he was finally placed under the care of the Red Cross. A humanitarian group had been responsible for his arrival in Canada that was to be his new home and eventually in the loving care of adoptive parents. But instead here, between the clean white, antiseptic sheets, and in one of the best of medical facilities, leukemia would triumph.

"We had hoped it would have lasted awhile longer." The "it" needed no explanation. The disease was well known for its remissions - the hope and despair it cast out to all those who loved and cared for all of its victims.

To lose Timothy was going to be devastating. Almost as much for me as it would be for Yvonne. Timothy had been her first candidate, before his disease had become as acute. He had expressed an intense curiosity about this new world and an inquisitiveness and eagerness to learn that had endeared him to the medical staff.

Whatever hurt and pain was to be inflicted he bore without a tear or whimper. In his nearly five years he had already learned those lessons well.

One by one I unhooked his fingers from mine as we said our good byes. He clung as tightly as he always did in his special way and I gave him a big hug, my voice already caught by the lump in my throat.

Outside his door I turned to Janet. "You'll call me, won't you if he if his condition changes?"

"Yes, of course I will." She was several years older than me and at the moment she was exhibiting a lot more professional composure than I was. I had little doubt she felt the same way. Five years ago she had lost her thirteen year old daughter to leukemia. She'd had a lot of practice in pain.

"And remember lunch we promised ourselves! Anyone living on this cafeteria's rabbit food deserves a reward."

Janet, I think, made a pretense of dieting out of sympathy for her nursing friends who attracted extra pounds by just the thought of food. Janet could hardly have weighed more than 110 pounds. Added to her inherent slimness, her dark shiny hair, always in the proverbial page boy, gave her the youthful prettiness of a teenager. I had met her on a number of visits with Yvonne when we'd come to visit Timothy and I'd grown very fond of Janet, but then anyone who knew her felt the same way.

You're right! Her response was enthusiastic. "When?"

We decided on the day, the time, and chose a small cafe, known for its excellent food and pleasant atmosphere. We waved our good byes at the elevator as I left. I was looking forward to our lunch. Janet was good for the soul.

The week had vanished and the brief exhilaration of the break away from Island View had quickly evaporated leaving a vague depressing taint to the days. There had been no word from Paul, and no sign of the Snow Goose. Though I hadn't expected to see either it only added to my depression and in the times I'd given it thought I wondered if I shouldn't have simply dismissed it all chalk up Island View and everything about it to an unpleasant experience – but the kind that makes one older, wiser, and sadder.

Sunday morning the Snow Goose was in her slip. I had walked out along the dock to set the crab pot and glimpsed her white prow protruding beyond the edge of the dock. I debated whether or not to walk over and find Paul but decided against it. He knew a great deal more about me than I knew about him. In fact, I was very aware of just how little I did know about him. Arriving on board Sunday morning uninvited, I concluded, would be to cross a threshold of familiarity I preferred to leave intact. Then, as if by telepathy, he phoned.

"Wanted to know if you liked your fish poached or broiled?"

"Broiled will be fine with lemon please." I was amused at the conversation and more than pleased to hear from him.

"Okay, but you'll have to bring your own."

"And what time are you serving la fish?"

"Now."

"Brunch is it?" I glanced at my watch.

"If that's what you want to call my breakfast, I don't mind."

"All right. Be over in a few minutes. Anything else you need?"

"Just you and your lemon."

I was pleased to be seeing Paul again. Very pleased. Which is why I was telling myself I was merely anxious to know the results of the analysis.

I changed my sweater and slacks, gave a quick brush to my hair, freshened my make up and then applied a liberal spray of my favorite cologne. I grabbed two lemons from the fridge which didn't seem like much of a contribution at all. I found a bottle of Zinfandel and headed out the door.

"Anybody afloat?" I stepped on board.

A voice greeted me from somewhere forward and below. "Make yourself at home. Just about finished."

"What are you doing down there?" I called back.

"Applying band-aids to a couple of hose connections. Nothing serious that a lifejacket won't save us from."

I wandered over to the edge of the stairs and peered down into the engine room. "That's reassuring. I've never had to tread water while eating brunch before."

He emerged from the engine room, the amused look in his blue eyes, a trace of a grin barely evident in the dark shaggy beard, the pipe at rest in the corner of his mouth. It had been a long week. I wished I'd had an excuse to greet him with more than a casual quip.

I started to say something just as he turned off the lights in the engine room and closed the door. Instead I shut my mouth. Just beyond him I had had a glimpse of the engines. They were different. They were bright green with white lettering and with shiny pieces of metal. Even the black hoses seemed to be shiny reflecting the overhead light. Was the shape of them different as well? I couldn't remember. But I did remember seeing the engine room. If they had been replaced that must have been a major job and expensive. But he'd been away fishing on board the Snow Goose

His hand on my shoulder startled me. "You were saying?"

"Oh, nothing."

"Good. Anything I can't stand is a yakking woman."

A moment later Paul handed me a steaming mug of black coffee. I sipped the black liquid pensively and tasted the bite of whiskey. He'd returned to the galley and I was alone with my thoughts. I was beginning to feel more of the same frustrations. Was I becoming a doubting, untrusting soul, poking into corners and questioning every motive by everybody? I never had before. Why was I now so preoccupied with such simple things that didn't make any sense? There could be a thousand reasons why Paul would have neglected mentioning the engines. But I had a hard time thinking of even one.

He returned to the wheelhouse and I watched him place the beginnings of our meal on the table. Presumably he found the wheelhouse more spacious and comfortable than the galley below. For a big man, his movements were precise, efficient. He seemed to exhibit the necessary skill to cope, to survive, which I began to think he did very well. Strangely, as I studied the wheelhouse, there was very little evidence of who or what he was, as there had been just as little in our conversations.

He caught my gaze. "Don't judge the meal by the table setting – Plastic plates and forks can make anything appetizing if you're hungry."

And I was. The aroma from the small galley was having its effect. By the time Paul returned with the two plates, I knew why. Fresh cod, seasoned and broiled in butter with fried eggs and potatoes. And cold white wine. Conversation dropped off as we devoured the food. It was my turn to pat my stomach as I leaned back from the table. We sipped our wine ambling through a half dozen subjects, all casually impersonal. I'd helped clear the table and put things away. "That really was good! I bet it didn't even come from The Granville Island Fish Market! He hadn't mentioned the fishing trip and I half hoped that with a little prodding he might. But it wasn't going to work that way.

He laughed as he got up and retrieved his pipe from the ashtray by the controls. "And you thought peanut butter and jelly sandwiches were my specialty?"

"No but then I thought that would spare me from having to tell you how good it was. I just can't stand one upmanship."

"I wouldn't let it worry you." He struck a match and sucked on the pipe, slowly and repeatedly, extinguishing the match only a moment before it would have died. "You may have enough to worry about." He was gazing very directly at me, his cool blue analytical eyes studying my face.

I was suddenly alert. "What do you mean?"

"I've received the analysis of the insecticide."

I felt a cold chill move down my spine. "What, what was it?"

He spoke very calmly, the pipe still in his mouth, his eyes steady and level. "The chemicals that one would find in a commercial insecticide."

"Nothing else?"

"You mean had there been any arsenic added?"

I was silent. If he intended his last statement to ridicule me, I hardly needed it. I already felt foolish. Paul wasn't exactly the man I wanted to appear to as the overly melodramatic female, an Encyclopedia on the Methods of Murder on her bedside table but then if, in fact, it was insecticide and nothing else, my suspicions were in error. Aside from my bent ego, I had nothing to worry about.

"I probably have watched too many episodes of CSI." It was a token gesture of dismissal. "They could stack up bodies like cordwood around that place and the cause of death would be attributed to dandruff!

"I wouldn't dismiss this just because you want to call it murder."

"Why not? If there was nothing in that analysis that would have killed him then he probably just... died of a stroke."

"I didn't say that. I said nothing had been added. What was in that analysis was quite lethal. Particularly if the concentrations had been altered."

I stared at him and stumbled over his words. "If the concentrations had been altered?"

He puffed on the pipe and continued. "What can kill a fly can kill an elephant for that matter a whole herd of elephants. The common aspirin can kill. One tenth of one gram of nicotine in tobacco which, incidentally, is one of the deadliest of all poisons, can kill a person instantly yet cigarettes are smoked by millions of Americans daily."

"But if the concentration was increased..."

"It was. But it's not unusual for a product to change its chemical structure over a period of time. That's one of the reasons people are cautioned against using outdated prescriptions. But proving that it was deliberately tampered with is another matter. And without a body or the bottle that contained the stuff, it reduces it all to suspicion."

"You mean that's it? Case closed? Forget about it?" I was exasperated. "You've just finished saying that the concentration had been changed just because we can't prove how or who...."

"Proof is a rather necessary ingredient in our judicial system. Without it you can scream bloody murder all you like! You'll probably get locked up in a place just like that one."

"Yeah and get fed an insecticide sandwich by some sickie who doesn't like my tulips!"

Paul's amused laugh was riddled with a very conciliatory tone. "Come now. That's being a bit melodramatic. You said you were going back there this week?"

"M'mm."

"Why not do what you have to do and just keep your eyes and ears open if anything else happens you think is strange and there's not likely to be then we can deal with that if and when that happens."

"You mean call when I've tripped over the next body?"

"If you like. I'll be around this week and I'll stay in touch, body or not."

I still felt disappointed, yet somehow reassured. I'd blurted out this whole business to Paul in the first place because I needed an objective viewpoint. The least I could do was to respect his advice.

"All right, I will. Thanks Paul, and it was a great brunch. I don't believe I even got my feet wet."

"I guess the Band-Aid worked." He slid the door open as I made the motions to leave. "Take care of yourself I'll call you later this week."

I waved a good bye and climbed the ramp to the upper dock and looked back down at the Snow Goose, resting quietly in the slip. She appeared almost ghostlike in the gray mist of morning. And like a ghost, I wondered where she had been and why. And as for her master, I wondered also about where he'd been and why. Why did I doubt that his week's absence was a simple fishing trip?

And now that I'd been given an indication there could have been something or somebody responsible for Mr. Abernathy's death, I was even more concerned. In fact, I was quickly surrounding myself with a lot of suspicions that were growing more and more complex.

They had penetrated my mood and for the first time I began to sense an undefined, elusive danger invisibly lurking somewhere nearby. The sea mist began to crawl over me like a shroud. And as if wearing a shroud, I must have dissolved, ghostlike, into the tomb of fog as I hurried along the dock, home.

MONDAY DECEMBER 11th.

But my Monday morning hadn't started at Island View at all. It had started at the Burnaby Health and Rehabilitation offices where an early morning phone call from his secretary had asked me to meet with the director. For all his having such an impressive name and title, Dr. Giles Mannering had turned out to be a pompous ass.

It was evident in the small cherub like, effeminate face, the thinning hair groomed strategically in all the right places, and the expensive and meticulous detailing of the handmade silk suit. Even the subtle glint of a gold watch and cufflinks suggested they, too, probably had a very unique pedigree.

His office looked like the library of a very private and exclusive men's club the kind of setting in which James Bond would find himself chatting to "M". Book matched dark oak paneling played background to an extensive library of books that seemed to have little to do with his profession and mostly to do with art, a collection of which was arrogantly displayed on the remaining three walls. What I knew about art suggested that any one of the oils had at least three or four zeros in their price tags. Sitting in one of the two velvet wingback chairs opposite the antique mahogany desk, I was having a hard time imagining that the petty details of British Columbia's hospital administration were ever permitted to invade such exclusive surroundings.

Perhaps they weren't. For the past five minutes I had been listening to his social and political bantering as he conferred with his secretary over the intercom. He was to address a luncheon meeting at a conference of psychiatric social workers on Thursday at the Vancouver Hotel, he had a staff meeting tonight at six o'clock, and he and Mrs. Mannering were to attend the Queen Elizabeth Theater with the Austin's on Friday. According to Janet, who had given me most of my information, Mrs. Mannering was a large, domineering, bible thumping Baptist, daughter of a wealthy Alberta rancher, who spent half her time arranging and running fund raisers for one cause or another, most of them resulting in proceeds she could have donated herself without ever missing. The rest of her time she spent extolling the glories of her husband's prestige and position.

If I was ever confronted with her as well as him, I was debating which one I would find more obnoxious. I'd decided it would be him, when he summoned my attention by clearing his throat delicately and fixing me with his cupid like smile.

"Now, Miss Daniels. I understand you've been working at Island View for the last while?"

"Yes, that's right." I still had not gathered the purpose of why he had asked to see me or what he hoped to gain. I was convinced, however, that his motives would be anything but honest.

"Have you had any success at all with the program out there?"

"It's contributed to our overall assessment of the institutions and facilities, if that's what you mean. As far as selection of any possible candidates for the program, no." If I sounded pleasant and civil, I was doing an academy performance of acting.

"Ah yes. I was afraid of that. You see we have ah some of our most unfortunate cases are out there. Really, there's very little anyone can do for them. Most distressing." He repeated the phrase twice for my benefit. He didn't find it distressing at all.

"But," his little cherub face beamed a smile, "we are making advances. In the last few years, just in drug therapy alone..." He paused long enough for me to be properly impressed. "But then, of course, I mustn't bore you with all the trials and triumphs of our profession." (Of course not, doctor. I couldn't possibly understand any of it, poor little mental incompetent that I am.) I returned an equally pasty smile.

"After all, you have a most challenging task and you deserve a great deal of respect for undertaking what must be a very difficult job." (Now that I've cleaned up my plate do I get dessert?) I continued the pasty smile, and for his sake I lowered my eyes and assumed a totally demure expression. It also camouflaged my disgust.

"However, if you've not found a candidate then I must assume you've concluded your work there?"

"Mostly. I have just the report to do it shouldn't take more than a few days. Is there a problem?"

Perhaps he was a little too quick to reassure me.

"No, no, of course not, my dear. As you know, I support the program entirely." He paused, again for effect. "It's just that some of our staff are, shall we say, perhaps a little less professional in their attitudes than they might be. They ah tend to view this sort of thing as, well, an unnecessary interruption in the normal routine of the hospital. I must admit, we do know that a carefully planned and maintained routine provides a safe and secure environment for our more severely disturbed patients." (Feed and water the vegetables three times a day is that it Doctor?)

"I gather Mrs. Rutherford has objected to my activities?" I was beginning to see the purpose of this polite little charade quite clearly.

"Mrs. Rutherford is ah a very dedicated woman. She's been with us many, many years, and through some most difficult times. Not an easy job, hers, as I'm sure you understand. She's a very capable woman; a bit, shall we say, antisocial perhaps, and doesn't accept interferences easily. But otherwise a fine woman, fine woman." (Yes, lovely person, Doctor. It's just that Frankenstein's mother gets a bit cranky is that it?)

"However, if you've really concluded your work there I see no reason why there should be any further problem, do you?" (You mean if I pick up my toys and go home?)

"I'm sorry, Dr. Mannering. I didn't see any problem in the first place. I hadn't considered my work to be construed as interference." I returned a very direct look and the pasty smile was gone. I paused fractionally to taste the full flavor of my insinuation, then continued sweetly, "It's unfortunate that it's been regarded as such. As I've said, I'm almost through and I don't anticipate any problem now either."

"Oh, I'm pleased you're a very understanding young woman, I can see that."

He rose from behind his desk and offered a dishrag handshake almost with distain.

"I'll be most interested in the results of the program." Lastly, as I was being led to the door, "I do hope you'll keep me informed."

"Of course, Dr. Mannering. Thank you for your interest. Goodbye."

Toad! A little slap on the knuckles don't meddle with our thirteenth century methods and stay out of our dungeons you've upset our Auschwitz matron. I was furious! Why that insincere, two faced bastard! Sitting preening his feathers in his fur lined nest! I wonder when you last 'meddled' in the affairs of the fifth floor. How convenient for you that you've had such competent staff. Do you have to supply the whip and chairs or do they buy their own? I'm sure Mrs. Rutherford probably makes effigies of all her patients as a hobby to stick pins in. That's silly. Why use an effigy when she's got the real thing? Why not rat poison instead of pins? Much more fun to watch!

    I marched down the hall and viciously poked the elevator button and rode down in a solitary rage. If Mannering had been a fly, I would have pulled his wings off!

MONDAY DECEMBER 11th.

"He's horrid! He sits behind this antique desk in this elegantly furnished office miles from the hospital and exudes this nonstop flattery and has the audacity to suggest that the sooner I leave that place the better. I'm upsetting everyone with my silly little project and the staff Mrs. Mean and Ugly herself doesn't like having her dolls touched."

This time he'd offered the martinis, the invitation being the note I'd found taped to the porthole when I got home. And I could think of nothing I'd needed more to help dispel the angry black mood I'd gotten myself into. Paul lounged back in the captain's chair on the Snow Goose, taking small sips of his drink, his pipe giving off gentle puffs of smoke. He was wearing his amused expression. I'd gulped most of my drink down and I was not amused.

"You're upset."

"Livid, actually. I don't know," I said dejectedly. "If Abernathy was murdered, there doesn't appear to be any way of proving it. But he's dead. Jennifer's alive! And I can't ignore the fact that if if she was asking for help then she can't be insane at least not entirely insane. Not enough just to be locked up on that floor for the rest of her life. And if I can't get to Jennifer I would at least like to look at her records but I don't see how I can go back there without Rutherford planting a knife in my back. Maybe several knives."

"What would the records prove?"

"I don't know maybe nothing. But another psychiatrist might have a different opinion. Maybe she's not hopeless. They're medieval out there. Maybe there are new kinds of treatments that could help her. Paul, she's only eighteen years old! She's probably going to live sixty or more years locked up in that place and most of it tied up in a strait jacket!"

"Can you ask to see her records?"

"I was told all records are strictly "confidential. They're not available to anyone other than the medical staff. Besides, those records are up on the fifth floor in the nursing station, so they might just as well be in a snake pit. Even Phillip doesn't spend any more time up there than he has to."

"Are they kept locked?"

"No, I don't think so. At least I saw Phillip take them out and put them back without locking the filing cabinet. But the floor itself is locked off from the rest of the hospital. He used a key to get us through the main doors."

"And where does he keep the keys?"

"He took them from his desk drawer. I guess they're keys to a lot of things that probably have to be kept locked. There was a whole bunch of them on a ring."

"Is his desk drawer kept locked?"

Suddenly the significance of his question penetrated my thoughts. "No! I couldn't... Paul, I can't just... How? What if I got caught? Oh God she'd probably crucify me." I had nothing left to drink but the ice cubes. He caught my glass halfway to my mouth and refilled our drinks.

"Don't get caught!"

"That's easy for you to say. I'm not a thief. I'd be terrified! Oh Paul, I just couldn't! It's out of the question."

For several silent minutes fear sent the thought into hiding. Then, like a mouse at a crust of bread, the idea crept back and began gnawing in my mind.

"But what if I do get caught?"

"I imagine you will be severely reprimanded and probably sent packing. I doubt even they would consider it a crime worthy of anything more. And I don't imagine they enjoy publicity."

"But if they discover her records missing...?"

"Why should they be missing? You can photograph them. You don't have to take them."

"You're suggesting I just scale the outside of the building in the middle of the night, saw my way through a couple of iron bars, leap over the counter in a single bound and photograph her records with my Brownie Instamatic? Combat training wasn't in my curriculum. Or do I do this by bringing a six man crew and television cameras with me?"

"If you want to get caught, yes. If you don't want to get caught, you follow the same method that would be considered normal in the main doors, opened with keys, and out again. Only you'll have a camera and it will be at night."

"Why night?"

"Do you know when and what goes on during the day? When meals are served and rounds made?"

"No."

"Then you can be reasonably sure you're likely to have less interruption at night than during the day."

"But they have a woman a night supervisor there. How do I avoid her?"

"A lot of night staff security and maintenance aren't that dedicated. If they were they'd be doing the same job or a better one during the day. She'll probably be asleep or more likely inebriated enough not to know what's going on. You did say she imbibed?"

"According to Phillip she kills a crock a night. I guess you could call that imbibing."

"Then you could probably take a television crew with you and she'd probably never wake up. I think a 35 mm with a macro lens would be simpler."

"I see. Remind me to show you my photo album some time. Marvelous collection I have of people's feet though occasionally I sometimes get a head too. It's just that they don't match the other end of themselves."

"Twit. You're not going to photograph anything that changes or moves. You focus and press a button."

"You have a rather uncanny way of making this whole thing sound so simple. Besides, I don't own a 35 mm camera. Of course, I can buy one. I'll drop in at Mendel's and ask them which one they recommend for taking illegal photos of hospital records."

"On the other hand," Paul chose to ignore my snipes, "I own several they're a pretty basic piece of equipment in my field for recording data. You're welcome to use one if you want to."

I hesitated a long time, then took a long slow breath.

"Okay. I'll do it." Obviously the martinis were having their effect. Maybe I really could scale the outside of the building. "Besides, what have I got to risk besides my reputation, a criminal record and probably my life?"

The next hour was spent with Paul showing me how to load and unload the camera, focus, use the cable release and adjust the light meter for readings. Then we went into the details of how and what I was going to do. The 'when' was resolved by choosing Friday night. Fewer staff, less activity and like most hospitals, reluctant to admit patients before Sunday night, less likelihood of unexpected encounters. When we finished I was emotionally drained. I'd had to force my mind through the hurdles of the details while it wallowed in fear and apprehension. In the end I really didn't know if I had the courage to do it. But Friday night was still three days away. Or three days in which to change my mind.

By nine o'clock I had reached the saturation level for the day, or for the night, or for what was left of it. The martinis had hit hard on an empty stomach and now that they'd worn off I was too tired to think of much else except sleep. Paul must have realized it because he got his jacket and my sweater coat and walked me back to my houseboat. This time I turned to him and he held me for several long moments.

"Promise to be careful?"

"Uh huh. Promise." I was already half asleep.

* * *

Though I'd be wavering on my resolution all day Tuesday, Wednesday morning arrived with the full reality of what had been discussed two nights before. It brought with it a kind of cold terror that left me convinced that I shouldn't, couldn't attempt such a foolish act. I would just have to tell Paul that I had reconsidered and thought it best to forget it, unless we could think of some other, more orthodox way of getting at those records.

It lasted half way through the morning. I sat at my desk and listened to the sounds around me. From down the hall I could hear Mrs. Wainwright chatter on like a child's windup toy chirping its way across the floor. She had never mentioned Mr. Abernathy again. I got the strange impression that anyone who ever entered this institution was in effect, never heard from again. An orderly wheeled an ancient cart past my door and down the hall. The wheels screeched out in need of repair but he shuffled behind it, as though oblivious to everything around him. I assumed he was staff but the empty eyes and the face, devoid of any expression, could well have made him a patient. Truly, this place was nothing more than a funeral home for the living. If they could put the patients in coffins and still keep them alive they would have achieved the maximum in care and maintenance. Yes, I had to admit, there were those patients who were old and removed from all reality. But then there was Jennifer. Once again I began to entertain and review the details Paul and I had discussed Monday night.

Thursday arrived cloaked in both dread and relief. I had teetered through all of Wednesday with the thought of abandoning the whole thing. But for courage I leaned heavily on logic and common sense, which reminded me that what I was going to do was hardly heinous wrong, underhanded and probably illegal, yes, but hardly the crime of the century.

Then, unexpectedly, I got a break. Phillip arrived at my desk out of nowhere in mid afternoon to announce he was leaving to spend the next three days at his cabin at Whistler for a skiing weekend. No more than a half dozen guests and I'd be welcome if I cared to join them. I tried to sound grateful and enthusiastic but managed to graciously decline. The enthusiasm wasn't entirely faked. With him leaving early, it suddenly left me with a lot more opportunity to get the keys. I wished him a good weekend and went back to my paperwork.

To my utter surprise, the first part was incredibly simple. I knew that Phillip would leave as he usually did, in a last minute rush of tidying up loose ends. I waited till nearly four, walked into his office, and slipped his desk drawer open. I had the keys inside my bag in moments. Once I had the keys, I felt suddenly very confident. Why not tonight? The thought instantly appealed to me. If something did go wrong and I couldn't get to the fifth floor, I would still have Friday night to make another attempt.

Now that I had made that decision, the hours dragged. I left later than usual near five and drove out of the parking lot and along the driveway that passed through the grounds and then through the main gate. Any number of people, had they cared to look out, would see my car as they would any car departing. It meant I would have to walk from the main road when I returned. Undoubtedly the main gate would be locked and even if I'd had keys to it my car returning that late could arouse suspicion. The main road from the direction I normally arrived was visible, which meant to go home and then return was also out of the question.

Instead, I drove a few miles along the narrow winding road till I reached a small rural pocket of houses and, then eventually an all-night mini market. In the deli section, I selected a ham and cheese plastic wrapped sandwich, a container of coleslaw and a large coffee. Back in my car I used my cell phone and dialed Paul's number. There was no answer. I wedged the Styrofoam coffee cup in an upright position and slowly drove back along the same way, then pulled over about a half mile from Island View to wait.

And wait was all I could do. I thought about trying to read, but a flashlight I kept in the car might attract a passing motorist and I much preferred not to have anyone remember me in a parked car. Instead I put it in my purse in case it was needed. I ate the sandwich and the coleslaw slowly, making each flavorless bite last as long as I could. I did the same with the coffee and still the hours dragged.

Sleep was impossible and so my mind turned over the details again and again through the dark cold hours, questioning, doubting, accepting and rejecting trying vainly to find answers that, like round pegs into round holes, would fit. I couldn't accept the words in Jennifer's book as coincidental. I'd tried but the haunting image of her clear blue eyes beseeching, begging, sane returned again and again. A patient who for years had accepted his circumstances and seemingly adjusted to them found dead in the basement – possibly poisoned. Why? And a woman, hostile and protective of her floor and her patients, quite beyond reason. Why? What was she afraid of? What was she protecting?

Phillip. Young, bright, presumably ambitious. Working almost as a custodian to the "vegetable factory." Hadn't those been his words? Where was his pride? His sense of professional accomplishment? But whatever, wherever the answers were, they remained as remote and elusive as Island View itself.

Midnight came, lingered and then slipped away. At one A.M. I gathered my scarf and raincoat, checked the camera for at least the fifth time, crawled out of the car and began the walk back towards the hospital. It drizzled fine, misty rain and I walked briskly, trying to shed the stiffness of sitting for so many hours. Ahead of me, at the entrance to the hospital, a twelve foot wire fence topped with barbed wire encircled the grounds. I had no choice but to use the front pedestrian gate. And I had no way of knowing if it would be unlocked. It also meant I was in full view of the hospital; the trees and shrubs dwarfed to maintain visual security. I took a deep breath and approached the gate with what I thought was a sense of purpose, then sighed with relief as I found it unlocked. I passed through and closed it as quietly as I could, only too aware that I must also make my movements appear normal.

The shadows of the hospital loomed dark and sinister as I reached the front steps. I followed the narrow walkway around the building to the staff entrance at the back. It was open, again as I half hoped, half expected it to be. I was now inside and climbing the stairs. If anyone moving from one floor to another took the elevator, I wouldn't be seen. But it was old and slow. More than once I'd seen the staff routinely choose the stairs. Still, I clung to the barely plausible story of having my car break down and I'd forgotten my cell phone ... but beyond the first floor, that alibi lost any credibility it ever had.

I got to the fifth floor, breathing heavily, and not just from exertion. My hands were icy cold and my body tense. Reluctantly now, I moved through the swinging doors at the top of the stairs into the naked light of the corridor. Clutching the ring of keys tightly, my fingers closed round the one most likely to fit. If it did, and the doors opened, I would be only feet away from my objective but in full view of anyone there.

Despite every effort to stay calm, my fingers trembled and I fumbled with the key, impatient when it failed to work, my nerves honed now to razor sharpness. I tried another key, and then another, and then back to the original, forcing myself to try and keep calm. Then suddenly it turned, and the bolt, as it released, sounded like an alarm. I waited a minute, maybe two, expecting a voice, a movement, while I fought desperately to regain what little control I had left.

I pushed the door open and the nurses' station came into sight. From the staff room behind I heard voices, which at first sent small shivers down my spine till my mind registered them as the slightly melodramatic overtones of a late night movie.

I stood now on the crossroads of the corridor. To my left, at the end of the hall, was Mrs. Rutherford's door; I could see it was closed, at the other end, the two simple chairs and table that constituted the lounge. The corridor was empty.

I don't think I made any noise as I crept round the edge of the counter and stopped before the staff room. It was darkened except for the television screen, which cast its images about the room.

Her breathing was loud and slow. In the dimness I could make out the heavy white uniformed body on the couch and assumed it was the regular night nursing aide, Mrs. Shirosky, her head resting awkwardly on pillows that had been propped for television viewing. There was a nearly empty glass on the table and an ashtray full of cigarette butts. There was no bottle, but then I guessed it would have probably been well hidden. I was satisfied that she was asleep, but for how long I could only guess.

The filing drawer protested as I opened it and my mind screamed at the noise. It took me several minutes to find her file the faded edges of the manila folder worn with age. It was thick and heavy and it seemed to take me forever to get the file open on the desk of the nurses' station and the camera focused and aligned. Gradually there began a semblance of order and I turned each page, squeezed the cable release, advanced the film and repeated the procedure. From the staff room her heavy breathing continued while car tires screamed above police sirens as the movie droned on.

Twice I stopped to reload film into the camera, my hands growing unsteady again as I tried to hurry. I was agonizingly aware of the time that had ticked by, my ears strained for any change in the heavy breathing, and tense now to finish the last few pages. Then suddenly the sounds of her breathing stopped and the springs of the sofa groaned in protest to the movement of her body. Terrified, I scooped up the file and clutched it and the camera and disappeared under the desk top. Crouched in only a few feet of space, I knew I would be visible to anyone approaching the nursing station and I cursed myself again, for taking as long as I had. No doubt it was time for her rounds, and she would get up, find me, call security, AND Mrs. Rutherford and I would have no choice but to confess my purpose. Caught red-handed with a camera and Jennifer's file in hand, there would be no way out of it. Minutes ticked by while I imagined the whole miserably embarrassing scene, until gradually a familiar sound seeped into my consciousness. Once again the heavy breathing had resumed and I took a great sigh of relief as I crept out from beneath the counter and with trembling hands began to resume my work. It took me several more minutes to set up the pages and camera from where I left off. I grew nervous again and began to flip the pages anxious now to be finished. Then at last I was done.

Carefully, I replaced the file and eased the drawer closed. I placed the camera in my bag and tiptoed back around the edge of the counter back to the corridor threshold.

I froze. My heart leaped into my throat and pounded in alarm. At the end of the hall the door was ajar and I watched helplessly as I saw it being quietly closed by shadowy movements behind it. How long had it been open? How long had she been standing there? I seemed riveted to the spot unable to move too terrified to think.

Something screamed in my head to move get the key open the door get out and dreamlike I started toward the main doors. I had to unlock them again oh God, why hadn't I been less cautious and just left them unlocked. Panic took hold. Cursing under my breath, ignoring the scraping of the bolt as it finally slid back and home again I slipped through the door. I reached the doorway to the stairs and crept down the steps before my mind began to work. If Mrs. Rutherford had seen me, and I was almost certain she had, she'd closed the door, not opened it. She hadn't approached me or stopped me. Why? Because she would get someone else to do that! They'd be down on the main floor. They'd check the doors and probably do a check of the floors. If I kept going I'd walk right into them.

I was trapped.

I fought desperately to make my mind work, to find a way to get out. I was certain she had seen me, but wait, could she be sure it was me? I still wore the heavy wool scarf, and the older (and warmer) raincoat I didn't usually wear. Still, she would report someone. They'd check the doors, maybe each floor, then what? Surely they wouldn't search the patients' rooms and the linen and storage rooms. That was it! Hide let them search give them an hour, maybe two. Then slip away. My memory raced backwards trying to remember the layout of the fourth floor. I had to move quickly, get out of the stairwell.

Wasn't there the supply room on the fourth floor or was it the third? I slipped through the swinging doors and moved along the corridor. I was right. There was the door! Desperately I reached for the door knob, only to find it locked. The keys yes I had keys which one? Would any of them be the right one? It was only a supply room. Would there be a key on this key ring? I had to try. How many seconds must have ticked away as I tried one after another? Then I felt one work. The door gave way and I slipped inside. At least for the moment, I was safe.

The room appeared to contain a full inventory of supplies and equipment. Shelves were lined with jars and bottles, boxes and packages all identified with numbers taped to the edges of the warehouse shelving. I retreated to a remote corner and huddled there on the floor waiting for time to pass. Tension had left my legs rubbery, and as I tried to maneuver to a more comfortable position my foot knocked something off one of the lower shelves. I cringed as it hit the floor with a dull thud and felt something like talcum powder. I risked using the flashlight as I replaced the plastic bottle on the shelf and swept most of the powder out of sight. It was bad enough to be in this place I didn't need to leave a trail of where I'd been.

I think every moment of the next two hours was sheer hell listening, waiting for voices, men, flashlights. I heard nothing. Once footsteps approached and I cowered, waiting to hear another key turn in the lock. But they hadn't slowed or stopped. Still it made my blood run cold at the thought of being caught.

My watch read four and I now began to fidget. What time did kitchen staff come on duty and the nurses change shift? I decided to leave while I could be reasonably certain of not encountering anyone else arriving or leaving.

I was very stiff now and my muscles protested as I moved to the door cautiously, opened it and checked the corridor. It was empty. The temptation to bolt was almost overpowering. Instead I retreated back into the storeroom for one final purpose, that only now as I was about to leave dawned on me. I had been lucky. One key had unlocked this sanctuary. I couldn't be sure I would find another. If I was forced to return to this one, I wanted to know just what security it provided. I flicked on the flashlight and meticulously guided it back over and around the shelves and walls, hoping somehow to uncover a hiding place that might remain undiscovered. It was absurd but in this great mausoleum of a building I knew of no other place that could offer safety.

Then the light picked up the faintest outlines of what seemed like a door frame. Cautiously I moved deeper into the storeroom and let the light trace the lines till it clearly revealed a door. I was puzzled. There was nothing on the door itself or its location to identify its purpose. I retrieved the ring of keys, selecting and trying one after another without success. Anxious to be leaving, I gave each key only a brief try, cursing myself at having to take the time now when I had spent two hours here already. I had the key I had used for the storeroom in the lock and it seemed to fit, though it wouldn't turn. I withdrew it and selected one that was almost the same. Delicately I worked it in place and then as I nudged it against whatever was resisting it, suddenly it gave way.

I turned the handle and opened the door.

For a moment I saw nothing but a jungle. Vines of tubing trailed from trunks of tanks lined against one wall. More snaked down from above and joined others. Above a long, stainless steel counter, chemistry vials sat waiting to perform whatever service was required of them. On the counter were trays that held long, glistening instruments. Vats and jars of substances lined another wall and more equipment appeared ready and waiting. A faint odor of disinfectant lingered on a trace of a medicinal or chemical smell which only served to confuse me all the more. That this was a lab of some sort I had no doubt, but I could not understand its purpose. Intrigued, I ventured further in and directed the flashlight along the walls, the ceiling and the floor.

The room grew in size to that of an operating theatre. Two gurneys occupied one corner and near the middle of the room a long, stainless steel operating table sat in cold anticipation. I could make out what seemed like large gas cylinders nearby and a trolley held a number of stainless steel tanks. Even more curious now, I turned the flashlight back to the counter and stepped closer to examine the contents of the jars. Was this some sort of lab for the treatment of patients? Phillip had never mentioned it and yet it seemed to suggest that purpose. I directed the light onto the labels and came back with what was to be expected chemical compounds whose names meant nothing to me. But if I could recognize even one, it might be helpful. The flashlight had caught what seemed like an alcove that appeared to contain more chemicals, and I turned my attention to these.

Something lurked in a vat of liquid. This time the label gave me only a series of numbers and letters and what appeared to be a Latin name. None of it was familiar. I turned to the next one and found it to be similar. I moved the flashlight along the row and was met each time with the same result. Frustrated, I turned to the other side of the alcove. Here the glass containers were very large, cylindrical in shape and secured by lids that were tightly clamped in place. The first seemed to contain several whitish fragments. Again the label was meaningless. The next one held only the hint of something I could not determine. I turned to the next. It seemed to contain a convoluted maze of roots, again whitish in color with black cob webbing. Something oddly disturbing began to play in the corner of my mind. The next one seemed even more intricate. I saw what seemed like a mass of spaghetti like filaments extending from a corrugated core. The cut ends seemed to float listlessly without direction or purpose. Again, this time growing more apprehensive, I turned to the next and saw only a partially exposed skeletal fragment. The rest was hidden by a fine floating seaweed of fiber. I was growing both more frustrated and yet more anxious by the moment. The next one appeared to be the same. Thin, white, almost translucent filaments all but obscured what the jar contained. My mind had reached an abyss, unable to remain where it was, unable to go on, unless it crossed what now was confronting it.

My hands had grown icy cold but unnaturally steady, tensed and ready, as I slowly reached out and touched the glass container. Briefly a small rivulet of relief swept over me as my sense of touch recognized the cool smooth familiarity of glass.

I hesitated only a second. With some effort I turned and tilted the container toward me, the flashlight now ready to expose whatever it held.

I was staring unmistakably into the blank expressionless eyes of the face of Mr. Abernathy. His severed head shifted in the liquid and the spinal stem, dark and ugly, bumped along the bottom of the jar like some dark, deadly sea creature before settling once more in a stupor. Lazy white worms of hair strands repeated the rhythm and then they too died. The seconds seemed like an eternity before the shock of what I was seeing had penetrated my own brain. When it did, revulsion suddenly overwhelmed me and I pulled away in terror. In panic I turned to flee, hit the counter and heard the terrifying crash of glass as the container smashed to the floor.

The sound came at me like a monster out of absolute darkness. The flashlight had gone out when it too hit on impact. Then the strange odor began to surround me and I felt the wetness of the liquid now on my legs. For a moment I stood teetering with shock, my hands gripping the counter like it was the last sanctuary of reality of sanity in this house of horror.

I don't remember if I screamed but the sound of breaking glass had wrenched me apart. Oddly, the sound lingered in my head, persistent and demanding. Bit by bit I began to recognize that the silence had been destroyed, that I had been dependent on that for my escape and that I still had to get out, not only of this room but also of the building.

I stood for what seemed an eternity, forcing my trembling body to be still, calming the nausea that had welled up inside of me, quieting my nerves, shutting out the darkness and what lay on the floor near my feet. For all of a fraction of a second I thought of groping for the flashlight on the floor. Revulsion quickly stifled the thought. With all the discipline I could muster I forced myself to forget what I had just seen and concentrate now on escaping.

Somehow I fumbled my way around the counter and, like a sleepwalker with arms extended, found my way to the door and closed it behind me. I stumbled past shelves, turned and retraced my steps in another direction until at last I was at the main door. Quietly I opened it enough to chance a brief glimpse of the corridor. It was empty. I closed it behind me too, but left it unlocked, half hoping the intrusion might be considered the result of a confused patient. Then I tiptoed to the doors leading to the stairs and flight by flight I reached the main floor. If I was going to get caught, now was the time. But again, mercifully, the corridor was clear. I approached the staff entrance and stopped as I caught sight of the aluminum cylinder of a flashlight, its magnetic holder hugging the metal locker. I had passed it, and a portable fire extinguisher below it, many times without giving either of them a thought. Instinctively, I grabbed the flashlight, putting it in my bag, slipped through the staff entrance, and felt the joy of the cold damp night air as it greeted me with welcome relief.

I paused for only a second, then tightened the scarf and bent my head against the pouring rain. I followed the path that led round to the front of the building and now again I was in full view of anyone inside. I'd considered following the fence. If there was a break in it, sheltered as it was by shrubs and trees, I could have had the benefit of cover. Instead, reluctantly, I moved down the walkway, the same route I had used nearly four hours ago hugging my shoulder bag, conscious of the weight of the camera and flashlight inside, and forced myself to keep the brisk walk from turning into a run.

My ears strained to hear voices; a shout behind me or from someone posted at the gate waiting for me. Would the gate now be locked? I glanced quickly across the grounds where the main gates extended into the ornate wrought iron fence a hundred feet or so on either side before turning back into the trees and shrubs in parallel lines. As far as I could tell, I was alone.

I don't know what made me look back but I did, half dreading, half expecting to see the lighted windows in the otherwise shadowy facade that would surely confirm they knew of my presence.

It was at that moment I saw them.

It had been only a slight movement at the side of the building deep in the shadows, half obscured by the shrubs. For a fraction of a second I thought I'd been mistaken, my eyes straining to catch another movement. Then, as if by command, they began to move like lean, low shadowy darts, two dark Dobermans, their heads low and their legs covering the ground now at incredible speed as they moved in on their target.

In the instant I watched, horrified, as they grew larger, closer, the shape of the lead dog now quite distinct, the other only a few feet behind. I turned and broke into a run towards the gate, which seemed yet so far away. My God, if it were locked fear bit deep into my soul and I pushed myself forward the gate fifty feet away, thirty feet....

I knew they were gaining. I could hear their feet in quick, rapid succession cover the ground behind me their panting growing louder as the distance between us narrowed. The gate fifteen ten feet away surely they were just behind me now would they attack first or wait to corner me then move in? My lungs cried desperately for more air, my head dizzy with fear and exertion.

Then suddenly my hands felt the cold, wet bars of the gate solid ironmongery. Open open God! Almost too late, I remembered it opened toward me I pulled back desperately and it began to swing toward me. At the same time I felt my right arm seized by viselike needles that sent pain riveting through my body and I screamed out in agony.

The glistening, pale eyes were less than two feet away from my face the first dog, with jaws like a steel trap had caught my right arm as the second dog now covered the last few feet of ground. He'd caught my arm from behind, forcing my body to turn.

It saved my life.

In that instant my arm was seized, my left hand had been clutching my bag and now, with the weight of the camera and flashlight, it was already caught in the momentum of the turn. It was my only chance. I guided its trajectory with every ounce of force I could manage and brought it smashing down on the dog's head.

It hit with a sickening impact! I felt the blow and heard the dog yelp with pain as my arm suddenly became free. I turned back to the gate, already on its homeward swing, slipped through and slammed it shut behind me. A second later the body of the second dog hurtled against the bars its gleaming eyes and teeth only inches away from my face and I felt its hot, moist breath on my fingers as I released the gate.

My blow had only temporarily stunned the first dog. It now began to sniff and pace the base of the gate, emitting a low, deadly growl, its tongue slipping between the canine fangs that gleamed white and deadly in the dark.

I turned once more and began to run, gasping for breath, my legs rubbery and threatening to collapse beneath me. If there was a break in the fence they'd find it I was sure of that. They had been trained well. How many minutes or seconds would I have? The safety of my car seemed miles away.

I ran blindly through the night, back along the side of the road, my feet sending loose gravel flying, my heart pounding and my throat dry and desperate for air. Twice I staggered and slowed to regain my balance, the pain in my side doubling me up and my body wet and hot.

My ears strained to hear the sound of the dogs' feet on the gravel behind me and my eyes searched the brush by the road, expecting two dark shadows to emerge at any moment and move toward me.

Then suddenly it was there the pale shape of my Mustang parked well off the side of the road. I no longer controlled my movements my feet moved like lead weights and my body staggered in the same direction. Lights flashed in my head and I was no longer aware of anything other than the car.

The metal was moist and cold as I pawed my way along the hood and the windows. I found the door handle and then in agony remembered that I had decided to lock it, even parked in such a desolate area. Seconds ticked by while I groped awkwardly for my key ring, pinioned in my bag beneath the camera and the flashlight. Then, barely able to turn the key in the door, I got it open and with my last ounce of energy I crawled in behind the wheel and pulled the door shut.

I have no idea how long I sat there my head down on the steering wheel, gasping for air, my heart thudding, my skin moist and clammy, my right arm hanging like a dead creature. Only then did I become aware of the pain, a deep, throbbing pain like spikes being rammed into my arm with a rhythmic pounding that seemed to drive them deeper and deeper.

I fumbled with my left hand for the car keys and awkwardly started the car. For a moment the engine only turned over. Again I tried. The third time it caught, and with my left hand I moved it into drive and pulled it back onto the road. The pain echoed in my head and I gritted my teeth. More than once my vision blurred and I saw the white center line disappear under the car.

When I at last turned into the marina parking lot, my mind was numb, my arm screaming at the slightest jar as I clawed my way from behind the wheel. It was dark, deserted, still a graveyard of empty boats that sat derelict in their watery tombs.

I couldn't seem to walk in a straight line the dock swayed beneath me, flanked on either side by the icy calm water. I'd gotten to the end of the dock and now turned right along the upper dock under the huge shed roof. The lights seemed to move and sway and more than once I staggered dangerously close to the edge. Then I saw the Snow Goose. I was almost there.

I think I half fell down the narrow ramp. I felt my knees more than once scrape on the wire mesh. I clung now to the deck railing and forced the sliding door open.

He wasn't there. My mind seemed to take forever to work. Of course, he would be there it was night- almost dawn. I blinked twice till I could be sure of what I saw. It was faint but I thought I saw a dim light coming from the engine room. I staggered over to the steps.

"Paul," my voice seemed inaudible my throat was so dry. I tried again. I got to the first stair and managed them one by one.

"Paul..." it must have been a whisper or maybe I just thought I called his name. The door of the engine room was open. It was empty. The eerie light illuminated the massive shapes of the engines, like two black hulks, and the wires and hoses slithered and snaked their way into the darkness.

From less than two feet behind me I thought I heard his voice. Drunkenly I reeled around to find Paul standing perfectly still in the shadowy doorway of the forward cabin. The dark sweater and blackness of his hair and beard made him only vaguely visible in the dim light. Except for his right hand. It was raised to waist level and calmly held the gun from the tool box.

It was pointed directly at me.

THURSDAY DECEMBER 14th.

I don't remember much about the rest of that night. Despite the shape I was in I'd protested long and loudly when it became apparent to me that I wasn't going to be allowed to remain at the foot of the stairs where I had evidently collapsed.

We were walking (Paul was walking, I was being half carried) back along the dock; then we were driving until we pulled up in front of a large building and I was deposited under a lot of bright lights and peered at by a young man in white.

After that I fell into a pile of black cotton batting - and then the bright lights, the man in white, and the pain all went away.

It was dark again when I woke up, and even then I did it reluctantly. But the smell of bacon and eggs kept nibbling at some part of me that said I should stay awake rather than slip back into my dark cozy retreat. I'd figured out I was in my own houseboat, my own bed, had a bandaged right arm that I would be happy to discover belonged to someone else. I was also wearing a sweater I'd never seen before. Then Paul arrived upstairs with a tray.

"Is it morning already?"

Paul set the tray down while I gently eased myself against the pillows he stuffed behind my back.

"It's 5:30 at night. This may look like breakfast to you, but you're going to have to call it dinner. Your cupboard looks like mine."

Bit by bit I oriented my fuzzy thoughts, as lightheaded as I felt, and began chomping at a piece of bacon. Humphrey jumped up onto the bed and approached the plate for a sniff.

"Don't believe a word he says." Paul reached out and gave him a tickle under the chin. "He's just polished off a can of Sardines in Cream and some Kitty Bits. About five pounds of them, I'd say. I was thinking of serving them along with some pork and beans for you, but then I found the eggs."

"Glad to save you the trouble." I sniffed in response. I snatched the second strip of bacon out from under Humphrey's nose and gobbled it down. It seemed even a bit of food made me feel nervy.

"Tell you what," I said as I tackled some buttered toast, "I'll tell you all about my adventure if you tell me about the gun."

"If you're going to crawl on board in the wee small hours of the morning that's the kind of reception you're going to get. How could I know it was you?"

"I called you - I called your name! I even tried to phone you. Earlier, that is, to tell you I was going to do it Thursday night instead of Friday night." I licked my fingers indignantly.

"So I gathered. Sorry I wasn't on hand to hear about your improvisational whims. When you'd agreed to Friday I expected it to be Friday night. As for your arrival on board, you weren't in any shape to do much of anything by the look of that arm.

"Tell me the rest."

"You don't remember?"

"Only vaguely." I mopped up an egg with a piece of toast.

There's not much to tell. You needed medical attention. That's what you got."

"There's something else I don't remember."

"And that is...?"

"This sweater. It's not mine."

"That's because it belongs to me."
"I don't think I have anything on underneath...your sweater."
"I know you don't have anything on underneath...my sweater."
"Oh. Could I ask...how I got that way?"
"It was very simple. I took your clothes off."
"You took my...clothes off?"
"Well, you helped."
"I helped?"
"Just with your clothes."
"I see."
"I had to bathe you."
"You had to bathe me."
"You kept falling asleep."
"Of course."
"They'd given you a sedative."
"I see."
"And you wouldn't have wanted to go to bed as wet and messy as you were..."
"No! Of course not."
"I didn't think so."
"It's just that...I'm glad I was so...co-operative."
"Oh you were. Very co-operative."
"I was?"
"You couldn't wait to get your clothes off."
"Oh my God!"

He enjoyed every minute of my embarrassment and his chuckle only made it worse. Then for a moment he was serious. He reached out to hold my good arm before he spoke.

"Mia, I put you to bed. I didn't take you to bed. I think I know when the difference is important." Then the grin was back, the blue eyes forcing me to look up at him.

"Just don't tempt me with any more serious medical emergencies. The next time you have a hangnail, my discretionary powers may not be as good. I can't pretend I didn't like what I saw, but I didn't have to see you to know that. All right?"

I smiled back a little sheepishly. "All right."

I polished off the rest of the breakfast. Then downed the two pills Paul handed me with a glass of water before I settled back on the pillow.

"A dog bit me."

"I assumed that. Some dog."

"What do you mean?"

"You have seven stitches for some pretty deep puncture wounds. A few more bites like that one and you would have been hamburger."

"Yeah?" I was a little shaken. "I guess I was lucky."

"If you call that luck." He glanced at the exposed part of my arm below the sweater that had been mummified in white gauze.

"Care to tell me what happened?"

He made himself reasonably comfortable sitting near the foot of the bed and as he began his pipe-lighting procedure I settled back - feeling actually quite mellow, except for my arm, and related the details of the night. I told him when I'd found out Phillip was leaving early for a long weekend at Whistler, I had decided to take the initiative and go up to the fifth floor Thursday night. I told him again about trying to call him and about finally getting up to the fifth floor and taking the pictures. Then I told him about Mrs. Rutherford and about the fact that she must have seen me. "So instead of leaving the building I hid in a storage room. I was there for almost two hours. Then just as I was about to leave I thought that maybe I had better just see what kind of a hiding place the room really was, in case I couldn't get out of the building and I had to return to it." I paused before continuing. "That was when I found the door."

"What door?"

"The door inside the storage room that opened into...some kind of treatment room. It had gas cylinders and gurneys and an operating table." The memories of that room were flooding back in ghoulish clarity. "They had specimens in jars.

Paul...they had his head, Abernathy's head in a jar." The words suddenly spilled forth.

"Why? What could they possibly want with his head? He died. Suicide. Murder. Call it what you will. And they have his head preserved like some sort of...laboratory animal?" I shuddered with revulsion. Oddly, it didn't seem to have much effect on Paul"

"Well it may not be quite as bizarre as you think. I imagine that they receive a fair number of tissue and organ donations from their patients. Research and study must still have to go on, even in hospitals like that one. I don't know what the legal parameters are for that kind of thing but it would appear that no one is questioning the practice, at least so far."

"Well after last night someone is going to be questioning who was in that room. I...when I saw the...his head, I dropped the container. I also dropped the flashlight. Paul, it was a very horrible experience. I just wanted to get out of there. But someone's going to find the jar broken and the flashlight. I just couldn't bring myself to do anything about it."

"That may not be a problem. It might not be discovered for some time and when it is they're likely to assume that perhaps it was one of the patients. They may just question the staff. And they may not even do that. Particularly if they're doing anything without authorization. Tell me now what happened after you left the room."

So I did, first about the dogs and finally my escape. When I had finished he continued to puff rhythmically on the pipe, staring at some invisible target, preoccupied with some facet that held his attention.

"You're wondering why the dogs attacked me?"

"No, I know why they attacked you. They were ordered to kill you. I'm wondering who gave the order."

I snapped to attention.

"Kill me? Paul! They were guard dogs! Isn't that what guard dogs do? I don't mean kill people - but they chase them and catch them."

"Exactly. They corner their prey; hold him on the ground until the dog handler takes over. Even when they're ordered to attack - they are trained to disarm a person - to bite to hold an arm or leg…"

"Maybe - maybe they just got too rambunctious," I said lamely. The memory of those pale eyes and snarling fangs didn't make me sound too convincing.

"Look, Mia, there's - what - thirty acres of grounds out there? Very logical that dogs would be used to patrol that kind of area. They must have had several patients over the years try to escape and even they must get their share of vandalism and petty theft. But those dogs were not ordinary guard dogs."

"But how can you be sure?" I don't know why I was arguing the point. Those gleaming fangs were still all too clear in my mind.

He continued. "You said there were two of them. Tracking and guard dogs work alone or with their handler. Dogs trained to kill work in pairs. One dog disables the prey, the other moves in for the kill."

I kept quiet.

Paul continued, "Were they barking?"

"I... I don't remember... no."

"Doesn't that seem unusual that a dog chasing its target wouldn't be barking - particularly when you'd gotten away only seconds before?"

I remembered their panting, their hot breath so close to me - the deep growl as they'd prowled the fence. But they hadn't barked, not once.

"What I don't understand," he extracted his pocket knife, selected a small blade and stirred up the coal in the basin of the pipe, "is why they didn't kill you."

That seemed so simple that by the time I offered an answer I'd turned it into a question. "Because I got away?"

"More likely they hadn't been released soon enough."

Or maybe the dogs didn't run as fast as they should have."

"Dobermans have been clocked at over fifty miles an hour. How fast were you running?"

"Sixty."

Suddenly I seemed exhausted. My nice black wooly retreat was beckoning me.

I let my head fall back on to the pillows and somewhat sleepily asked, "Paul?"

"Yes?"

"You've just told me someone tried to have me killed."

"Yes."

"Why?"

He gave me a very long and steady gaze. "I don't know. Do you?"

TUESDAY DECEMBER 19th.

Janet was already seated at the table amidst the hanging ferns and the Art Deco posters that adorned the white plaster walls. The restaurant was small, quaint and pleasant with gentle sounds of a guitar blending with the passing fragrances of tempting entrees. Janet poured me a glass of wine from the carafe as I settled into the bentwood chair. I let a few minutes pass in pleasantries before I felt compelled to ask.

"How's Timothy?"

"Not well." She gave me a quiet look - the kind that seemed to understand that I needed to ask.

"How - how long do you suppose he has?" I tried to keep my voice casual.

"That's hard to say." It was a nothing answer - except that I knew it was the truth. "I don't suppose he'll be with us at Christmas."

I sipped my wine to help the lump in my throat go back to wherever it had come from.

"Perhaps it's just as well. I don't suppose he even knows the meaning of Christmas or has ever seen the snow fall or even gotten...." I stopped. Tears filled my eyes and I tried vainly to blink them away. Janet's hand reached out and covered mine. Conveniently, the waiter arrived and Janet discussed the luncheon menu until I'd regained enough composure to join in.

After that the mood seemed lighter and we chatted about the usual things I suppose women talk about. Maybe I was trying too hard - or I'd missed a cue. Once or twice I caught Janet gazing at me when I glanced up from my plate.

Onion soup, a crisp green salad with avocado, sprouts and nuts, and a healthy wedge of Quiche Lorraine had constituted lunch - and I was more than full. I sipped my wine as I watched Janet finish the last of her lunch and debated whether I had the right to abuse our friendship.

When coffee came, we juggled to make room for the cream and sugar and the coffee cups on the small table.

I took a deep breath and plunged in. "Janet, I have a favor to ask."

"Ask." She smiled back at me.

"It's, ah, professional advice I need," I began.

"Something other than I think you look a little tense and perhaps you should get more rest?"

"A little more than that." I ignored her subtle suggestion. "Psychiatric advice I guess you could call it – only it's not for me." I added hastily and grinned, "Not that I probably couldn't use some."

"I'll admit you've been looking rather preoccupied."

"I guess I am. You see, I have a problem."

Awkwardly, I tried to phrase it so that it made some kind of sense. Without the details I purposely left out, it sounded rather questionable as to who really needed help. But she wasn't entirely unable to follow my thinking.

"So you want a psychiatrist to review this patient's case to see if there is anything unusual?" I liked her wording. She was being discreet.

"That's right."

"Do you have the records?"

"I have copies of them."

She avoided asking the obvious question.

She knew I had been working out at Island View. Her next question was a verbal thought process.

"So you... don't want to involve the staff psychiatrists either because they are involved or because you want a second opinion."

"Right."

"A second opinion of what?"

I took a deep breath. This was the test.

"Of whether or not this patient is insane."

"I see."

It was quite clear that she saw. I was some crazy person who'd come unhinged and went around thinking that people locked up in mental institutions had all been misunderstood, misdiagnosed and really were perfectly normal. I was preparing myself for a lecture precisely along those lines.

"I think I know just the person."

I was elated. "Janet, you're a doll! Who?"

"Dr. Pedersen. He's pretty old and doddery - but he was a practicing psychiatrist at our hospital two days a week up until five or six years ago. Rather a dear old soul. I think actually he practiced common sense more than psychiatry. That and vitamins. One of those healthy body, healthy mind types. I'm sure if he was willing he could give you his opinion."

I'd heard the obstacle.

"If he were willing?"

"I think you'd better let me be the go-between. Give me the records and I'll stop by his house on my way home and give him an explanation. Less chance that way of us both being considered nuts."

Janet, in her own way, had a way of calling a spade a spade.

The next day she called. "I saw Pedersen." She skipped the details of whatever reasons she'd given for such an unusual request. "I left the photographs with him and he said if you'd call him tomorrow he'll have reviewed them by then. I think you're better off going out to see him in person. For one thing, he's hard of hearing, and he might be more helpful if he's talking to you in person."

She gave me his telephone number, address and some general directions on how to find his place.

I took her advice and Thursday afternoon, I was on my way to see him.

In Janet's usual understatement, Pedersen was more than hard of hearing - he was deaf - a device I soon realized he used simply to ignore anything he didn't care to hear. It was, I assumed, a privilege of his age which, with his stooped and unsteady walk, the arthritic and trembling hands, and his slightly unkempt appearance, put him somewhere in his eighties.

I'd found him in his little lean-to greenhouse, potting plants.

"Dr. Pedersen?" I'd first tapped, then knocked, then rattled the greenhouse door before I'd aroused his attention.

"Yes, yes - you must be Miss Daniels."

"Yes, Dr. Pedersen. Mia Daniels."

"Eh?"

"Mia Daniels."

M'mm. Come in ... come in."

He shuffled to the door and ushered me in.

"Mustn't chill my beauties."

For a moment I was at a loss, till I gathered he must have been referring to whatever exotic varieties of plant life he was growing. He turned back unsteadily and continued clipping away at some kind of plant while I tried to occupy as little room as possible in the tiny jungle of greenery.

"Known Janet long?"

"Quite awhile. I met her when visiting patients with Yvonne Yuen. She's the di…

Apparently he neither heard nor cared to hear about Yvonne.

"Fine woman, fine woman. Good nurse, too. Like the kind we had in the old days, when they really cared. Too bad about her daughter, Kate. They should have had another child. Told her that. She was a damn fine mother."

I was beginning to feel even more in debt to Janet. I doubt that he would have given me the time of day had he not had a very deep respect and admiration for her.

"So you been tryin' to bring a little schoolin' into the hospitals." He turned his back on me and continued to putter with some pots while I tried to make myself even smaller. I told him briefly about S.P.A.C.E. but whether he listened, whether he heard or cared, I had no idea.

"Tea time." He'd finished whatever he'd been doing and I gathered now we were to leave the greenhouse. I already felt warm and damp and hardly reluctant to leave.

The house was only slightly cooler but was in contrast, dark, almost dingy, and somehow caught in a time trap of some many years ago. There were afghans and embroidered doilies layered in dust, a collection of Dresden china scattered about, and plants that had been placed in everything from sardine tins to jam jars.

And cats.

He took the end of his cane and poked one awake.

"Aggie - move."

Reluctantly, the cat yawned, stretched, and left. The spot, I gathered, was for me. While he hobbled back to the kitchen, I amused myself surveying the contents of the room. I found another cat curled up in a pile of newspapers in a darkened corner, one asleep upside down in a chair and another, this one a big ginger, reposing majestically on the desk, enjoying the few rays of daylight that crept through the dusty curtains.

He made several rather slow and awkward trips back and forth till he had the cups and saucers, biscuits, teapot and cream and sugar all laid out on the coffee table.

He slurped some tea and spoke.

"Gotta cat?"

"Yes. I like cats. Why?"

"Too bad."

"Oh?"

"Got too many."

"I see."

I'd seen three. Then, as if by some cue, two more, no more than ten-week-old kittens, charged in one door, across the room and up the back of an armchair in the old "I'm the King of the Castle" game.

I had to agree. But we'd finished with cats now.

"Strange case."

"Oh?" He caught my full attention.

"Too bad. Such a young girl."

I waited for him to continue.

"Can't tell a thing without seeing her, though. Nobody can."

I'd suspected that. But still, I had to persist. I was about to when Pedersen interrupted.

"You know anything about medicine? No - I suppose not." He took another slurp of his tea. "She's what's been diagnosed as a manic depressive - that means she's withdrawn into her own world - detached herself from the rest of the world, so to speak.

"Every once in a while she comes back out - not in what you'd call a normal way - it's not. It's what we call manic - often a hostile, aggressive, sometimes dangerous behavior pattern."

"What causes this change from one state to another?"

"Stimulus of some kind or another - a change in environment, a chemical imbalance, neurological damage, who knows? Some people can survive poverty, famine and pestilence. Others break under little or no stress." He bit into a biscuit, ignoring the crumbs that fell down his shirt front.

"A lot more they can do for them nowadays than in my time. Still, it doesn't always bring them round." He continued, "According to her background, she exhibited a number of neurological symptoms as a child - crying, headaches, dizziness, nausea - which could have been a contributing factor or simply symptoms of another disorder."

I voiced it more as a question than as a fact. "But then after the fire, she never recovered."

"Called trauma. It's like a trigger. In severe cases it can push a healthy, normal mind over the edge. In other cases, the mind is already disturbed - fear, anxiety, depression- a traumatic shock only aggravates the condition to a point of intolerance. When there's not much left of the mind..." He had only a small piece of his biscuit left in his gnarled fingers. "It can slip away like this!" He held it out in front of one of the plants. For a moment the delicate striped flower head of the plant swayed ever so lightly. Then, seemingly, it lunged at his finger tips - a second later it was reposing exactly as it had moments before. The biscuit had disappeared.

I stared incredulously.

"Dionaea Muscipula, ancestor to the snapdragon," as if that dismissed what I had just seen.

My wide-eyed gaze traveled round the room at the exotic jungle of strange-looking plants. He'd read my mind.

"Don't worry - they don't care much for people. I think, young lady," he mumbled, "Miss Daniels, wasn't it? – that you like a lot of people who first are exposed to the mentally ill - get caught in the same trap. The patient looks sane -speaks and acts in a sane manner, and in fact is sane."

"I don't understand then."

"Because they may have been insane - for only a few moments in their life - long enough to do themselves or someone else great harm. Or they may actually be insane - sometimes for minutes, days or even a few years at a time. But the rest of the time they are as rational, normal if you like, as you and me."

I watched Pedersen as he spoke - feeling a strange depression, coupled with relief, overcoming me. He'd confirmed my "second opinion." The medical records had indicated nothing unusual to him. And he'd certainly diagnosed my own problem. It seemed very clear to me now that I'd seen Jennifer in those few moments when indeed she may have been sane. Only not sane enough.

"Dr. Pedersen. Just one more question. What chances are there for someone like her ever to recover?"

"None. Most times anyway. Patients today are usually treated and able to resume their normal lives within weeks - months at the most. Chronic long-term patients are usually those with little or no hope of ever recovering."

"I see." I stood up, feeling quite defeated. He'd been a kind old soul not to have embarrassed me with my cloak and dagger suspicions. But clearly I had reached the end of the road.

I would have to accept his "diagnosis", whether I liked it or not.

"Dr. Pederson, you've been very kind. I appreciate your time."

He chose not to "hear" me. Instead he rose and hobbled awkwardly over to the desk to retrieve the photographs. Then he put two well used books on top of the manila envelope of photographs.

"Here, you might want to poke through these. They're in plain talk, not gobbledygook you won't understand. You can give them to Janet when you're through with them. They'll get back to me. Pity about the young woman. Not a relative?"

"No, Dr. Pedersen - just a friend."

"Friends count sometimes as much as family."

He held open the front door for me. "You sure you don't want a cat?"

I gave him a brave smile. I hoped it didn't show just how defeated and depressed I felt. "No, thanks just the same. But if I ever do, I'll remember you have a couple to spare."

THURSDAY DECEMBER 21st.

"So that's it." I'd wrapped all of Pedersen's comments in a nice neat package, tied it up with a ribbon and presented it to Paul.

"And that takes care of Jennifer." I added with a sigh of resignation. "As for Abernathy, maybe he really did have a stroke, and as for my episode with the dogs, I'll never know. Maybe they're just a little more security conscious than in most places. Certainly those dogs would deter anybody from trespassing."

I sipped my brandy laced coffee, curled up on the corner of the seat of the wheelhouse of the Snow Goose and waited for Paul's comment.

He remained silent.

He sat in the cockpit chair, the pipe making only the occasional puff of smoke to suggest it was still alive, as he gazed out into the grayness of the thickening fog. I heard the fog horn sound its lone and eerie warning from the Point Atkinson lighthouse and I followed the wake of a harbor tug turning towards its moorings its radar scanning head rotating above the mast while the red port lights appeared only as blurs in the dense fog. The Snow Goose rolled almost imperceptibly as the wash from the tug reached her hull.

Fog, as it inevitably did, brought almost an unnatural calm to the water, a deathlike quiet as the thick, wet grayness pressed down on the sea. Maybe the fog seemed to creep into Paul's mood and his mind. It was some moments before he answered, as he turned his attention back from the harbor.

"Then you're through out there? he asked. You're calling it quits?"

His last comment slightly ruffled my feathers.

"I'm not calling it quits I'm just through out there, that's all. There's nothing more I can do. As it is I've put in more time there than was ever required. I've still got loose ends in other places to take care of for Yvonne and I don't have that much time left. It's nearly Christmas. The S.P.A.C.E. program my part of it, the evaluations are to be completed by the end of the year."

"I suppose uncovering the odd murder and the attempt on your own life makes a satisfactory conclusion."

"Paul!" I was more than a little miffed. "I did everything I could to clear up or at least clarify what I thought had happened. Remember, you agreed with me when I said there was no point going to the police without proof. And as I recall, it was you who suggested that little midnight escapade that nearly got me killed. The point is I was wrong. Pedersen may be old and doddery but there's nothing wrong with his head. He was very thorough. He spent a lot of time going over her records, her history, her diagnosis, her medications, and he didn't find anything wrong. He's not involved. He doesn't know the patient, so he can't be biased. Paul, I didn't want to believe him because it made it all seem so futile. I've always trusted my instincts my intuition whatever you want to call it and I genuinely felt there was something strange not only about her, but about the whole place. But I'm prepared to admit I was wrong. Even you suggested I wouldn't find anything wrong with the records. And you were right. I'll probably go on thinking it's a strange place but maybe mental institutions are always strange. All I know is that I've got to get on with what I have to do. I'll chalk up Island View as an unpleasant experience and, in time, probably forget all about it."

"Are you trying to convince me or yourself?"

I took a deep breath ready to fling an answer back, but paused when I saw him smiling.

The smile extended into an invitation. "Then this evening should be special. I don't know what you can do with a can of pork and beans but I have a bottle of white wine to go with it."

For some reason he seemed distracted, as if the suggestion was an obligation rather than an invitation. But ignoring the thought I replied testily, "Do you always get mean and hungry at the same time?"

"Always." He was still smiling at me.

"By the way, did I sound convincing?"

"Why aren't you?"

"Absolutely. I just wondered why you were making me jump through a hoop."

"Just interested in your rationale."

"For that you deserve pork and beans."

I threw it back in jest as I went down the steps to the galley.

The can wasn't difficult to find alongside a dozen of its other cousins. I poked around until I'd managed to put together a meal of corned beef, pork and beans, potato chips, and pickles. But beggars can't be choosers. My own cupboard had little that would have been more promising on such short notice.

I carried the loaded plates back upstairs to the wheelhouse just as Paul was returning from the engine room.

"Now not a word of this to anyone promise," I hissed. I folded sheets of paper toweling into facsimiles of napkins. "...or we'll have every chef in the world hounding me for the recipe."

Like a well trained dog, I waited expectantly for my praise. I doubt that he even heard me.

"Sorry but it's going to have to wait." There was a tone to his voice that had suddenly grown serious. "I'm going to need your help. A little matter that appears to be premature."

I looked down at the two hot plates of food and back at Paul but he was already at the door. He disappeared momentarily and then reappeared carrying two fins, a face mask and a wet suit, all of which he dumped in the middle of the cabin floor. Then he began to unbutton his shirt. I was still standing in the same spot, obviously looking quite baffled.

"I know you don't understand. It's better this way." He put a hand on my shoulder and looked down at me. "Now I want you to make a promise."

I hesitated while I tried to make some sense out of the last two minutes. I couldn't, but nodded solemnly anyway.

"Promise not to ask any questions. I don't have time to answer them now and I don't intend to later."

"Okay...." It came out rather meekly.

"And promise to do exactly as I ask nothing more, nothing less."

I nodded this time but as I felt the pressure of his fingers increase I added, "Okay, Okay!" He let go and continued to unbutton his shirt.

"Go below to the forward cabin. You'll find a coil of line, and a flashlight. Bring them up here and then turn out these lights."

I did exactly that. When I returned he was standing naked to the waist, broad muscular shoulders pale in the yellow light, a cell phone in hand, his voice muffled and abrupt. Then he turned, dropped the cell phone on the table, checked that I had what he had asked for, and then proceeded to undo his belt.

"Now outside. Turn this light off and put those things in the Avon, and then go back to your houseboat. And remember to lock your door."

His words came like a slap in the face. Don't ask any questions, just go home. Well, we'd see about that! Maybe it was about time I wasn't quite so obedient. For the moment however it seemed best to comply with his wishes. Stupidly, I had been about to ask what an Avon was, but I heard the zipper of his fly being undone so I left. He'd already told me not to ask questions.

My question was answered soon enough. A large rubber raft was tied to the starboard side of the Snow Goose. At the bow end a tarp lay sprawled over an unidentifiable mass while at the stern, an outboard motor canted itself in readiness, the prop hovering above the water. Quickly I returned to the Snow Goose, grabbed his floater coat, which I learned lived on a peg just inside the door, and called back to him in the darkness. "If you don't mind, I'd just as soon not freeze to death while I carry out your commands. Call me when you get back from fishing. I wouldn't want to be caught without a lemon on hand." I didn't wait for his answer. Back outside I lay the coil of rope on the seat and nestled the flashlight inside of it. Then quickly and quietly I stepped in and wormed myself below the tarp, squeezing myself into as small a space as possible. I was competing with what I assumed was equipment normally stored in the boat. Hopefully I would remain undetected as long as none of it was required, at least till we were out to sea. Beneath the rugged contours of the tarp I managed to create a tiny peephole, just enough to let me see what he was about to do.

As if to answer my curiosity I heard him leave the Snow Goose. A minute or so later, he lowered an air tank and weights into the bottom of the boat and when he climbed in, the black rubber skin made him little more than an approaching black shadow.

I held my breath. Then, with a sigh of relief, I heard the outboard cough to life and settle down to a low purr. We slipped out into the harbor and the Snow Goose became only a phantom in the hazy, receding light of the marina, and I was left to my thoughts.

We were now in the inlet. To the east and ten miles from where we were it would become the familiar view I'd seen often from Island View. To the west was Vancouver harbor the north side even now reflected only a hazy dimness of the metropolitan skyline. Beyond the city stood world-famous Stanley Park, some several hundred acres edging down to the open sea. Very near to us but to the east, the Second Narrows Bridge loomed high above in the fog, its concrete pilings, one on either side of the channel, forcing ships between their massive loins. About thirty yards further to the east, the C.N. railway bridge also crossed the harbor, the centre span a lift bridge, allowing the shipping traffic to pass beneath. I knew somewhere up there in the blackness two men occupied the bridge tower, raising and lowering the center span. Their visibility tonight would be reduced to zero. With no traffic, I wondered how they could while away the hours.

I'd expected us to move either up the inlet or west into the harbor but instead we went South, across the inlet. I sensed rather than saw our direction. I could make out the enormous bulk of a freighter docked at the Alberta Wheat Terminals, the grain destined for some far-off country. Only the closest of the huge sodium vapor lights along the piers glowed with any brightness, and even they cast an eerie green halo that did little more than illuminate their tombstone stance.

We were now almost beneath the ship her sea ravaged belly rising out of the blackness to tower above us. I could hear the faintly decipherable sound of machinery against a steady low hum of engines.

Paul cut the engine suddenly and lowered an anchor over the side, paying the line out hand over hand till presumably it touched bottom. Then he reached for the coil of rope. He lashed one end to the gunnel and maneuvered the air tank into position. The fins were on his feet and he held the face mask briefly over the side before he put it on.

The time had come.

I pulled the tarp back and sat up. "Pass the worms please. I hear the fishing's pretty good in these here parts."

"Jesus Christ!" He spat the oath out in surprise and anger. "What the hell...I thought I told you..."

"To pick up my marbles and go home? I believe that's what you had in mind. In my mind however, I thought I'd come along for the ride. Is this it or is there some purpose in us bobbing around in the sea in the middle of the night?"

"I don't suppose it ever occurred to you that what I wanted you to do was for your own bloody good!" He spat out the words then lowered his voice to a menacing whisper. "I want you to listen to me and listen to me carefully. This time do exactly what I tell you to do. Your life as well as mine may depend on it." He didn't pause for a response. "There isn't much time. I'm going down to look for something. I want you to pay out the line as I need it and only as I need it. Don't let it go slack. Understand?" I nodded. "The escort tugs are going to arrive very soon there'll be four of them and two of them will be heading for exactly where we are now.

"I want to be up and out of here by then. We can't be seen and you won't see them until they're practically on top of you but you can hear them. When you do and if I'm not back by then tug the line three times got that?"

I nodded once more. I wanted to blurt out, "But what if what if I don't hear them, what if it isn't a tug, what if..." a hundred things. But it was too late. He adjusted the mask and with his hand still in place fell backwards over the side.

For a moment I clung to the side as the Avon dipped under the release of his weight, and then I was alone. I sat peering first into the blackness of the water, until the stream of tiny bubbles either ceased or moved beyond the scarce few feet I could see.

I'd been told what I had to do but why? The questions gnawed at my mind. What was he doing? And why? Paul Montgomery the marine biologist? What was he involved in? Why now? There were always freighters in the harbors endlessly plying their cargos from port to port. What was there about this freighter? Were they doing something illegal? Or were we? Why the suddenness the secrecy? Was there something about her cargo? Some kind of contraband? Then why wasn't he on board? Did it involve customs? Then why wasn't he using normal procedures whatever they were for that kind of thing? Each question only prompted another.

I huddled deeper into the oversized jacket, frightened and confused while my mind tried to find some semblance of sense. A foghorn moaned again and appeared to muffle a more distant sound. It seemed this time to come from a different direction. I grew uneasy. Fog distorted sounds I knew, and except for the freighter I had little orientation in the almost zero visibility. Was it my imagination that the freighter seemed further away? No there was no wind, no waves, just an unnatural calm; but the tide was moving. The Avon was drifting and I was moving imperceptibly away from the freighter.

Oh God, the line had ceased to slip over the side and I now held it tightly, gauging its tension. Was it slack? Was it taut? I didn't know! Was the tide pulling on it? Was it caught? How long had he been down? Two minutes, five minutes, ten? My ears strained to hear the first sounds of a boat, and my eyes searched the blackness of the water for some movement, some hint of his return from the depths. Nothing. Again I searched the steel carcass of the ship and the pier beyond desperately trying to judge how far the raft had drifted.

Something moved. Something near the edge of the pier. Through the grayness of the fog, my eyes riveted themselves to the location, trying to fathom, to focus. It was moving again and then I saw the black outline, the tank. It was Paul. But that couldn't be. How long had he been gone? He couldn't have gotten there, there hadn't been time. Then the figure moved almost directly under the flood lights and I could make out the movements. Suddenly he turned and began to climb down the rungs of what must have been a vertical ladder leading into the water. If it wasn't Paul, then it was another diver. Who? Why? A deeper apprehension began to grow in my mind as the seconds ticked by. Was he going to Paul to help, to do whatever he was doing? Did Paul know? My mind swung quickly back to the moments before we'd left the Goose. It had happened so suddenly – one moment I'd been holding our dinner plates and the next moment we'd left. No, he had made a phone call. But did that have anything to do with this sudden appearance of another diver? There! Was I mistaken? Had I heard a boat somewhere off in the distance? For several seconds I sat absolutely motionless, until I had convinced myself of what I was hearing. Then I wrapped my bare hands on a length of the line and pulled long and hard it eased back into the water and I pulled again and then finally once more. I scanned the darkness of the harbor and the water waiting my heart now beginning to thud in my chest now fearfully aware that I had drifted further back into the inlet. Would he follow the line back to the boat or would he merely surface? My eyes and my ears stabbed the fog and the night waiting, searching, hoping. Distant, unrelated sounds floated out of the blackness to tease my ears. Did I hear a boat? Was that an engine? No longer was I sure. My nerves were stretched beyond their limits.

Then it came closer than I had expected. The water now agitated, rolled and boiled and then a hand broke the surface and reached out for the boat. Paul's face mask appeared from below and then, almost instantly, I saw another face mask appear briefly only a scant foot away.

Suddenly, I caught the glimpse of a knife blade, a second before it disappeared beneath the surface. I must have screamed out a warning I can't remember, but I watched Paul turn to meet the knife as it thrust toward him in a powerful downward plunge. Frantically, helplessly, I watched the water churn and move torn by the struggle of the men only barely beneath the surface. Again, sounds now came from everywhere boat engines distorted by the gurgling of the angry sea. Terrified, I glanced up and saw nothing my eyes returning to catch only a glimpse of a face mask as it broke the surface and disappeared beneath. There was something out there moving through the water coming closer. I watched, with nothing I could do as the sounds around me grew louder and louder. Then suddenly a figure broke the surface and I recognized Paul and then again the second man broke the surface this time in a slow, uncaring way, movements uncoordinated and useless.

"Paul, Paul," I screamed above the roar. I was crouched at the side of the boat extending my arms to reach his. I couldn't get my balance. His hand grabbed mine and he shouted something over the noise.

He pulled and I toppled over the side into the frigid sea. I came up gasping with the shock of the cold, blinking against the salt water in my eyes.

"We're going down. Don't fight me." He had his arms holding mine as he shouted at me, his face only inches from mine. Then he tore his floater coat from my body. The sound now was deafening and seemed nearly on top of us. I turned my head in abject terror; I saw the gray knife like bow of the tanker looming out of the water, only yards away.

Already I felt the tug of the displaced water pulling at my body as tons of steel bore down on us. As surely as a torpedo, we were a target. At that distance there could be no stopping, no slight change of course. The bow even now loomed almost on top of us.

I felt something shoved in my mouth, my hands forced against my mouth and nose, and then Paul pressed my body against his. He plunged and we were under the surface moving down away into the deep. I heard the sound suddenly reduce to a hum, while a rhythmic thump; thump began to grow in my ear drums.

I was being forced down, down. The pressure grew on my chest, my face, my body. I was being squeezed and I began to panic, while tons of steel and metal now filled the very place we'd been moments ago. My lungs ached and my head pounded with the thuds.

Louder and louder, closer and closer we were rolling, out of control the pain was becoming excruciating. I felt Paul's body against mine his strength, his movements seemingly taxed beyond endurance. I had to breathe oh God this was it! My lungs were bursting! I gulped. Miraculously there was air! I fought the panic as the noise grew unbearable. The thudding was now almost on top of us. Even in my fear stricken mind suddenly came the horrifying realization. The propellers! Giant steel blades cutting the water cutting anything and everything sucked into their path. This would be the end. In the blackness they couldn't be more than a few feet away the blades as deadly as a shark moving in on its prey.

My mind and body grew senseless waiting for the final tearing apart. I clung to Paul desperately while the pressure built steadily and my mind exploded in an agony of stark terror.

We were tossed, we were being pulled and buffeted the water screamed in my ears and I closed my terror ridden mind against the end. Paul was still moving. Somehow we were still alive. The noise yes it was leaving it was going away. The water grew less savage and I felt Paul's body against the force moving, moving. The pressure in my lungs and in my head was changing. We were moving up back up through the icy depths.

We broke to the surface he gasping, choking my lungs gulping for air my mind dazed unable to comprehend the miracle of being alive. Then I turned in the direction of the sound to catch sight of the stern of the freighter now a rapidly blurring image. Only moments ago, she had been nearly on top of us and was now plying her way through the fog out to the open sea.

I don't know if I was laughing or crying. I was numb. Shivers shook my body and my arms thrashed uselessly as I tried to keep above the water.

I was being pulled. I felt his movements this time slow and weak, to keep us afloat and moving, where, I didn't know or for how long. The cold took over the panic in my mind and turned to pain, and then to a numbing finality.

Suddenly I felt the edge of the raft and ever so slowly I began to understand. It took the last grains of strength but I managed, with Paul's help, to claw my way over the side. I lay exhausted, panting, too weak and numb now to help him. He pulled himself up and over the edge slowly and awkwardly and then I heard his voice low and urgent on his cell phone. Minutes later I heard the motor start and felt the motion turn my body to ice. I was slumped like a pile of dirty rags tossed in a corner of the raft my body shaking spasmodically my teeth chattering uncontrollably.

How long it took us to reach the Snow Goose I have no idea. I remember the engine being throttled back, the gentle bump as the raft edged back in the slip. Then I felt Paul's arm under my shoulder as he half dragged me out of the raft. My legs were numb and useless my body stiff with cold and pain and uncontrolled shivering. My feet missed half the steps before I was deposited in the rear cabin.

Except for an eerie halo of light seeping in the windows from the dock lights high overhead, the boat was dark. Whether in the dimness or by instinct, it was sufficient for Paul to go about the tasks at hand. I stood unsteadily where he left me, shaking uncontrollably, and I heard him move to the head, heard the shower being turned on and then he was back. His hands moved over my body removing my clothes and then his own and then I was being led into the shower and I felt the biting pain of hot water and his hands on my body, soothing, massaging, working at my neck, my back, my legs until the shivering and pain had ebbed and was finally replaced with an ache that seemed to be a part of every bone and muscle in me. Then, silently and in the darkness, I was led out of the shower and dried off. Then there was the softness of lamb's wool being pulled over my head my arms poked through armholes and then I was placed in bed under an eiderdown quilt.

Briefly I was alone, and then his arm slipped under my head and I was being made to swallow something hot and biting. Coffee. Quite liberally laced with brandy. When I had finished that, I felt his body beside me, his arm cradling my head on his shoulder, and I sought out his warmth, his strength in the last few moments before the brandy and the exhaustion took over and spread throughout me like warm black molasses closing out the cold, and the terror of the night.

FRIDAY DECEMBER 22nd.

I don't know how long I slept but I woke up with the light of dawn easing through the windows and pain creeping through my body with the slightest movement. I'd once read somewhere that shivering is the body's life support procedure to stave off death by hypothermia. It utilizes every single nerve and muscle in the body and in severe cases survivors have been crippled with pain for days and weeks afterwards. From the way I was feeling, a few days in a dungeon stretched out on a medieval rack would feel like a therapeutic massage.

I was lying on my side, my hand across his chest. My fingers played with the corner of the towel on his shoulders.

"Paul..." I whispered his name very quietly, somehow knowing that he wasn't asleep. Then, painfully, I raised myself to lean on my elbow and suddenly I was wide awake.

The towel was soaked with blood. He opened his eyes when I moved and looked up at me. His face was pale, while deep lines of exhaustion had etched themselves under his eyes and across his forehead.

"You're awake." I'm not sure if he meant that as a question or merely an observation. "Get some rest - you'll feel better in the morning."

"My God, Paul, what happened?"

I lifted his hand away gently to remove the towel. I didn't need an answer. The memory of the knife in the diver's hand flashed to mind.

"I must have been mistaken for a dogfish." He winced as he spoke and the smile was cornered by pain. Under the towel was a two-inch dark and ugly wound near the top of his right shoulder. I had no idea of how deep it was but it had bled profusely.

"I didn't know you were hurt," I blurted out. "All the time you were looking after me..."

He closed his eyes briefly, opened them and spoke with some effort. His words seemed to drift through a layer of numbness.

"Not really," he smiled weakly. "Water's forty-two degrees. Twenty minutes in it and you'd have been unconscious. Another twenty and you'd have been dead. I didn't think either of us needed another body at the moment, particularly yours."

"Well, my body is in considerably better shape than yours right now." It had as much life and flexibility as cast iron - but I wasn't going to admit it.

"This needs medical attention which, for some strange reason, I think you're going to reject."

"You're right."

"Then tell me where you keep the first aid kit."

"In the head."

"I'll be right back."

"Don't forget my medicine." I was half-way out of the cabin. I turned back puzzled.

"What medicine?"

"This." He glanced down towards the floor at the empty coffee mug. "Only leave out the coffee this time."

It was the best that our combined efforts - my limited medical knowledge and the contents of the first aid kit - could offer. But he accepted what I did, which was to clean the wound and apply an antiseptic powder and gauze dressing. The medicine he took more willingly, nearly a half bottle of brandy followed by the reheated dinner from the night before. Maybe the brandy was sufficient to numb his stomach into accepting the beans and corned beef at what was now six a.m.

He dozed then and I tried to, unsuccessfully. An hour later I gave up. I stayed in the sweater but climbed back into the rest of my still very damp clothes - and tiptoed out.

Had I been observed coming home at dawn after a night out, one might easily assume I had been wined, dined and royally seduced. Instead, I'd been half drowned, nearly ground to pieces by propeller blades, and almost frozen to death.

I would have been quite content with just the pork and beans.

* * *

I spent an hour soaking in a very hot tub; then for the next hour I curled up in bed and tried to sleep. But though my body cried out for rest, my mind nagged at all the events that had happened in the last few weeks. In frustration I forced myself to focus on things I needed to do. Christmas was only days away and while cards and gifts had long been delivered, there was the tiny silver tree to put up and the usual last minute errands to be done. I thought about stopping by the Snow Goose to check on Paul but thought better of it remembering the last time I had arrived unannounced. Reluctantly, I bundled myself into the warmest of my winter clothes and headed out, the weather cold, and the wind biting. By early evening, errands accomplished, I had just enough strength left to light the fire and carry my dinner and a glass of wine - back upstairs to bed where, I concluded, it was the only civilized place to spend the evening.

I mulled over the night's adventure and my episode with the dogs a little over a week ago and a lot of other thoughts. About Jennifer and Mr. Abernathy, about Mrs. Rutherford and Dr. Mannering, and Phillip and now Paul. I might just as well have tried taking a spider's web apart. I had ends that led nowhere, wrapping in and around others without any apparent connection and ending in knots that were impossible to unravel. Twice now I'd been nearly killed. Was I simply an unlucky and unintended victim - or was I the prey?

I'd propped Pederson's Encyclopedia of Psychiatry open and was just about to tackle my dinner when he called.

"How are you feeling?" His voice seemed the same, his tone casual, as though last night had never happened.

"As they say, "as well as can be expected." The important question is how are you?"

"About the same."

"How's the shoulder?"

"Okay."

Silence.

The conversation had reduced itself almost to a monologue. I found myself suddenly getting exasperated that he seemed so unwilling to offer some kind of explanation for last night's near disaster.

Then as if he'd read my mind he said, "I'm sure you've got a lot of questions you'd like to ask."

"But that you're not going to answer?" Just by the way he'd said it; I knew what his answer was going to be.

"It's better that way."

"If you say so." My words were tainted very slightly with a queer mixture of empathy and hostility that I hadn't quite sorted out. He had, after all, saved my life. But then he had also nearly gotten me drowned. The fact that I'd put myself in the position in the first place was something that for the moment, I chose to ignore.

"Mia?"

"Yes?"

"Keep your doors locked."

"Paul..." This time the exasperation came out in my voice."Why...why are you telling me this?"

"Because you don't, and you should. Just on general principles."

"Particularly on general principles, is that it? The Boogey Man might get me?" I was sharpening my words like darts. The empathy was quickly disappearing.

"If I were only concerned about the Boogey Man, I wouldn't care if you ever locked your doors."

"You have a strange way of caring, probably only topped by your peculiar idea of an evening's entertainment. What may I ask would you do for an encore? Fire me out of cannon? Take me snorkeling in a fish pond full of piranha?" The darts were fast and furious and very accurate. "Sorry to be such a rotten sport about it all. That just wasn't my idea of a romantic little midnight cruise."

"Then perhaps the next time I tell you to do something, you'll do it, for your own good. Don't you suppose I care just a little bit about what happens to you?"

"I suppose."

"I'll be in touch."

I had one more dart inside me. What the hell.

"By letter bomb or a hit man?"

"Good night."

I was miffed. To say the least. "Good night!" I dropped the receiver into its cradle in disgust.

I opened the Styrofoam container and picked up a duck leg. As a treat, I had stopped in Vancouver's famous Chinatown where golden brown ducks hung in so many restaurant windows despite the attempts by the health department to forbid the practice. They were a tradition among the Chinese and a delicious one at that. The crest of my anger had peaked. It plunged me first into remorse for the way I had acted, and then self pity, and then back to anger till finally, though still very frustrated, I was back on an even keel.

I took a sip of wine, munched on another piece of duck, paper toweled my hands and returned to the page I had begun.

I must have read it four times before my focus "…affecting one in four and now believed to be the generic cause of several major diseases bringing the statistics of those occupying hospital beds to a staggering one out of two. While mental disturbances may have a detrimental effect on a person's health, this usually results from a behavioral pattern.

Diagnosis and consequent treatment are often difficult because of the lack of abnormality in a person's physical condition or in their behavior. Many of those seriously disturbed have, in fact, maintained an apparent normalcy in their work family and social circumstances for many years, exhibiting none of the physical, mental, or emotional symptoms to suggest the presence of an illness."

I nibbled another slice of duck while I continued to absorb the page.

"The illness has usually become known in these cases by deviation in behavior which in some cases may be aggressive, violent and often extremely dangerous. In other cases, deviation in behavior may be so subtle as to be almost undetectable, the victim displaying great cunning and no remorse at committing acts involving torture, murder, sadism and violence. It must be remembered that these victims often are of higher than average intelligence, some considered to be brilliant to near genius intellectual levels. Detection in such cases as psychopathic behavior have been brought about to police investigation, through intensive laboratory and field work when the medical authorities involved have discounted any such possibility."

I scanned the rest of the page between a few more bites and began the next.

"Dr. Christian Von Braun, the renowned psychiatrist, addressed a conference of his colleagues in 1875. In it he described the victim of mental illness in a rather literate way:

"To be a victim of insanity is to be a victim of self-imposed sentence in hell. It is to become the devil himself, to walk with demons and dragons, to breath fire and pain, to play with life and death, to be infected with the hideous, to worship the depraved, to masquerade inhuman form, to wait to devour others, to feed one their flesh and mind - and to beat upon their quivering, helpless souls.

"It is to walk this earth forever condemned to shadows and whispers, obediently serve the urges and needs that rise out of the body, to delight in the taste of blood and tearing of flesh, to infest with one's disease the minds of one's loved ones, and violate all that they hold sacred and precious.

"It is to grovel naked in slime and stench and feed on human waste. It is to slither into graves and like a rat, chew at the living and the dead. Insanity. It is the cesspool of mankind."

I stopped reading and shut the book. Goosebumps covered my arms and I shivered at what I had just read. I sipped the last of my wine and stared into the few remaining flames among the glowing embers. Then I turned out the light and pulled the covers tightly around me.

I lay awake for some time and watched the reflections of the fire as they danced across the ceiling, undulating as if enacting some primitive ritualistic dance.

Through my mind, like puppets, came the images of Jennifer - the strange, haunted eyes silently pleading - the discarded body of an old man - the watery grave that I had almost known and the knife rising out of the water on its deadly mission. Then came more images – the propeller blades as they moved closer and closer - the icy cold that had nearly crucified my body and soul - and finally -Timothy - a small boy with brown almond – shaped eyes waiting for the night shade of death.

Sanity, with its logic, with its reasons and purposes, with its humanity and goodness, its justice and tolerances, seemed as fleeting and elusive as the shadows on the ceiling.

FRIDAY DECEMBER 22nd.

Eventually I must have slept. When I woke again the fire was nothing more than glowing embers. I heard the fern brush against the windows, the lamp creak as it swayed above the downstairs coffee table, and the wind as it buffeted the house with increasing strength. In the distance I could hear the moaning of the docks albatrossed around their pilings and the whinings and groanings of the tugs opposite me and the pleasure craft alongside, as they fidgeted restlessly in the choppy water. For all the prevailing mildness and temperate conditions on the West Coast, the weather had an unpredictability about it that could turn its pleasantness into a sudden, savage force.

For the better part of an hour I tried to ignore the movements and sounds. It was building, and sleep soon would be impossible. And sleep, if for no other reason than to provide a refuge for my mind, I needed badly.

It must have come. At least in fragments. The sleep that I so desperately needed should have continued through the night.

It didn't.

I awoke slowly, with persistent sounds gnawing at my semi consciousness.

Outside, I heard the slap of the lanyard on a nearby sailboat, and the tugs as they heaved in the water and pulled at their moorings. The wind slammed against the windows and the house creaked as it pitched and rolled. The storm had strengthened considerably and through the intensity of its anger it seemed to take me a long time to detect the sound that was wrong, the sound that had awakened me.

The grating! What was causing that? I sat up and listened more closely, puzzled even more. Something was wrong. I crawled out of bed and in the dark fumbled around for sweater, slacks and shoes. I don't know why I didn't turn on a light. Somehow it would only have been a distraction. I padded downstairs, opened the door onto the deck and stepped outside, staggering against fierce winds that ripped against my sweater.

It was worse than I had expected. In the pale yellow lights high above the docks, I could see the masts of the sailing boats doing an inverse pendulum swing of forty-five degrees. The docks heaved in the water and the pleasure boats thrashed against their moorings like young children in a temper tantrum. Somewhere metal screamed against metal. The high winds were coming from the southwest through the unobstructed valley of the harbor, hitting the marina full force.

I was already chilled to the bone. I slipped back inside and retrieved a windbreaker, gloves and a flashlight, and headed back onto the dock. I felt it move under my feet. It was an uncanny feeling. Then I saw it in the yellow beam of the flashlight the blue, frayed edges of the one inch polypropylene mooring rope, caught under the edge of the deck flashing of the houseboat the twisted metal, razor like edge bearing down on the line with each heave of the house sixty-eight tons cutting into the few remaining strands.

Alarm suddenly gripped my mind. If the line broke, the tension would go to the power cable leading into the houseboat and the 100 amp line would be suddenly torn loose! The circuit breaker was inside the house, but to cut the power in the cable I'd have to go to the main electrical box. I watched the flashing bear down again on the line while indecision hammered in my head. How much longer would it hold? Five minutes?

Fifteen? Or maybe it would go with the next gust of wind.

I clutched my collar up around my face and began to move out along the dock. Even on the main dock I had to fight to keep my balance. The docks heaved under my unsteady footing while I was caught in gusts of wind that seemed to come from every side. I had to move from the main dock to a finger dock. Barely two feet wide, I stepped cautiously onto it, now very alarmed at how little stability remained. The dark choppy water lapped at either side and with my arms extended like a tightrope walker I moved one foot at a time, swaying dangerously over the side. If I slipped, if I fell, I could never crawl out the dock was eighteen inches above the water I'd have to pull myself out and be forced to use my right arm, which still ached from the teeth of the dog. With the rest of my body already stiff and exhausted, I would have little hope of succeeding. How long would I last in the water? What had Paul said? Thirty minutes maybe forty at the most? No one was around. No one would hear me.

I crept even more slowly agonizing with the need to hurry. God, why hadn't I called Rob? Was he even at home? I didn't know but I could have tried to reach him. I cursed myself for my stupidity and then stopped short. In the wavering beam of the flashlight three feet ahead of me was water. In the pale beam of the light the rest of the dock five or six feet away tossed in agitation the connecting chains now hanging downward into the blackness.

I swore in frustration angry with myself and all too aware of the time that was so precious.

I was now down on my hands and knees as the dock I was standing on leaned violently in the increasing storm. I turned and crept back along the way I had come standing for only moments at a time, then reduced once more to crawling. I inched my way back to the main dock and then onto another finger dock, it too, perilously unstable. Then, finally, I saw the electrical panel only a few yards away. I clawed my way desperately toward the box and forced down the lever.

The tiny clock like faces ground to a halt, frozen in place. I was knocking out all the power to this entire section of the marina. Rob and myself and Paul aboard the Snow Goose were the only ones living in the marina and, only the heaters in the pleasure boats left on by their owners would be affected. I was hardly concerned at the moment with them. I turned and crept back along the way I'd come now on my hands and knees in the growing turbulence of the storm. The minutes had ticked by ten minutes? Twenty minutes? I had no idea it had been too long. I tried to hurry. I stood precariously and inched my way along, fighting desperately to keep my balance.

"Rob? Rob?" I banged loudly at his door and it opened by itself. "Rob?" I took a few steps inside and called again. No answer. Once more I shouted as loudly as I could. Was he at home? I didn't know. Still no answer. I couldn't waste any more time. I left, went back to the deck of my houseboat, grabbed a coil of extra line, and crouched down at the edge of the deck. Miraculously the line was holding, only now the strands were almost threadlike. I threw my gloves off as I began a loop in and around the dock cleat and then ran the length of line to the far corner of the deck. Almost instantly my hands were numb with cold and the line twisted and coiled un-co operatively the more I tried to hurry. I lay down on the deck, extending my shoulders and body over the edge in order to reach the bracket. Awkwardly I got the end through and began to tie a knot. My hands dipped into the icy coldness and I gritted my teeth against the pain that crawled up my arms.

Then something nudged my left hand, something in the water. I recoiled in apprehension and turned awkwardly to peer into the water. Vaguely I could make out a shape part of something soft and cloth-like. As I stared at it the cloth became a shirt with the vague shape of what could be a human form. Fingers of fear began to claw at my insides and trepidation gripped my mind. My right hand groped along the deck where I'd left the flashlight my eyes remaining fixed on the object tossing in the angry water. Ever so slowly I extended my frozen, trembling hand toward the shape. Gingerly my fingers pulled at the edge of the cloth and the thing, as if in some ghoulish greeting, rolled over and surfaced, brushing the edge of the float. My heart pounded in my ears and already I felt my voice weak and useless caught somewhere in my throat. My fingers

numb and paralyzed with cold, seemed incapable of pressing the flashlight switch. Then suddenly the yellow light exposed what I now recoiled from in horror.

The mutilated remains of Rob's face and body lurched up from the sea. I could hear the water gurgling as it ran in and out of his hideously gaping mouth and I could see bones protruding through his torn flesh. It was a thing no longer human.

My voice came distantly in a low agonizing moan that grew to a shriek of utter horror my eyes riveted in shock at what I was seeing.

Too late, in my state of mindless agony I caught the movement behind me, the shadow that darted suddenly out of the dark, and the hands that reached out for me.

* * *

The water was closing over my head, sucking me back down into the icy blackness. I thrashed and struggled desperately trying to stay afloat. I pleaded with them and screaming and choking, my eyes wide with terror, I looked up at their laughing faces. They were all there. Their faces distorted, leering. Rob, Jennifer, Mr. Abernathy, Margaret Rutherford, Phillip, Mrs. Wainwright and Paul.

He was holding me, forcing me down, down into the water.

Then I opened my eyes, blinking at the daylight, and I felt his grip slowly relax as I sank back into the pillows.

"That's better how do you feel now?"

For several moments I just lay there. Slowly I began to orient myself to reality and to my surroundings. I was on board the Snow Goose. I guessed it was morning. Through a porthole I could see the sky was clear blue, unblemished by even a trace of cloud, the sun smiling as if in apology for the night's misbehavior.

But my head throbbed with a dull ache that started somewhere in my forehead and ran down to the very base of my skull.

"Awful."

"I'm not surprised. You've been sedated it will take a while for it to wear off."

"But...." My voice slurred in the feeble attempt at the question.

He was sitting on the edge of the bed looking down at me with more concern than his voice reflected. It was an attempt to sound casual and conversational.

"You were hysterical or pretty close to it when I found you. I was worried about your moorings with the high winds so I called you but there was no answer. When I tried a third time the line was dead. So I came over. Your phone's still dead, by the way. I've called repair service for you but it will be sometime before they get out. You slept through the worst of it but that was quite a storm last night. Lines are down everywhere, trees have been blown over, several boats have been destroyed and roads washed out."

I'd had to struggle to try and keep up with what he was telling me. My mind was groggy and my brain numb. "My houseboat...?"

"You were lucky. Your repair work came in the nick of time. I'd suggest you get all your lines checked. Polyprop won't stand up to repeated abrasion if ..."

Suddenly out of nowhere a hideous image rose in my mind. "Rob...my God. What happened....?"

"It's been taken care of."

"Rob...?"

"I expect he drowned." He turned his head and reached for a mug of coffee from the tray on the footlocker and handed it to me.

I tried to raise myself up on an elbow, ignoring the coffee but my head throbbed with the movement. I lay back and looked up at Paul. "But his face... he was so ... he didn't just drown."

"Water has a way of distorting things." He stood as though the conversation was concluded. "I suggest you get some rest. I have some things to do. If you feel up to it later on, make yourself something to eat. I'll be back later this morning."

I didn't say anything as he started to leave.

"By the way," the familiar grin was back, his eyes roving over another one of his sweaters I found I was wearing, "you appear to be making a habit of finding yourself in my bed. A guy COULD get the wrong idea..."

The pillow I weakly tried to throw at him missed, of course.

It had been a split second only of lighthearted teasing and it vanished as quickly as it had occurred. After he had gone, I propped myself up with some effort, and slowly sipped the coffee, conscious only of the throbbing in my head as I tried to come to terms with the tragedy of Rob's death. The horror of seeing his face in the water came back to haunt me and I fought to shut it out and accept what in Paul's words must have happened. When I'd finished the coffee, I lay back, closed my eyes and apparently the pills did the rest.

They must have had some medicinal effect, because, two hours later, I felt better; at least enough to ease myself out of bed and into another cup of coffee and some toast which I carried out onto the deck.

The sun was bright and the breeze brisk. I sat basking in the wintry warmth. For a long time I stared out into the harbor, idly watching the tugs with their barges in tow, a few small pleasure craft skimming along the surface, and a freighter plodding its way up the inlet. How normal everything looked. Blue sky, gulls, ship traffic. I seemed to be looking at it all from another world, like a soul departed from the living. How strange my world had become.

For perhaps an hour thoughts ebbed and flowed through my mind, lingering only long enough to echo the faint dull throbbing in the back of my head. Finally, I roused myself from my deteriorating mood, grabbed my jacket, "borrowed" a couple of quarters I found in a nearby ashtray and went out for a walk.

An hour later the fresh air and exercise may have helped my head but it had done nothing for my mood. It was black, ugly and very angry.

Paul had returned with a bag of groceries, shed his jacket and had so casually offered to make brunch.

"I don't want anything to eat. I want some answers."

He turned around slowly and repeated the word, "Answers," as if not understanding the phrase.

"Yes, Paul. Answers. See this?"

The Vancouver Province newspaper I'd gotten from the paper box lay neatly folded, showing its front page headline story covering the storm and detailing the damage.

"I've been through it page by page, in fact line by line. There's no mention of Rob's death. Anywhere."

He sat down slowly in the cockpit chair and began the procedure of lighting his pipe.

"Not every drowning makes the newspaper."

"Rob's should have." I was seething. "Because it wasn't just a drowning which makes it all the more reason why it should have been in the paper."

"News coverage may not be as efficient as you'd like. It may have missed the deadline."

"It didn't miss the deadline." My voice was ice. "Because it was never reported."

"How can you be sure?" He was surveying me too casually as he tamped the tobacco.

"Because I stopped at the marina office this morning to pick up the mail. The guys were saying that not a single owner had even bothered to come down to check their boats. Everybody figured theirs was still afloat or they would have heard from the marina."

"So...."

"I said, 'Well, at least they must have had a visit from the police.' They both looked at me as if I had rocks in my head. No, the police hadn't been down. Not the North Van. police, the R.C.M.P. nor the harbor police. No one. Let alone an ambulance or a vehicle from the coroner's office. And I want to know why. Rob didn't just drown! Something else happened to him something awful."

"You didn't mention it to the guys?"

"No. I thought at least I'd give you a chance to explain what's going on."

"I'd like to but I'm afraid I can't." A small cloud of smoke drifted lazily upwards.

"You mean you won't."

"I mean it's better for you if you remain shall we say uninvolved."

"Paul I am involved. Rob lived next door he was a good neighbor and he was a friend. I want to know what happened and why. And..." I got up from the table, "and if you're not prepared to give me an explanation, then the police will."

"That's not very wise."

"Wise!" I exploded. "Wise! Paul I don't give a damn if you don't think it's wise! First you decide suddenly to go diving around a ship, at night, in the fog and not only does someone attack you with a knife, but we practically get ripped to shreds by a freighter and incidentally," my voice became low and threatening, "there's no mention of a body of a diver being found in the harbor either. And then last night. Your obvious reluctance to involve the police suggests some implication on your part I neither like nor am going to accept."

"If you believed that you wouldn't still be here."

"Up till now I've considered myself a reasonably good judge of character. You don't strike me as being a criminal but I've been wrong before," I hissed, "as you will recall." Angrily I reached for my jacket.

"Where are you going?"

"To the police! My phone doesn't work, remember? And by coincidence, I noticed yours doesn't either."

"Then I'll drive you."

"Don't bother. I can drive myself." I started for the door.

"I'm afraid your car doesn't work either."

I turned back in surprise.

His lips parted in a thin hard grin.

"You don't think I didn't anticipate you'd go to the police sooner or later?"

I sat sullenly in the passenger seat of his car and watched the traffic thin out around us. I wasn't there by choice. He'd simply taken me by the arm, led me up the dock and very firmly pushed me into his car.

At midday, the flurry of last minute shoppers filled the stores and boutiques, crammed with merchandise dressed in tinsel and glitter. In contrast to the Christmas spirit my mood was angry and depressed. Silently I chastised myself for being such a fool. Why hadn't I simply gone to the police this morning instead of returning to the Snow Goose? Where was he taking me?

If I had had even half a hope that for some diabolical pleasure he was, after all, taking me to the police, it quickly evaporated. Police headquarters were down on Pender Street. He had turned onto the Grandview Highway, leading past the few houses holding out against the commercial and industrial spread that now consumed most of the area. It was not remotely in the direction of the police station. I was about to protest when his signal lights blinked on and the car paused momentarily before turning off the highway into a large industrial park, its name discreetly screened by the landscaping under the pale garden spotlights.

I was alert and wary. I wanted to know where we were. If there was even a fraction of a hope of getting away, I was going to take it. Again the car paused briefly, this time in front of a large industrial overhead door that began to open quickly and quietly as if on velvet ball bearings. We headed inside and downwards, maybe three floors, and stopped at what must have been a designated place. With three empty floors of parking, only one other car on this level was present, which did little to dispel my growing apprehension.

He parked, came around to the passenger side, took me by the arm and helped me out of the car and the short distance to the elevators. Then as the elevator door closed behind us and I watched Paul press the button for the 14th floor.

Interesting. In reality was it the 13th floor? Most new buildings mis-numbered the two floors small concession for superstitious employees. If the 14th was the 13th, then the 15th was the 14th. I don't suppose that mattered to anyone except me. But given half a moment to get away, I was going up. I would be expected to go down. They'd have to methodically search the building for me floor by floor.

By the absence of cars in the garage, whatever security staff there was, was minimal. As far as I could tell, the entire building was unoccupied. It was worth a chance.

I was dragging behind Paul by only a few steps as we headed down a long carpeted hall, flanked on either side by nameless office doors. I'd seen the fire stairs to one side of the elevator doors. If it was still open I'd take the elevator, if not the stairs.

I moved rather I turned as quietly as I could, my first steps tiptoeing before I broke into a run. The elevator door was still open. Then, suddenly, no more than five feet ahead of me a wall descended across the width of the hall, silently and effectively blocking my only exit. I slammed into it, my fists hard against the same coarse covering that I'd seen on every wall. I backed away, stunned. For all intents and purposes, one could assume that it was merely the end of the hallway. What had triggered it? Had there been a signal of some kind? From Paul? I turned to face him. He was standing idly waiting for me as one might patiently wait for a lagging toddler. Then he spoke.

"Coming?"

SATURDAY DECEMBER 23rd.

The eyes protruded frog-like in their sockets and looked out sleepily from under the hooded eyelids. He sat unmoving behind a great dark desk in the dimly lit office – an enormous man, probably 250 pounds and mostly fat, on a framework designed for half that load. His gray-green jacket and shirt did little to conceal his bulk, other than to blend into a background of a similar color. The only contrast was the pale, pink, shiny skin on his face and his neatly folded hands. A thin, pointed tongue darted across his lips and disappeared. The eyes rotated in their bulging sockets to fix me in their cold, unchanging range.

"Come in, Miss Daniels. We've been expecting you."

The voice was a coarse, rasping whisper, and seemed to require great effort.

Paul pulled one of the two chairs back from the desk and motioned me to sit. I didn't bother to thank either of them.

"You'll forgive me if I dispense with the pleasantries." The tongue darted across the lips and slipped back in its cave. "I understand you're concerned about the recent, ah, incidents that Montgomery here has been involved in?"

I glared back at him. "Touching. I don't call murder and drowning "incidents".

He continued ignoring both my retort and my hostility.

"If you're referring to Montgomery's activities involving the freighter, that was... unexpected."

"The freighter we visited," Paul interjected, "was not scheduled to depart for another four hours." He was lounging on the corner of a credenza opposite both the "frog" and myself. Presumably he thought an explanation might evaporate the hostility that was boiling inside me. "A captain can order a departure at any time." He continued. "Ships' pilots are reluctant to take a vessel out with visibility less than one mile but the final decision, however, remains with the captain. Their radar is next to useless in the harbor – but there's nothing in the Navigation Act making it unlawful for them to depart with little or no visibility."

"I find it fascinating," I said sarcastically to Paul. "That explains the movement of our harbor traffic. It hardly explains your activities."

He glanced toward the frog behind the desk and I caught the almost imperceptible nod he was given.

Paul retrieved his pipe and tobacco from an inside pocket and began the routine of lighting it, which I had now come to recognize as a commencement exercise.

I sat sullenly, glancing warily from one to another, waiting for an explanation.

It was Paul who spoke.

"Mia, you might just as well sit back and relax because this is going to take awhile. To begin with, what do you know about drugs?"

I was taken completely by surprise. But I was not prepared to acknowledge that.

"Which kind? Legal or illegal?"

"Illegal."

"Very little." Then sarcastically I added, "But I'm a fast learner. Breaking and entering, murder at midnight, bodies that just disappear. I should be a natural for smuggling." I flashed him a kewpie doll smile.

He preferred to ignore my remarks and instead puffed on the pipe until it reached some obscure level of satisfaction. Only then did he continue.

"Let me give you a brief history. "Opium as you probably know comes from the opium poppy. Smoked for centuries, much the same way as this," he directed his gaze to the pipe resting in his hand. "Morphine - about one-tenth of a grain is found in each grain of opium."Heroin is produced by heating morphine in the presence of acid.

"Up until the late 1940s the use and trafficking of drugs were more or less restricted to those three." He continued, "Then in 1943 came LSD - 25 - lysergic

acid diethylamide. The 25 comes from the twenty-five compounds in the lysergic acid series synthesized."

I sat sulkily and listened with most of it going in one ear and out the other.

"It was discovered to be hallucinogenic. In other words, unlike the state of euphoria that users of heroin reach when they begin taking the drug, LSD users 'experience' great philosophical and emotional insights with a kaleidoscope of sights and sounds. By 1962, black market use of this so-called mind-expanding drug had spread from the typical university student to the general population. The formula is available to anyone who wants it, for fifty cents from the United States Patent Office and the chemicals are almost as easily obtained. Beyond that, any moderately bright chemistry student can produce it in an ordinary laboratory. Quantities that were produced many times exceeded the demand. One-quarter of a milligram is a very substantial dose. Most drugs are measured in milligrams - thousandths of a gram - LSD doses are measured in micrograms - millionths. In other words, an amount of LSD weighing as much as an ordinary aspirin would be enough to affect 3,000 people.

"At that time, and up till 1967, the street price of heroin was thirty-five dollars a cap - while LSD sold for as little as a dollar.

He tapped his pipe bowl and for a moment gave his attention to adjusting the mixture and then satisfied, continued. "The longer it was sold, the more users were cultivated and more of the hazards became known.

"Dosages were inaccurate, often contaminated, as could be expected in an illegal operation. Many were adulterated - combined with amphetamines. Stories of bizarre trips, suicides, flashbacks' began to turn the tide. For many, the report of suspected genetic damage - chromosome damage - caused even more rejection.

"By the seventies, users had turned to marijuana. Or, more precisely, turned back to marijuana.

"Operation Intercept was not only an unmitigated failure, it gave birth to what may well be the greatest threat to mankind we've ever had to face."

His monologue had let the fire go out. He stopped long enough to stir the pipe bowl with the end of a wooden match, then lit it and puffed till it caught and glowed.

I couldn't have sat and listened to him without beginning to understand he was giving me a background to circumstances that, while unrelated, seemed infinitely more critical than my own. His last statement had left me on the edge of the cliff. I waited impatiently for him to continue, while my mind began to vaguely grasp the motives of his actions.

"Though it failed to stop large-scale smuggling, it did put a dent in the quality and availability of marijuana sold on the street. Some users reverted to LSD. Still others, seeing a multi-million dollar business, have been enterprising enough to develop a new drug. This drug is called Narcon-62. It is, from the user's point of view, the best of all three. It's euphoric, mind-expanding and hallucinogenic without the hangover or withdrawal pains of heroin or the hazards of LSD.

"There is only one problem with Narcon-62. The `62'. Dictoride chloro-cyclohexane or DCC-62. It's a distant derivative of the same chemical family as the oregano chlorine insecticides found in DDT. It's now believed to be deposited in the cells of the body in minute traces. When this accumulation of DDC-62 builds up, or when a major change in the body metabolism takes place, it breaks loose, with devastating results both physically and mentally."

Out of the corner of my eye I caught the movement of the frog's hands. They slipped below the desk top and returned with a file folder, which the frog pushed towards Paul. Then he rebuilt them back into their neat little structure.

Paul reached for the file and extracted an 8"x10" photo which he handed to me. It was a picture of a smiling freckle-faced youth - the kind of school picture that proud
parents display on top of the television set in the living room.

"Richie Sommers. Honors student in his graduating year from Delbrook High. Responsible, well liked and with a great future."

He handed me the next picture. A body lay sprawled out on the ground. Black rivers spread from great blotches across his chest. It was a black and white photo. If it had been in color, I know there would have been a lot of red.

"He turned a shotgun on his parents. No motive, no reason, no provocation. He was killed by police when he turned the shotgun on them."

He handed me another photo. This time a group of young men lounged on and by the hood of a late model car. Someone had circled in red the face of an ordinary looking guy, probably in his early twenties.

"Sam Portafino. Construction worker. Considered to be a reliable, trustworthy employee by Belmont Construction. Married, one kid, enjoyed a few beers with the boys Friday night and coached Little League Baseball Sunday afternoons."

I expected the next picture to be the bloody violent conclusion. It wasn't. It was a morgue shot. The white sheet was folded just under his chin. I wasn't going to ask why he was there.

"Took a hunting knife to his wife, daughter and son and was threatening to kill a third child before the police shot him.

"There was no motive, no purpose, no explanation for their sudden, violent actions. But there was Narcon-62." He paused, his voice seeming to sadden slightly as he continued.

"The body metabolism changes when a woman becomes pregnant."

He gave me a quick, hard look and handed me the next picture.

It was grotesque.

An almost embryonic infant stared back, devoid of the features that should have been there. There were only black, gaping holes where there should have been eyes.

The nose and mouth were underdeveloped, and misshapen, like nylon stocking that had been pulled tightly over the face. Deformed arms and legs extended in an unnatural direction with the remains of what may or may not have been toes and fingers.

"What you've seen was found abandoned in a garbage container a couple of months ago by an old man called Joe Romano. The rats had already done their work by the time he retrieved it. Romano did what he thought he should do at the time. He dug a grave, buried the infant, and prayed to God to take the baby's soul to Heaven. But it didn't ease his mind.

He went to Confession. Still he couldn't forget. Couldn't sleep. Yesterday he went to the police and told them the story. The preliminary pathology report indicated the baby was probably born late October. Where it was born, who the mother was, why it was abandoned, all have yet to be answered. The gross deformity, however, bears a striking similarity to several other cases in the U.S. of babies born recently with similar mental and physical deformities. Doctors believe the cause is Narcon-62."

I suddenly felt sick. "Oh God. Paul. I can't believe - I can't believe any mother would take a drug that could do that to a baby."

"Most mothers wouldn't, knowing that it could cause genetically defective children. But there are those who don't believe it, those who don't care, those who are willing to take a chance, and those who take it unknowingly. But, it really doesn't matter. It produces almost instant addiction. There is little or no chance of recovery – even after as little as half a milligram.

There was a long, dismal silence.

"Paul, is that what that was all about – Thursday night?"

"Yes." His expression was hard. "More precisely DCC-62. The ONE ingredient that as yet they've not been able to synthesize. You see, it's a substance that is found in the Copra root. It's grown in the forests of East Asia, then collected, dried and pounded into a white powder. A great number of organic substances come from trees, roots, fungi, cacti, but they only continue to be used because a synthetic compound hasn't been developed to replace them. It's only a matter of time before they will and you can bet they're working round the clock on DCC-62.

In this case the DCC-62 was and is our only lead. We know it's coming in on a freighter. Freighters try to unload and reload their cargo in the shortest time possible, hence there's a lot of crew and dock workers on and around the ship. But just before she's ready to get under way, when the crew is all on board and the dock is empty, the drug is lowered over the side to be picked up by a contact. After that, it's taken to a lab where, through a fairly involved process, it's made into Narcon-62, ready for distribution."

"If you could find out where the lab is, couldn't the police seize the drugs there?"

"Seizing the drugs is only part of it. The key people involved have to be caught. If they're not put out of action, they'll only go underground even further. That creates a bigger risk. They'll be more cunning than they were, and they have already indicated they're anything but rank amateurs "

I was still left with pieces of the puzzle that didn't seem to fit.

"And Rob's death?"

"We don't know. Yet. He could have been implicated in some way."

"Rob? I can't believe that. He was an artist – a free spirit - just a decent, honest sort of guy. Not all artists are hippies and into drugs just because they are apt to do their own thing. I'm not that conventional either, remember. You might just as easily have suspected me."

Unexpectedly, the dry, whispery voice of the frog spoke.

"We did."

I'd almost forgotten about him. For a moment the shock left me speechless. But it only took a few seconds to bring to the boil a brew of righteous indignation and pure venom.

"Me? Me?" I spat at him. "Even if I did invite myself along, I didn't expect to be taken out into the harbor and almost killed! If we hadn't been almost run down by a freighter, we probably would have drowned! Then because I want to find out what had happened to Rob, I get dragged down here by force to this place, whatever it is, and told by you – whoever you are - that I'm suspected of being a criminal. You have your nerve! You really have! May I be so bold as to ask just how you arrived at such a preposterous assumption?"

The frog's tongue slithered briefly across his thin lips before he spoke. His eyeballs fastened themselves on me with a look of cold detachment.

"You have just recently returned from East Asia."

"Most ordinary people call that a vacation." I replied curtly. He ignored my sarcasm.

"You volunteered to work in the S.P.A.C.E. program."

"I was asked by a very close friend to volunteer while she was away on her honeymoon. Besides I wasn't aware that to briefly volunteer one's time to a humanitarian cause in this country is a crime - or for that matter that it should even be of particular interest to you."

I threw it out casually. But my mind had focused on the fact that this person knew a great deal about me - knew it precisely and knew it well. There'd been no file folder produced with my name on it. No sneak looks at facts or figures. He'd more than done his homework. He'd memorized it. Again he ignored me.

"For the past week or so you have spent a good deal of your time in and out of a hospital. Earlier this year you had a floating home built for you which is moored at C slip in Lynwood Marina. Claymont Towing occupy moorage directly adjacent to you for the Harbor Queen, The Harbor Venture, The Harbor Ranger. They're under a two-year contract with the Harbor's Navigation Escort vessels - to the ships moving beyond the First Narrows Bridge up the inlet. You have clear visibility of all marine craft as well as tugs, tankers and freighters moving in the harbor.

"The floating home is precisely one thousand, one hundred and eighty-six square feet, comprising two floors built on a concrete barge..." He continued on precisely, thoroughly and completely. Each fact was exact. There was no hesitation, no pause to search for a fact, not even a minute inaccuracy. I wondered if he would name the titles of the books on my bedside table or the color of Kleenex in the bathroom.

"You forget one thing."

He remained silent but one eyebrow wormed its way up a half inch.

"The porthole." As casually and as glibly as I could manage, I continued. "You see I have this marvelous porthole in my front door. Paul here gave it to me - actually gave it to me and installed it even. He brought it up from a freighter wrecked off Vancouver Island years ago." The sarcasm drenched the words like honey. "I'm sure you'll want to include that in your files - that is, of course, if you haven't already."

I pressed my lips together in an overly sweet smile to them both.

The frog's bulbous eyes seemed even more remote and inhuman as they focused on me.

"We have. To be more precise, it came from Jason's Marine Salvage, 1126 - 6th Avenue in New Westminster. It was purchased November 20th for $227.75 dollars. Originally, it came from a navy training vessel that sank in 1936 off the coast of Oregon. It was installed for you on Saturday December 2nd. Where upon you lunched on..." the eyelids lowered in a sleepy half blind over the eyes, "steak sandwiches and beer. Molsen's."

Paul sat casually gazing in my direction, wearing his amused expression. He didn't even have the decency to look the least apologetic.

If I had felt outraged before, I now felt absolutely humiliated. Too many female thoughts flooded into my head as I recalled that first scratched arm episode, the dinner, the afternoon when he'd installed it. It had all been planned, premeditated and calculated. I'd suspected something the day I'd met him. Then, like a fool, I had merely assumed that this tall, rugged man, new to the marina, would be an interesting person to know. I felt used. God knows, I thought I was a little too old to suffer those pangs. Apparently, I wasn't. My thoughts retreated to regroup somewhere between cold anger and a very bruised ego.

The frog continued his monologue.

"If you recall, I mentioned we..."he paused to impress the tense on me, "had" considered you possibly to be implicated. We believe now, in the light of other events, that to be no longer a probability. However, it is a concern that you wished to involve the police in this matter. That would be unwise. Let's say, `Too many cooks spoil the broth?' I believe we can trust your understanding and the need for discretion in this matter?"

He had a clever way of telling me he wanted me to keep my mouth shut. It was phrased as a question veneered with politeness. Underneath, it was a statement. An order.

I remained sulkily silent.

"Where you are, Miss Daniels, is of no importance. You will not be brought here again. What we do, I believe, is obvious."

The fingers of his hand unfolded and pushed the small white business card towards me. I saw the lions' faces in the emblem of Her Majesty's Service. His name and business address below and the four words, `Royal Canadian Mounted Police.' Then two more.

`Narcotics Division.'

I took a long, deep sigh. Hostility, humiliation, embarrassment. Those emotions didn't leave much room at the moment for the respect and admiration for those dealing with what was surely a difficult and dangerous job. Indignation still prevailed. I studied the words casually and turned to Paul.

"Just one thing, Paul?"

"What's that?"

"Should you ever consider a career change, you might consider acting. You're very, very good at it."

The ride home was done in icy silence. I'm not sure which served to make me feel worse. That I had actually been suspected of being involved with drugs or that I had been "used" by Paul to apparently determine my involvement if any in the whole rotten business. And all the while I had ignored my suspicions, remained blind to reality, and dallied in foolish flattery.

I suppose this will end up in a report too." I dished up the rest of the chow mein and the fried rice from the cardboard containers Paul had insisted on buying on our way home despite my protests. There wasn't much left. We'd already devoured the beef and broccoli and sweet and sour pork. "Mia Daniels now suspected of masterminding an international network of black market fortune cookies." I plunked them on the table.

"No. You've been demoted. You're considered no longer of interest."

I gave Paul a rather wicked glance while I gnawed a sparerib.

"You mean I'm no longer of interest to the frog. And to you?" Two bottles of beer on an empty stomach had made me quite outspoken. Nothing wrong with using a shriveled up ego as a harpoon.

He avoided my question. "James Justin Decotis - `The Frog' as you refer to him - is a genius at his profession. He's masterminded some of the major busts in the history of narcotics. Here, in Hong Kong, Marseilles, Beirut. To be dismissed by J.J. as a suspect is to become a born-again Christian."

More seriously, he added, "As for me, I don't have any suspicions, but I do have some concerns. And for what it's worth," he looked very directly at me "my interest in you has been a lot more than just professional." He continued before I had time to ponder his last remark. "Your experiences out at Island View had me worried. We've had an interest, don't forget, in hospitals, industrial labs, and chemical plants. What we're after is a fairly sophisticated setup, not a basement chemistry lab."

"Well, that would have to let Island View out. The most sophisticated thing that's been in that place was your camera. I suppose the pictures of all those medical records were also scrutinized by him?"

"They were scrutinized by a psychiatrist from the University of B.C. If there had been anything unusual found we would have followed it up, but there wasn't."

I'd devoured my food and now chased the last few grains of rice with my chopsticks, sneaking a finger over the edge of my plate to corner them.

"And now?"

"Now we just carry on. You do your job and I do mine. You wouldn't normally have been informed of any of this, except for the fact you were going to the police. It's imperative that everything remain as routine as ever. Having this place crawling with police is the last thing we need."

I sighed in agreement. The effects of food and beer had somewhat soothed my disposition. "Will you ever tell me what happened to Rob? And why?"

"Yes - if you want to know - when we find out."

I collected the cardboard containers and organized our plates one on top of another, then retrieved my jacket from the nearby hook and zipped it up. Paul did the same thing and walked me back to my houseboat.

I'd been angry, frightened, shocked, humiliated and embarrassed. Now I was just tired.

"Well, I can't say it hasn't been fun." It was a grim remark but I tempered it with a smile.

"Bye, Paul. Take care." I turned to go inside.

What else was there to say?

His arm slipped around my shoulder and he turned me back to face him.

"Not good-bye. Just so long - for now."

Unexpectedly, he kissed me and then held me to him for a long time. I felt his beard brush the top of my head and my face press against the cold, vinyl surface of his jacket

He released me and turned back along the dock quickly, slipping into the shadows of the late afternoon.

Whatever had prompted that response left me more than a little confused. If I was no longer a suspect was I still being cultivated for some useful purpose? Was it a chauvinistic form of an apology, or was it just a token display of the male on the make?

Another time and place I might have entertained that idea with a little more enthusiasm. But at the moment, I had something more urgent to do. Something that somehow had surfaced through all the horror and tragedy of what I had listened to this afternoon. There was little chance that it might work out but it was worth a try.

Nearly four hours later exhausted, and still not able to confirm what I had planned, I fumbled my way upstairs and undressed in the dark. The moon was playing hide 'n seek with a half dozen clouds and now and then slipped enough light in the windows to make me prefer it to anything else. I crawled between the covers, hugged them up around me and snuggled down into a great furry blackness.

I must have fallen into a very deep sleep for the sound was so loud and so persistent, I sat bolt upright. I held that position while my sleep-drugged brain connected

enough circuits for me to figure out the only way to stop the noise was to answer it.

"Hello?"

"Mia! You're home! I've been trying to reach you for hours. It's Janet..."

"I've been out, I guess."

"Well, you must have just gotten in because I've been calling every half hour."

"They must've just fixed it then."

"Fixed what?"

"The phone - it was the storm the other night." I yawned, trying to wake up. "By the way, I have the books for you."

"What books?"

"Pedersen's books. You know."

"No, I don't know." She was being very patient.

"Oh yeah. That's right. Sorry. He loaned me a couple of books to read. Said I could return them to you."

"Fine. Bring them over Christmas Day. You're still planning on joining us for dinner aren't you?"

"That's just it. There's been ah, a slight change of plans, I think."

"A better offer?" she teased.

"Not exactly..."

"Well, why don't we have lunch tomorrow, same time and place and you can tell me then, all right?"

"All right."

"Mia?"

"Are you still there?"

"Yes."

"Are you awake?"

"Mostly."

"Mia?" There was a quiet shadow hanging over her voice. A cold dread crept into my senses.

"I called, I'm afraid, with some rather sad news."

"What? Oh no - not Timothy?"

"He passed away this evening - around nine. I was there with him, Mia. There was no pain. He was actually very peaceful and content - as if he knew all along that this was to happen. Children seem to have an uncanny way of understanding life sometimes. Timothy was a very exceptional child in that way."

I could feel tears forming and swallowed hard.

She continued gently, "The chairman of the South Asian Refugee Center and his wife were here. You remember, you met them once. They gave me a gift for you and asked me if I would please see that you got it. It's quite lovely. A small hand-carved ivory pendant like that of Pele - I think she was the

Hawaiian Goddess of Fire - or something. Anyway, it was a token of their gratitude for the love and attention you and Yvonne gave Timothy while he was with us. I said I would make sure that you received it.

"I'll bring it with me tomorrow then - all right - and I'll see you then. Good night, Mia."

I heard the receiver click, tactfully as always. Maybe she'd heard the sobs I'd tried to choke back. Numbly I replaced the receiver, drawing my knees up as my head bent on top of them, the tears streaming down my face and my mind reeling with the loss of a tiny, frail boy of five, whose life had been so ill-fated and untimely. I cried out into the night asking, like thousands of others who lose a child, why? Why now, must a child with everything to live for die so early before he had even tasted the goodness of life, before he had romped through mud puddles and chased butterflies and laughed at funny clowns and tasted cotton candy and gazed at tinseled trees and ribboned presents.

Instead, he had survived war and seen death. His mother and father, his brothers and sisters. He'd known pain, cold, starvation and exhaustion. He'd lost his

family, his home, his country, and with disease, at last his life. I played the game of reason and fate and denial and I could find no answer. Exhausted, physically, emotionally, I lay back with the words of Dickens drying my tears, `It is a far, far better place that I go than I have ever known.'

Oh God, I hoped for the sake of that dear little boy, it was.

SATURDAY DECEMBER 23rd.

I don't know why I didn't sleep. Emotionally spent, I lay on my side staring out at the water reflecting in the moonlight, my mind dull and drifting, my head echoing a distant throb. Like Shakespeare's MacBeth, snatches of the past events, the people, would "Fret their hour upon the stage and then were heard no more." In a medley of confusion they tripped through my mind, like some peculiar game of charades. Whatever meaning was to be found escaped me.

The night ticked on.

As if to console me Humphrey settled himself by my pillow and wheezed his rusty purr like a lullaby. Eventually his obligation performed, he returned to his woolly retreat under the loom to sleep out the rest of the night.

Had it been an hour or maybe two? I wanted desperately to sleep now but shrouded in her black veil like a phantom, sleep remained beyond my reach. Another hour must have ticked by before I finally gave up.

Somewhere, at the foot of the bed, I found my dressing gown and padded down to the kitchen. In the yellowish cast of the dock lights seeping in the windows, I plugged in the kettle, scraped a measure of hot chocolate into a mug, and when the kettle had reached a point I considered adequate, filled the mug, stirred and carried it into the living room by the window.

I sat for a long time curled up on the sofa, sipping the hot liquid. Quietly moving through the night as she always did, the Harbor Ranger came home to her berth opposite my houseboat. I heard the engine reverse as she was brought to a standstill, snug against the dock. Already her navigation lights were off and there were a few brief, faint words as one man tied the lines. They collected their gear and strolled back along the dock to waiting cars. All done so routinely. For a while I envied them their jobs, despite strange hours and often long and routine work. It reminded me that in just a few days this job would be over and in a few months I would be back once again working in my own field. Despite the problems and worries of field design, at least it didn't have the frustration and anguish I was experiencing now.

I saw it then, or thought I did, the hot chocolate almost gone and sleep now tiptoeing closer as I gazed idly out toward the tugs. A shadow seemed to be in a different rhythm to the rest. Was it near the stern of the tug that had come in or was it on the dock? I couldn't be sure. Then it lengthened and with sudden awareness creeping back into my head I saw that it was the shape of a man, and I saw what now snapped my mind instantly alert. The black rubber skin, the face mask poised on his head, the tank on his back.

Paul? No it couldn't be. Even at that distance, the build of the man was much different from Paul's shorter and broader. But then if it wasn't, who was it and what was he doing? They'd mentioned these tugs, hadn't they? What I was seeing began to have a very evil meaning. My hand crept out to the phone beside me and I darted quick glances at it as I began to dial Paul's number. The figure had slipped into the water I could almost be sure and then a small disturbance in the water by the dock confirmed it. In the dimness I very carefully pressed each number 9 7 4 1000. Glancing back out the window I could see small eruptions of bubbles reach the surface. I waited anxiously for the first ring. Then the second. Then the third. Paul – wake up if you're there –answer. The fourth ring.

Under my breath I pleaded with him answer you have to be there! Please answer. The fifth ring the sixth. I must have misdialed. I broke the connection and started again. I peered at the keypad and urged my trembling fingers to move precisely. It had to be right this time. I waited for it to ring and turned my eyes back to the water. Fear began to move in on me. The stream of bubbles was very evident and it was moving closer. Whoever it was underwater was moving towards the houseboat already half the distance had been covered. How many more feet? Seventy-five one hundred? It couldn't be much more. My mind seemed caught in an icy cage of confusion. I heard the first ring and then the second panic now edging closer. The third ring. The bubbles floated closer how many more minutes did I have? The fourth ring. Paul please! Please answer. Once more. Nothing. Trembling now, I managed to get the phone back in its cradle. I groped my way back upstairs and crept closer to the window. I didn't need confirmation. The tiny trail of bubbles couldn't have been more than twenty-five feet away. Could I get away? I moved to another window and looked along the dock and up towards the parking lot. Unmistakably, the shadowy figure of a man stood silently looking towards the houseboat.

I was caught, trapped. For whatever reason, the circle was growing tighter. Could I slip past the man near the gate, blunder my way through? If I tried and failed I would have placed myself in their net. I had only minutes left.

There was only one place to go. With the horror of it creeping through my mind I had no choice. I remembered Rob's maimed features only too well. Whoever they were, whatever it was they wanted, I wasn't going to wait to find out.

Very quickly I tossed off my dressing gown and nightgown not wanting my movements to be hampered, and threw on a long pullover sweater and slacks and slipped back downstairs. I grabbed a heavy screwdriver from the kitchen, and then moved to the shadows by the window. I had to know for sure exactly where he was if, in fact, he would use the deck. For a moment I saw nothing. I searched the black water again and again. There! The little telltale blossom of bubbles! They were so close to the houseboat, I'd been searching too far away. Suddenly the water erupted and I saw the black head and face mask break the surface. Two hands reached forward in contact with the side of the houseboat. I pulled back in the shadows and waited.

He began to move along the edge of the houseboat to the deck. Now no, wait. I had to be sure. Through the blinds I saw the figure lift himself over the side and turn to sit on the edge of the deck. A new kind of fear seized me. There was no doubt this man wasn't Paul. He was even shorter than I had first thought, but with a great barrel chest and powerfully built, heavy arms and legs. This man was a stranger. I had little doubt that his purpose was as evil as the panther like image he projected.

He raised the face mask and then leaned forward. That was it. His fins. He was taking them off. That's what I needed to know, to be sure at least for a while, he was staying out of the water.

And I was going in. My mind stumbled back to the months when the houseboat was being built. Against the advice of other houseboat owners, I had insisted that the center of the barge have a 6'x6' opening directly to the sea to handle holding tanks should new building codes require them. And the marine architect had agreed reminding me the sewer and water connections would be there and yes, you'll want access to check for possible leaks or damage. So accessing that space was a 3'x3' hatch door. Didn't I want a brass strip and a marine latch put on it? No. Then why didn't I get the carpet layer just to lay the carpet uncut over the top. After all, you'll never need to lift it. No. So the wall-to-wall carpet had simply been cut. The rug placed over the top concealed the edge. That had been the solution. How ironic. Quick access all right. Never, not in a million years, would I ever have dreamed it might save my life.

Now there would be only moments because he would have some way of opening the locked door. He'd been quiet and, except for me, unseen, and most of all unexpected. But his methods of getting inside and getting to me if he succeeded would be equally as professional. If he was at the front door now, he was no more than ten feet from me.

My fingers felt the cut edge of the carpet, between the ends of the fringe of the small prayer rug that lay on top. I maneuvered the screwdriver in place and applied all my weight. The hatch lifted at its hinged side and my fingers clawed for a hold to keep it raised. God, it was heavy. Heavier than I had remembered. Awkwardly, I slipped my legs down into the hole my feet searching for a ledge a place to brace the rest of me. Twice they struck the icy cold water and I caught my breath. Then they found a footing. I turned and groped my hand along the carpet for the screwdriver. Where was it? I had to have it. There! My fingers felt the rubber handle. I grasped the handle and then held it in my teeth to free my other hand. The weight was increasing. I could feel my left hand holding the hatch trembling with the strain. My fingers eased under and out of the way and I lowered it down on top of me.

It was too quiet. And instantly I knew why. Once more I lifted the hatch. With my feet braced on a beam, my body contorted in an awkward angle, it took now nearly all the strength I had. My fingers worked the fringe of the rug back along the edge. They had to stay clear. When the hatch was in place the fringe would lay on top of the carpet as it should. Caught in the opening it would leave a telltale indication of what lay beneath. My arms trembled under the weight. My strength was gone. I lowered it in place and then heard, thankfully, wood meet wood on impact. I also heard another familiar sound.

A key turning in the front door and the door starting to swing open.

Perspiration clung to my body and I shivered in the cold dampness of this black pit. Grotesquely, I was wedged only inches above the water, a position I couldn't keep for long. Already my legs and back and neck began to protest their confinement.

I remained absolutely still, except for my breathing, which came in great gulps I tried to take as silently as I could.

Suddenly, no more than inches above my head, I felt the hatch give fractionally. He was standing now, directly above me, not moving. My heart beat wildly and I closed my eyes as fear paralyzed my body and numbed my mind. Why? Was he looking at the rug the fringe? Did he know all along the hatch was there?

I think I must have stopped breathing. My body was rigid. Silence. Absolute silence. The smallest noise he would hear. I waited seconds, minutes? Then came the almost imperceptible sounds of weight shifting from the hatch and I knew he'd moved away towards the stairs. I began to breathe again. For a moment relief spread in a great warm wave over me and I shifted ever so slightly. I felt the instant relief on the muscles that had started to scream in my mind.

I began to predict his movements. How slowly and quietly he'd move up the stairs. Then towards the bed where he'd expect to find me. But it would be empty. Rumpled, slept in, but now empty. Night clothes tossed carelessly at the foot of it. He would check the bathroom, and the closets. It wouldn't take long to confirm I wasn't there. Then what?

I waited, cramped and cold, the pain of muscles under stress reaching through the numbness in silent agony. No sound. Total absolute blackness. I opened and closed my eyes and there was no change. It was like death, in a cold, black, watery coffin.

Something moved a vibration and I caught my breath. He was back downstairs, moving quickly now. I felt, rather than heard, the footsteps grow nearer and then retreat off in the direction of the kitchen. Were they louder or was it my imagination? No, they were quicker, less cautious. I hadn't been found. The prey had escaped from the trap into thin air or water. Fear, worse than ever, clawed into my mind and body. He, they, would know I couldn't have escaped. They must have been watching, waiting. They must have seen me come home. They knew that I couldn't have left. I would have to have come along the dock. There were no nooks and crannies, no attics to hide in. If I was there and I had to be then where?

It seemed so obvious, so shallow and evident. The logic screamed in my head as I began to realize how futile my escape had been. Why hadn't I left the houseboat, tried at least to get away? Oh God too late, I remembered the gun the gun I'd found on Paul's boat. If he wasn't there, at least I could have tried to get it or to the phone, even if I had just moments to call the police.

Inches from my head the hatch shifted under sudden weight. My breath caught and my limbs froze rigid with fear. This was it, it had to be. At what moment would I begin to hear the sound of it being pried open? The beam of a flashlight appearing to search and find their prey? What could I do?

There was only one answer left. And it could kill me as assuredly as the man now hunting me down.

I was going to have to hold my breath and dive down and under the barge that the houseboat had been built on, work my way underwater and come up somewhere along the side. If I got tangled in the cables and wires that I knew lurked under the barge, I'd drown. And if I did manage to make it to the surface... what easy prey I'd be. Already my limbs were paralyzed with cold. In the water I'd have no chance to fight off an attacker and even less chance with someone who was already an accomplished and equipped diver.

I waited. Were there voices? I couldn't be sure. Footsteps moved away and then back. My muscles were straining beyond their limit. If I moved, could they hear it? Would they know instantly? How much longer could I endure this physical agony? Desperately I waited for it to end. It had to. No matter what, it would be all over. I'd tried and failed.

Numbly, I lowered my legs into the icy blackness as quietly as I could clinging to the edge of a joist. For a brief moment the pain swept away from my limbs, released from their prison of pressure. But the cold began to gnaw in its place. A worse, more paralyzing, more numbing agony. What had Paul said? Twenty minutes in these temperatures? If I got out and got to the surface, would they be waiting for me there? That I didn't know. But the alternatives left me no choice. Once I made up my mind, once I'd started to dive, there would be no turning back. There'd be almost no chance of finding airspace again in the pitch blackness. I also couldn't afford to change direction. I had no experience with this sort of thing. How long would one gulp of air last me? Even if it would get me to the edge of the barge I knew with certainty I wouldn't be allowed a moment's delay.

I decided to risk coming up on the same side of the houseboat that the diver had approached. Both ends were encumbered with lines and the dock side carried water and power lines beneath them, none of which would I have strength or even presence of mind to deal with.

I was ready. Twice I submerged my head for seconds, and felt the fear and cold and dread spread over me and the salt sting my eyes. Then, for the last time I gulped in as much air as I could and went under.

I'd intended to go down first, but instead I felt the rough barnacled bottom of the float scrape across my head and my hands claw into the wet slimy bottom that was home to the thick writhing sea worms. Revulsion came in waves as I grasped at the coarse bottom in an awkward attempt to pull myself along. Something rough and heavy dragged across the side of my face and along my shoulder. A strange sensation filled my ears, and my lungs began their demand for oxygen.

I was moving, but surely not more than inches at a time. I had no way of telling. I turned on my back and dug deeper into the barnacles and I felt this time I'd moved. Something hard and strong struck my shoulder and I squirmed past it. Panic began to rise in my mind as my lungs began to scream for air. My hands scraped at the bottom of the float searching for a hold. My legs were so numb that I was unaware if they moved at all. Then I felt a sharp object cross my chest. My hands searched and found the cable and in near panic it seemed like it was impassable. It refused to give. I forced myself to crawl around it, feeling the barnacles claw at my arms and shoulders till I was once more free again to move. What precious seconds had it taken? How much more? How much longer? My hands reached out again this time to nothing I rolled over in the water and my head struck a hard edge and then beyond it there was nothing. It had to be! I clawed my way up the outer edge and broke the surface of the water. My God, I'd made it!

I was desperately weak and gasping for air. I clung to the wooden bumper for several seconds with what little strength remained. The pain of cold had penetrated every corner of my body and I shivered uncontrollably. Now, I had to get out. I peered into the darkness and listened, getting my bearings, scanning the water around me and what little I could see of the dock. Under water, I had somehow veered off at an angle. I was very close to the deck, much closer than I realized. If he was still around, there was every chance as he slipped back in the water he would see me. I clung like a sea creature to the bumper and listened. Nothing. Inch by inch I pulled myself along toward the deck. Now, even the moonlight left me completely exposed. Still, I continued, slipping my hands through the slimy growth of kelp. Past the deck, round the edge and now near the dock and into the safety of the shadows. I hadn't needed to swim, thank God. My legs hung uselessly in the water and my hands, exposed to the cold night air, had turned to claws, frozen now into icy numbness.

Still I continued to paw my way along the edge of the dock, this time my hands searching for a grasp, from cleats, to wood, to lines. These were floating docks, the deck a mere eighteen inches above the water. I knew already it was beyond my reach.

I had no strength left. How much longer I could even cling to the edge I began to wonder. My mind was growing numb, my concentration wandering. Somewhere ahead of me I saw the pilings. Maybe there I could try to crawl out, if I could find something to get my feet on.

I don't know how long it took me to reach them or how long I clung to them. Something writhed and moved out from under my hands, leaving me only vaguely aware of the starfish clinging in their sloth like way by dozens of suction cups. I felt another spasm of revulsion as the slimy, mucousy movements of a jellyfish slithered across my face and through my hair, back to open water. My feet scraped the coarse barnacled pilings, uselessly searching for a toehold. My awareness was reduced to only the cold; the numbness had crept into my mind as well as my body. For a moment I thought I was dreaming. Then consciousness returned and aroused my efforts.

Maybe I'd heard the sound before. It had gone on in my head for so long. Or was I remembering it from some time before? It was the sound of the night watchman's cane far away and above me the shuffle of his walk. I wondered idly, as I had so often before, why anyone with arthritis would want to be a night watchman, particularly in cold, damp air, walking the docks all alone at night. But he did, and had for years, long past retirement. Something kept nagging at me as my mind slipped in and out of a dozen fragments of time and space. I forced my head up and for a moment saw the same familiar figure with hat and heavy overcoat with the turned up collar leaning heavily on the cane as he shuffled along the upper dock a distant figure in the eerie yellow light under the shed roof. Then my mind was washed with cold as I lost my grip and slipped beneath the surface. Slowly and with almost sleepwalking movements I pulled myself back out of the water. It took me seconds, maybe minutes for reality to dawn that the man shuffling along far above me could help. Then, with all of the strength I could find, I screamed out at the figure again and again. Once more I lost my grip and I sank below the surface. For several seconds I remained submerged until one small shred of instinct to survive forced me to again reach out to cling to the dock. Only half conscious now, I looked up and saw him stop, alert, to listen. My God, help was coming! Hang on, hang on just a little longer.

    I did just barely my eyes watching the figure begin to move hurriedly along the upper dock that would lead him towards me. Hurried, but in a fashion, now unnatural. Unnatural for an elderly man with a cane and crippling arthritis. This man moved with speed, strength and obvious agility. Too late, my mind focused on my very deadly mistake.

SUNDAY, DECEMBER 24TH.

If it was a hospital it was far too extravagant. Plasma TV, plush carpet and black and red armored knights and horses on the bedspread that rode right over the edge of the bed to the floor. If it was heaven, I was worried. The sign on the back of the door said in big black letters that checkout time was one o'clock.

I was still digesting my whereabouts when a familiar bearded face appeared.

"You're awake." He held the smoking pipe and some newspapers in his hand, which he must have been reading for some time. He looked rumpled and weary.

"How about some lukewarm coffee?" The hotel's restaurant doesn't open till 7:00. I glanced at the bedside clock which told me it was 6:37 AM.

He put down the pipe and papers and pried the plastic top off a Styrofoam cup. There was something transient about it that seemed to match the surroundings.

It wasn't until I'd tried to prop myself up hat became aware of how terrible I felt. My limbs were stiff beyond belief, my throat was sore and I seemed to have almost no strength. Paul noticed too. He propped pillows behind my head and arranged the covers snugly around me.

Rather unsteadily, I held the cup and sipped at the coffee. I also saw for the first time dozens of red, angry looking cuts on my finger tips and the backs of my hands and arms. I inspected them with curious interest till I foggily remembered the razor blade barnacles that I had clawed at under the docks and on the pilings.

"Care to tell me what happened?" His voice sounded casual but it didn't match the expression he was wearing. He looked decidedly worried.

"I guess sleepwalkers shouldn't live on houseboats." I said lamely. Apparently someone I'd concluded that whoever had decided to pay me a visit by water had to be part of Paul's involvement. My proximity to him and the Snow Goose had begun to have some deadly implications. The events of our last episode though unanticipated, had practically gotten me killed. Last night's had been premeditated.

"I gathered that. When Gilbert hauled you out of the water you were practically unconscious. When he got you partially revived, you fought him off like a tiger!"

"Gilbert?"

"One of our men. Jim Nesbitt, the night watchman, is... on vacation. Temporarily."

I didn't seem to have energy for anger - sarcasm was easier. "Touching! Nice to know when you're not around someone's on hand to deal with these `inconveniences.'"

"I was around. Obviously so was he."

"Well then, why the hell didn't you answer your phone?" Apparently I'd managed to get rather angry after all. "A girl could get herself killed waiting for you to answer your bloody phone!"

He gave me a very direct look and spoke very quietly, his patience tightly reined.

"I didn't answer the phone because it didn't ring. A dial tone doesn't necessarily mean a phone works. Making it sound like it does though is elementary mechanics for someone with an unhealthy motive. Now will you tell me what happened - from the beginning?"

I did that - with every last detail of the fear and cold and terror I'd experienced. When I finished, I lay back on the pillow, exhausted and depressed. There were questions I wanted to ask, but I was just too tired. As for the answers, at the moment anyway, he didn't look like he'd give me the time of day.

"I think you should get some rest - I've got to leave but there's another man next door who's going to keep his eye on you. If there's anything you need, he'll get it for you. I'll be back later - and we'll have something to eat."

He walked over to the closet and retrieved a windbreaker, zipped it up and headed for the door.

"Paul?" Guilt was nibbling at the edges of my self pity.

"Yes?"

"I'm sorry for getting angry. If Gilbert hadn't gotten me out of the water, I'd probably have drowned."

"Grimly, he replied. It might have been a more merciful death than whoever it was had planned for you."

"I shuddered. By the way, where are we?"

"The Timberwood."

"Could you - would you feed Humphrey? I managed a small smile.

He glanced back, puzzled.

"If you insist on feeding and caring for me, you have to feed and care for Humphrey too. It's a package deal. He gets a can of Kitty Delight each day, and chopped liver three times a week."

"And I suppose he always get a special treat for Christmas?"

"Of course. A catnip mouse every Christmas under the tree - gift wrapped, with a card."

I rolled over and pulled the sheet over my head.

For a long while I just lay huddled under the covers trying to sort out the range of emotions that had swept through me over the last couple of weeks. It seemed I had experienced them all. Initially, I had been attracted to this man, I had enjoyed his company, his quiet strength and his resourcefulness. But then it had been invaded by suspicion, resentment, anger, frustration, humiliation. Coupled with the events at Island View, and what little time there was remaining of the day, the rest I so desperately needed would have to wait.

At 10:00 I moved from the already physically battered to something like the walking dead - all of it between the bathroom and the bed. I found my slacks, sweater and shoes in the closet. The clothes had been washed and dried. The shoes still a tad damp. For the moment I wasn't going to ask how they ended up in a closet or how I'd gotten to the Timberwood Inn and then into bed. I'm sure the answers to those questions would be the same. Dressed now, and having done the best I could by "combing" my hair with my fingers, I was just about to leave when Paul returned.

"Do you think leaving is wise?"

"No, but I just realized that tonight is Christmas Eve. I have a lunch date today with a friend and then I have one more thing I want to do. Both have to be done today, because tomorrow I'm leaving."

He gave me a look that seemed to spell hurt and disappointment. "Just be careful ...at least until tomorrow. I'll see that we have someone watching your houseboat." Without another word he turned his back on me and walked out of the room.

* * *

"You look dreadful! And you sound even worse!" At that, Janet was being kind. I could have easily passed for an animated corpse. The animation due entirely to the two vodka martinis, the first I had ordered while waiting for her,
the second to keep her company while she sipped a Dubonnet.

"That's a fine way to greet a friend!" The quick stop to shower and change apparently had made little improvement." I don't go around saying nasty things about you!"

"Friend or not - have you seen a doctor? Mia, I mean it. You're haggard and pale, and look at your hands and your arms. What happened to you? And you've lost weight and never mind the quips about that - you look positively ill!"

"It seems a lot of people have been concerned about my health lately," I mused. "Actually, I feel better than I look, though I couldn't have said that this morning. Just my usual ability for getting into trouble, I suppose." Then I sneezed. "Probably serves me right for getting my feet wet." I munched an olive and gave Janet a grin. "Anyway, since you're so concerned about my health, you'll be pleased to know this sickly soul here is taking herself off to Hawaii for rest and recuperation. Long lazy days to catnap through and Mai Tais by the swimming pool in the evenings."

"Oh, Mia - how marvelous!" She almost glowed with pleasure. "How did you ever manage to get reservations at this time of the year?"

"One phone call is all it took. That was the best piece of luck I've had in ages. My travel agent who had booked my previous trip through Asia had a cancellation a few minutes after I'd called him. It means I leave tomorrow, Christmas Day which is a bit of a rush and it does mean I won't be coming over to your house for Christmas dinner, either, I'm afraid. But it was either that or not go, except for one problem."

"What's that?"

"Humphrey. Normally I would have asked Rob to feed him but well, he's ... not available." I felt a twinge of guilt at my response but the truth would have required more than I felt I was prepared to handle emotionally. Though I had asked Paul to feed him this morning, it was a favor that I didn't want to be indebted for. Somehow I suspected that by the time I got back from Hawaii, neither he nor the Snow Goose would still be there.

"So I was wondering if..."

"We'd love to! It will give the old boy a chance to dry out in case he's gone over the side again. Why don't we have Jack pick him up in the morning?"

"That would be wonderful Janet! You sure you don't mind?"

"Of course not. He'll probably even have time to get the salt out of his whiskers. Besides I wouldn't let a cat, even if he is a precious old soul, stand between you and a vacation. It will do you a world of good, Mia. You've been under a great deal of strain. I think that program is taking its toll on you."

Dear, sweet Janet, I thought to myself. Attacked by dogs, run down by a freighter and stalked in the dead of night by a killer. I should be the one they keep locked up on the fifth floor. Who else but an absolute raving lunatic could get themselves so involved in madness and murder!

"Just a tad."

"You're almost finished aren't you?"

"Except for a final report, which I've just about completed, and a couple of loose ends, you're right." I pointed to Pedersen's books that occupied a third chair. "Apparently you visit him occasionally. I didn't know that."

Janet lowered her eyes and stirred the ice slowly with her swizzle stick. "Pedersen was like a grandfather to Kate. He even used to come and stay weekends with us and we had a grand time. Neither Jack nor I ever had much of a family and there's really only cousins left now. After Katie died, we just sort of continued the relationship. I get out to see him about once a month. He has his cats and his greenhouse but no family either. I think he misses people. Was he able to help you?"

"Yes, in a way. At least he cleared up a lot of doubts I was having." I took another sip of my martini. "I'm afraid I was getting myself caught up in what you'd probably label unprofessional involvement. It's a long story I'll bore you with some time but there is part of it that might involve you." She listened patiently as she always did while I gave her some background and briefly outlined what I had in mind. I had anticipated her response. She was wonderfully enthusiastic. Then when we had dealt with the details I returned to sum up the job. "Anyway, it's over, soon to be forgotten, and I'll be moving to home ground soon."

"What part of the world will that take you to this time?"

"A tiny island out in the middle of the Pacific. Used to be a leper colony." I grinned. "I could come back looking even worse than I do now. Can't exactly say though, that volunteer work hasn't had its risks, so to speak. But some time in the sun will help get me ready for crocodile soup and dried piranha, if that's what it's to be." I teased. "And speaking of food, shall we order?"

That was the nice thing about Janet. She was a patient listener with lots of empathy, and never pried. That's probably what made her both competent and admired at her job.

She had a knack of making people feel good about themselves. At the moment I felt good enough about my appetite to order a salad, hot crab and cheese on an English muffin, and cheesecake. She ordered the same and then reached into a compartment of her purse and carefully extracted a tiny box which she handed to me.

"I told you it was exquisite. Go ahead and open it."

She was right. The small ivory pendant couldn't have been more than an inch in length, yet it was precise in every detail. It depicted the figure of a woman with her arms raised above her head, flames licking at the folds of her gown, while the outlines of volcanic mountains formed a backdrop. I felt very honored to have been given such a lovely gift by people who hardly knew me, and saddened too by what had been the occasion.

"Here, let's see it on." Janet very carefully undid the tiny clasp, placed it round my neck and closed it again.

"Perfect." She must have caught my sudden sadness. "Well, you have to admit. It's much more flattering than a chubby Buddha!"

It was a good lunch and probably good for me. I enjoyed the food and even more so the company. My mood had lightened considerably.

We were walking back to the parking lot when I asked her a question.

"Janet, do you remember the big Panda bear I bought Timothy?"

"Yes - why?"

"Is it ... still around?"

"Yes. I was going to take it to the children's ward. Why?"

"Would you mind - I mean, do you think they would mind if I took it? I'd like to give it to a very special person. It's probably the only gift - the only toy she's ever been given."

"Of course. He could probably stand a bath but otherwise he's in pretty good shape. Do you want to go by now and we could pick him up?"

"Janet that would be great! Do you mind?"

She squeezed my hand. "He's going to a good home, I can tell."

Twenty minutes later while I had waited in the car, Janet had retrieved him from the ward, propped him up in the passenger seat of my car, fluffed his ears, and pronounced him good as new.

"He'd probably been the most mauled, squeezed, hugged and loved Panda bear in the world."

I felt a lump in my throat. "Guess we're never too old for toys. Thanks, Janet."

She gave me a quick hug. "Merry Christmas and have a terrific vacation, Mia. And spare me the postcards with setting sunsets and sandy beaches. Jack and I will be spending the Christmas season right here in the rain. I don't need to be reminded of tropical paradises."

"Okay. If you say so. I'll bring you back some Macadamia nuts." I winked. "They're terribly fattening."

I drove away with a wave and left her standing by her car with her nose all wrinkled up - playfully trying to make me feel sorry for her.

SUNDAY, DECEMBER 24TH

Paul must have been waiting for me. He arrived only a few minutes after I got home.

"Hi!" I greeted him cheerfully, my mood effervescent after my lunch with Janet. "You're in time to pour us rum eggnog, that's if you don't mind bartending." I removed the carton of eggnog along with some crackers and cheese from the grocery bag.

"This morning I didn't think I'd ever see you eat, let alone drink again." His mood seemed almost somber compared to mine. But then my day so far had been exceptional. Not a single life-threatening incident. I suppose I could have choked to death on an olive, but I hadn't. A day like today was practically a cause for celebration.

He slipped off his windbreaker and I planted glasses on the counter in front of him.

"He continued. You must have had an enjoyable lunch?"

"I did, as a matter of fact. With a friend of mine - a nurse who, by the way, went to great lengths to tell me I looked like something that belonged in a coffin!"

"With all the care and attention you were given?"

He poured the rum into the glasses and topped them up with the eggnog.

I added a dash of nutmeg and took a sip while he put the carton of eggnog in the fridge.

"The care and attention was first rate but I've decided that just being here is hazardous to my health. So I'm leaving. Besides, I need some rest and relaxation and time to think."

A bell tinkled and I retrieved the Panda Bear from the dryer, propped him up on the counter and arranged his brand new ribbon into a bow. Paul watched it all very calmly.

"Would he like a drink too, or do you think he'd prefer milk?"

"Neither, he's soggy enough as he is. If you squeezed him right now he'd probably wet his pants. But at least he doesn't feel wet and he'll dry out in time. Coming upstairs? I just lit a presto log. I don't mean to rush but I should get some packing done later on."

He settled back on the floor cushions after he stirred the log into flame.

"Your travel plans sound rather sudden. Were they?"

I took another sip of my drink and curled up close by the fire.

"Yes, very. It was a cancellation of a booking to Hawaii. I leave tomorrow at afternoon at three. As for Humphrey. I've arranged for him to stay at Janet's while I'm gone. She's the gal I just had lunch with."

Well, it will give him a change from falling overboard. That means you've concluded everything at Island View?"

"Yes. I'm turning in my final report and bidding my farewells. Oh, and I'm giving the bear to Jennifer and I'm returning her little blue book."

"You're satisfied with leaving things the way they are?"

His question made me just a little irritated.

"I'm leaving things ... as I found them, yes. I'll say my good-byes to Wainwright and Phillip though he'll probably not even be around. Anyway, I was probably wrong about Abernathy and about Jennifer and her book. I can't explain why the dogs were sent after me. But that combined with that night out in the harbor, Rob's death and the episode last night, which I suppose involves you somehow, just makes me want to get away for a while."

"Are you afraid something else will happen?"

I was getting a little irritated with the cross-examination. "I don't know, really. All right, maybe I'm frightened - but I'm also tired, really tired - and I just think it would be a good idea for us both - for you - to go on about your business - without having to be concerned about what may happen to me - and for me just to get some rest."

I squirmed into a tight little ball and added, "Look, I may have sounded ungrateful - getting half drowned, finding floating bodies and having someone hunt me down in the middle of the night in my own houseboat, but actually it scares the hell out of me, Paul. That's not my kind of business, remember? I'm the do-gooder - death and drowning and drugs are your business."

I swirled the eggnog around in the glass, took a sip, and continued.

"I just want you to know that I respect you, and the kind of work you do. It's dangerous, it's lonely and it's probably a pretty thankless job - I guess this world would be in a lot worse shape if it weren't for people like you, who are prepared to risk their lives so the rest of us can grab all the limelight for doing all the wholesome and virtuous things. It's just that I don't want to die being an innocent bystander.

"I know what you've told me - but I still don't know what happened to Rob or why he was killed or who it was that tried to kill me last night which I assume had to be his intention. And I know that you won't, or can't, tell me. I just don't like the idea of lying awake nights wondering where and when somebody's going to try again."

I stared down at the glass in my hand and shivered at the memories that too readily flashed through my mind.

Several moments passed in silence before he spoke.

"I did tell you you would be told - when we had the answers."

"I could be dead by then."

"Then maybe you'd like to know something that's just been uncovered."

Now I was instantly alert. "What? Tell me!"

It was his turn now to pause - long enough to take two long sips of his drink.

"You remember the photo Decotis showed you of the infant the police dug up?"

"Oh God yes! It was horrible."

"That infant was born October 26th in Vancouver General Hospital, delivered by an obstetrician by the name of Dr. Christopher Choo."

"I don't understand. The baby was found in a garbage container by an old man who later buried it."

"You're right. But remember the police dug it up and they have now traced it to the General. It seems the baby's deformities were the result of drugs taken by the mother early in pregnancy. According to Dr. Choo, two pediatricians and the Chief of Surgery, all of whom had seen the baby, it was considered medically hopeless. It was born almost without a face. Most of the features had never developed. Its lungs were impaired, it had a defective heart, the limbs almost non-existent and it was severely retarded. Even the brain cells were abnormal. It was a miracle that that it ever survived long enough to be born.

"My God!"

The mother was unmarried, on welfare, and had already been picked up twice for possession of drugs - once when she was four months pregnant. Hardly expresses much concern for her unborn child."

He paused and gave me a long hard look.

"The infant was sent to Island View."

I was incredulous.

"Island View?"

"To be specific, the fifth floor of Island View. It was going to die. Nothing the doctors could do to save it. They say that it might have lived for days, maybe even a week. Not any longer than that. According to the Hospital Chief, in cases like that which, he pointed out, fortunately are rare, and with either the consent of the parents or social services, an infant is sent out there till it dies. It spares the staff and parents."

"But then if it was sent to Island View - to the fifth floor, it would have been under the jurisdiction of Mrs. Rutherford. She's practically fanatical about her patients. So how did it end up ... where it did?"

"Maybe Mrs. Rutherford is more than fanatical. Or maybe the baby never arrived. As yet we don't know, but we're trying to find out. The ambulance driver, the man who was on duty that night, is visiting relatives somewhere up in the Kootenays. We're attempting to track him down now."

"But can't you just ask someone at Island View? Surely they must have records for this kind of thing?"

"We can, but we'd rather not. If there's anything... unusual about that place, we'd just as soon not tip our hand.

"Paul, are you saying that you actually believe something's wrong out there?"

"That episode you had with the dogs was ... unusual. Let's say at the moment we're doing some routine investigation of both the staff and the operation."

"But how does the baby fit into the picture?"

"That piece of the puzzle doesn't fit anywhere, yet."

"And I thought I could go out there this afternoon with a clear mind and not be finding skeletons in the closet." Suddenly my mood was tainted with all the old suspicions.

"At least you can be reasonably sure they dispose of the skeletons. Whatever else they keep in closets is what we'd like to find out. When are you going out?"

"Later this afternoon, probably around 4:00. I've some last-minute errands to do first. I have a report to turn in to Dr. Woodcroft and my things to pick up and the Panda to deliver."

"To deliver?"

"To Jennifer." I took a deep breath. "I gave the Panda to a five-year-old refugee boy at the Vancouver General. He was one of the first patients in the program and one of the brightest. He died last night of leukemia. He loved that bear very much.

"Anyway, you remember the little blue book Jennifer gave me? I want to return it to her. I know that I was all upset about what I saw - or thought I saw - in the book, but I'm just going to have to convince myself that it was a coincidence. I felt she should have the Panda Bear. I don't think she's ever been given a toy. So - I'm going to take the bull by the horns - or Mrs. Rutherford -same thing - and give the Panda to Jennifer. After all, I'm leaving, I've nothing to lose and, despite her hostility, I'm hardly doing anything that can be considered against hospital regulations. Even Scrooge became a pussycat in the end. And it is the season for miracles!"

He drained his glass and stood.

"I'll be curious to hear about your reception. You sure you feel comfortable going out there again?

"Through the front door and in the middle of the day, just fine. My after hours sojourns are history, thank God.

By the way, thanks for making that duplicate set of Phillip's keys but I have no intention of using them. Nor do I have any intention of ever seeing that place again, after this final visit!"

"All right, then. I have to go - we're hoping to have a lead come through this afternoon or tonight. And you did say you wanted to pack?"

"You're right!" I brightened. "Two bikinis and a pair of sunglasses." Then I added wickedly, "I always pack more than I need."

SUNDAY DECEMBER 24th.

It was after three o'clock, when I left the house boat. Already the traffic seemed snarled and poky, as if encouraged by a bleak, gray afternoon to annoy those last minute Christmas shoppers. Even the staff cars in the parking lot at Island View were scarce, as if they too wanted to rid themselves of the place and get on with the holidays.

I found Mrs. Wainwright in her office, chatting on the phone in her usual diplomatic tones, profuse in her compliments and niceties, as always. She could probably have sold the Black Hole of Calcutta as the Garden of Eden. What had Phillip called it? A vegetable factory. Yes, maybe it was. Mrs. Wainwright could do very well selling tickets at the front gate.

She concluded with generous thank yous and good byes and yes, that would be lovely, and replaced the receiver.

"My dear I'm so sorry to see you go. You've been a breath of fresh air around here."

I was being cynical I knew, but I thought to myself, yeah, about like prying the lid off a coffin that's been nailed shut for a century or so!

"I'm disappointed that you've missed seeing Dr. Caine. He left not more than twenty minutes ago." Very knowingly, she confided, "I think he wanted to get away to Whistler tonight. He's so fond of skiing."

"Yes, I'm sorry to have missed him, too," I lied. Outside of the typical male interest in me, he had treated me with remote detachment, a wary kind of aloofness, as if he, too, preferred like the rest of them to have me leave their sanctuary. I continued courteously, "Please pass along my thanks to him for his cooperation. I've left a copy of my report on his desk. I'm just going to deliver these things and be on my way. You've been very helpful, Mrs. Wainwright. I wanted to thank you and say good bye."

She stood and came around from behind her desk, extending her hand in a warm and friendly handshake.

"Good bye, my dear. And I do hope you continue your work."

I shook her hand, returned the niceties and left.

For a moment I slowed while I reassessed my decision, then I moved toward the elevator. I had considered phoning up to the fifth floor first but decided against it. It was too easy to get refused that way.

The elevator hauled itself tiredly up to the fifth floor, the doors slid open, and I stood for a moment outside the locked doors. I hoisted the Panda Bear firmly under my arm, took a deep breath and pressed the buzzer that would summon someone to answer.

I waited a long time before I heard the lock being slid back and then a small Philippina face appeared.

"I'd like to speak to Mrs. Rutherford if she's available."

I glanced at my watch and began to move past her through the door. It worked. Now that I was inside I would have to be asked to leave. Or told. That would come next.

I moved briskly towards the reception counter and then began to pace restlessly back and forth.

The Philippina's green pantsuit identified her as a nursing aide. I watched her move down the hall to the door that I knew was Rutherford's. She tapped and I continued my pacing. The next time I turned I could see her talking to a figure that was only barely visible in the few inches the door had been opened. I remembered seeing that door open the night I'd been there. I would never have believed then that anything would have ever made me return.

The next time I glanced up, Rutherford was moving very slowly towards me along the hallway, using a cane to support her weight. For a moment I was puzzled. Had she fallen, twisted an ankle perhaps? It sapped the aggressive stance I'd been mentally preparing. I had never been very good at kicking someone when they're down. But a minute later I discarded such humanitarian thoughts.

She made no attempt whatsoever to disguise her hatred. Her face was contorted in a great ugly thundercloud that would break in a fury of vengeance as soon as she'd reached me. I wasn't going to give her that chance.

I turned suddenly and approached her.

"Mrs. Rutherford, I'm leaving Island View today and I won't be back. In fact, I'm also leaving on vacation tomorrow. With your permission," I stressed the words very carefully, "I'd like to give this to the Drysdale girl. It's a Christmas present, if you like, but I would personally like to see her have it."

She regarded me with cold snake like eyes that looked out from the thin ugly face. Great shadows lurked beneath her eyes and her lips were stretched back like a leg hold trap, ready to spring.

"Patients on this floor have no need of toys." The words curled forth, low and intimidating.

"You may be quite right. However, I can see no harm in giving a stuffed toy to someone like Jennifer Drysdale. It will take only a moment. I believe she's in 507?"

I don't think I'd changed her mind. I think she reconsidered her refusal because it was easier in this instance to give me my way and be done with me. But then that's what I had banked on.

"She's been sedated."

The phrase, I gathered, meant permission was granted. She lowered her voice and spoke to the nursing aide while her eyes remained fixed on me in cold shafts of ice.

"Go with her."

She lay pale and frail in bed, her hair limply spread over the pillow and her eyes open, unmoving.

I sat cautiously on the edge of the bed and called her name quietly.

"Jennifer? Can you hear me? I've come to see how you are. I've brought you a present."

Moments seemed to pass while I looked for any response that might suggest the words had penetrated her dulled senses.

I waited. I spoke again.

"Jennifer, you gave me a present, remember? Now I've brought one for you."

Very slowly the blue eyes wandered listlessly, then stopped and stared vacantly up at me. She was obviously heavily sedated and I wondered why. I looked up at the Philippina girl and asked.

"Very excited." Her limited English was aided by expressive hands. "Her head..." She imitated by tossing and pounding it in the air..., "crying very upset."

"How long has she been like this?"

"Two, maybe three days, ma'm. It begin Friday, yesterday, today very bad."

"Has Dr. Caine seen her?"

"Yes. Yesterday, today too. He give her...," and her hands indicated an injection. "Excuse please," she gave me a little smile, "I be back soon." She left the room.

I leaned over and pulled Jennifer's hair away from her face. Her expression reflected the effort she was making to climb out of her semi conscious world. She blinked slowly and her focus seemed to sharpen fractionally.

"M m me?" For a second I'd forgotten the charm. She raised her hand slowly and drunkenly towards the small white charm still around my neck and then, inches away from it, her hand fell back beside her. I held it for her to see.

"That's a Goddess, Jennifer ... an imaginary person. People long ago used to worship her. Isn't she pretty?"

I don't know if she heard or understood. Her eyes remained fixed and she seemed to study it a long time. Her lips parted with great effort and she again said, "M me?" Was she asking for it? I didn't know. I would have loved to give it to her but I knew it would only be taken from her.

"Ch a ." She tried again to speak. I could see the exertion had caused small beads of perspiration on her forehead. She closed her eyes for a moment and then opened them again. They were wide and bright and seemed so distant.

"Charm? Yes, Jennifer, it's a charm." While I had her attention I continued quickly, "Here, look what I've brought you."

I took the Panda and placed him sitting up in front of her on the bed. Her eyes had closed again and her breathing seemed more rapid. She opened her eyes slowly and I watched them fill with fear. If she'd had the strength it would have been a scream. Instead, it was a low, agonizing moan of fear. Her eyes grew wide with horror and remained fixed on the bear. Her body became rigid.

Quickly I grabbed the Panda and put him down on the floor, shaken and very upset. Something about it had terrified her.

I tried to calm her and slowly her eyes gave way under the pull of the drugs. I spoke to her softly and seemingly for a long time until I felt she had again relaxed. Once more her eyes opened and she said the word "W a ter."

I stood, anxious to do something for her. I went to the nearby bathroom and found a small plastic glass and turned the tap. Nothing happened. I tried the hot water tap. Again nothing happened. Silently I cursed the decadence of this place. The Phillipina aide returned and she too adopted a blank expression at why there was no water, then she brightened. A moment later she'd retrieved a heavy metal jug from a bedside table and filled the glass.

"Jennifer, here's some water. Would you like a drink?"

She'd sunk deeper into the half world of consciousness and stared vacantly with glazed eyes towards the windows. I watched two large tears roll down across her face and then she seemed to slip away. Nothing I said or did produced a response. Maybe in time she would sleep. Perhaps a veil of unconsciousness, at least, would give her peace.

I picked up the Panda, prepared to go, and took my last heart wrenching look at Jennifer's frail young body, composed as she was in some mindless world. My hand slipped into my bag and I placed her little blue book on the bed beside her. It looked as small and forgotten as Jennifer. The aide straightened her covers; then she flicked off the light and together we left the darkened room.

I didn't stop to say good bye to Mrs. Rutherford. I saw her standing there, a triumphant, evil look on her face, another victory she'd won. And I'd been defeated. Already, I could feel tears forming.

I stayed upset for a long time through the long and tedious drive home and the routine of making a meal out of what I found in the freezer that I only poked at and then discarded. Even Humphrey regarded it with obvious distain, choosing his kibbles instead. I puttered about in the kitchen until it, at least, looked respectable enough to leave for a couple of weeks; then I ran a bath, soaked for a half-hour, and climbed into my dressing gown and stretched out on the bed.

It was eight o'clock. I'd hoped that Paul would have been by. I'm not sure that I just wanted a shoulder to cry on or whether I was curious as to what he may have learned. Earlier I had stepped out on the deck briefly while I debated whether I should walk over to the Snow Goose, but it had started to rain again, and somehow I didn't think he'd be there. Somewhere outside, I imagined, there would be a man posted to watch over me should I need help. It did little to reassure me. Instead, I dialed his number, but it rang repeatedly until I concluded he simply wasn't there.

In the shadowy light from the television screen I lay on the bed staring up at the ceiling, my mind kaleidoscoping on the afternoon's events. I wished I hadn't gone. I'd done nothing but upset Jennifer, when evidently she'd already been severely upset and that made me feel even worse. The Panda Bear had been something very special to me because of a little boy who had died and who had loved it so much. I wondered how honest my motivations were. Was I trying to replace Timothy's loss with Jennifer? I'd been hurt because she'd rejected the bear. Maybe in reality it was because I felt it was a rejection, somehow, of me.

I listened to the rain beat against the windows in response to the wind and it stirred even more depressing memories of Island View. I wondered what it would be like to lie in bed on the fifth floor, listen to the rain, and know that you'll spend the rest of your life there, a bleak, lonely, isolated ghetto. An endless routine of nothingness, an eternity of emptiness, of any stimulus, emotion, involvement. I wondered if Jennifer still remembered her childhood. Or had the charm only served to remind her of her own fate?

My fingers found and held the small, smooth carving of the goddess of fire. Fire that for Jennifer had barely spared her life and yet had sentenced her to a far worse fate. But then reality intercepted my thoughts. She was insane. Why couldn't I accept that? She had to be sedated because she'd become uncontrollable the worst she'd ever been isn't that what the nurse's aide had said? What had triggered her mind in the depths of insanity to drive her to such an emotional state? What stimulus in that sterile world could possibly have caused such a reaction, to bring back to haunt her a nightmare of fire, death and destruction?

I wondered if she was remembering the night, like a diabolical anniversary nightmare. Maybe a date? A calendar maybe that's all it had taken that could have been the stimulus. But hadn't the fire been in the late summer?

I got up, retrieved the manila envelope from the desk beside my computer, propped myself back up in bed, and clicked on the bedside reading light. I turned the photos of her medical records, skimming them as I went till I'd hunted down the date. Yes, August 17th. I was right. Late summer. It was a year of drought. That's why the fire had been so devastating. But it was December now Christmas eve. A shadowy thought danced across the stage of my mind, leaving only a trace of something evil. No more than a teasing, taunting fragment. Another date tripped hauntingly into the limelight and then slipped away into the shadows. I turned the photos slowly, methodically, for a long time till I found that date too. And now more dates boldly came to mind and I turned back slowly, expectantly, and found one more. For a long time I sat staring out into the night and the rain, the water and the wind, and then back to the hungry flames of the fire as they licked at the firewood. Then suddenly beyond the flames, the fragments began to take their places ready for the final act of a play far more insane and diabolical than could ever have been written. A plan of depravity and horror that surely must have been conceived in hell. And even now, as my mind tried to reject the images with reason and logic, it lost. Already the curtain was rising on the final act.

    I dressed without thought or reason but with a desperate urgency. It took no more than a few brief seconds to scribble the brief message and tape it to the front door for Paul to find. Then quickly I hurried along the dock and I was in the car and driving, too fast, too recklessly for the wet, slick and winding road. The miles ticked away as did the minutes. Cars passed with great splashes of blurred lights. Once I veered onto the white line and a honking horn tore through me as I careened away, hugging the edge of the road, the car barely in control. I needed every minute. I took a chance, glancing away from the road to my watch, sick to find it now almost ten o'clock. Then the dark, ominous building took shape and I slowed as I entered the gates, and followed the driveway to the parking lot.

    Desperately I scanned the building for movements, for lights, but there was nothing. It was the same route I'd used before and now I used again. Only this time I didn't care who saw me. I took the stairs two at a time, my breath soon gone and my heart pounding with exertion and with the growing fear of what I was going to find. I reached the fifth floor and for a moment clung to the wall, perspiring and gulping for air. Then, shaking, I took from my pocket the duplicate set of keys Paul had made and my fingers closed on the one I'd remembered by heart.

The moment the door opened I knew I'd been right.

Already the smoke had veiled the upper half of the corridor in its deadly fumes. It caught in my throat as I gulped for air and the tears began to form in my eyes, a useless defense against the sting. It was a heavy, dense smoke that forced me to move by instinct rather than by sight. I half ran, half staggered along the corridor to the door to Julia Fairchild's room and my hand grabbed the door knob. It was locked. I tried it again and again, fighting the panic. The keys! I wiped away the tears and tried to peer at the keys in the hope that somehow I'd know which one. First one and then another. The third one worked. I felt the door give way and I staggered into the room searching for the woman.

She was in bed. I could see the gaunt, hairless head, the face contorted in nothing more than a skeletal structure skin stretched like rice paper over the bones. Her claw like hands seemed poised like talons in defense and her eyes stared wide-eyed and vacant back at me.

"Julia." I choked out her name. I reached out for the frail hands. They were like chicken feet, stiff, retracted, cold.

She was dead.

For a moment I was stunned, frozen with disbelief, as the truth grew more ominous in my mind.

I stumbled to the next door, where I had seen the haggard old woman singing her lullaby to her `child.' I found her as I had expected, sitting in her chair, the old blanket still clutched in her scrawny fingers. The head had dropped back on her shoulders, her glazed eyes staring vacantly up at me. Her mouth gaped open in the hideous last grin of death.

In desperation now, I turned and groped my way out of the room and along the corridor to the door I knew was Jennifer's. I'd expected it to be shut, even locked. I half fell through the doorway and sank for a moment against the wall. Then I turned and saw what I had so desperately tried to reject.

Margaret Rutherford stood by the bedside, her left hand grasping Jennifer's wrist, the other holding the hypodermic poised inches above Jennifer's exposed arm, her eyes fixed steadily and icily on me.

"Oh, but you see it's too late." Her voice now was slimy and sweet the lips curled and the eyes glittered in their madness. A low evil laugh began somewhere in her throat and rose above the crackling of flames that licked the doorway.

"No!" I lunged at her awkwardly and from too far away, and caught the force of her left arm as she swung at me. In the dark smoke filled room I lost my balance, half tripping, half falling against the bathroom door jamb. Slowly I crawled to the foot of Jennifer's bed and eased myself up.

I saw her framed in the hint of orange light behind her. She held the hypodermic like a knife now over Jennifer's face and slowly raised it above her head, laughter vomiting forth louder and louder in sheer madness her eyes reflecting utter depravity.

I inched my way towards the head of Jennifer's bed and towards the bedside table. Any second she'd made her move, still by Jennifer's bed, still holding her wrist. Any second the hypodermic would reach its pinnacle and begin its downward plunge.

This time I didn't move. I gripped the cold metal handle of the water jug my groping hand had found and hurled it at her with every ounce of strength and control I had in me. It caught her shoulder and I heard the sound of something hitting the floor. She staggered backwards against the doorway out of balance, her hands, clawing the air and then, in horror, she turned, unseeing and in the thickening smoke fell into the flames. The laughter turned to insane shrieks, louder and louder and then great agonizing screams as the flames turned her into a burning stake that melted into the wall of fire.

Then, through the smoke, the hungry sickly noise of fire, I heard Jennifer's low moan. She was alive barely somewhere on the brink of unconsciousness or even death.

"Jennifer, Jennifer!" I shook her violently and again heard a low moan. I yanked back the covers and pulled her into a sitting position. She was frail, like a rag doll. I put her arm around my shoulders and pulled her, half dragging her as close as I could to the doorway. It was a gamble but it was also the only way out. I steadied myself and supported her as much as I could and then threw us out of the room.

We fell heavily to the floor, and in those first few inches, the air was almost breathable. The fire had been planned well. The main door would soon be consumed in flames, the only access to both the elevator and the stairs. But now, too late, in the final sadistic twist, as I heard the beginning of a low, evil growl, I suddenly knew what our fate would be.

The low animal like sound came closer from somewhere in the smoke and I heard the rattling of the chain that kept Samuel Louis Johnson restrained. In terror, I saw a great shadowy hulk grow visible and move towards us.

Desperately I caught Jennifer's arm and put it around my shoulders, as I tried to crouch beside her. Terrorized, I watched the creature move even closer to us. It was impossible to think of this brute as human for suddenly, the low animal sound turned to a scream and my heart beat wildly as I hugged

Jennifer's limp body closer. I could hear the flames roar and crackle, the heat pressing nearer, and the smoke growing denser. Again, the chain rattled even closer then stopped. I could make out the dark, hulking shape of its head and body and for the first time the eyes, that seemed paralyzed with confusion and pain. The light! Of course! The fiery orange of the flames now filled the corridor .We could, just maybe, get to the main door. Very slowly now I crawled a few feet forward, then braced my feet and pulled Jennifer's limp, prone body after me. Once more – the creature let out its low blood curdling growl seemingly only feet away. Again and again, I crawled and pulled her after me, closer and closer to the doors gasping for breath and choking until I could begin to count the feet I had yet to go. Fifteen feet away, ten feet. Dare I stand and try to drag her that distance? No. Again I crawled five feet, then once more. Now, staggering to my feet, I dragged Jennifer to her feet and with her limp body against me, I threw us at the door and with one hand got it open. We were through. We were safe!

I stood now with my back against the door, swaying with the dizziness and nausea that swept through my body, choking and gasping for air. I had to get help. Whoever was still alive behind the door I had just shut would soon be devoured in the inferno.

I propped Jennifer up against the wall as best I could, staggered a few feet and then fell, choking and gagging. I gulped for air and vomited. Weak and trembling I crawled along the corridor and unaware that I had reached the end of it, toppled down the stairs. I landed in a heap that left me stunned and senseless. Pain charged through my head. The coldness of the concrete floor clawed its way into my brain and my tongue tasted the thick warmth of blood. Seconds, maybe minutes passed before my head cleared and again became aware of the desperate need for help. I had to find someone. I crawled again, not willing to risk standing, to a door and beat my fists on it till it suddenly gave way.

Vaguely aware of my voice, I seemed to have been crying out for help. Where was someone, please anyone? Couldn't anyone hear me? Was I making sense? I thought I was. Then between my pitiful cries I heard footsteps.

Suddenly, I felt the impact of a hard slap across my face and Phillip's voice seared into my brain. Dazed, I saw the alarm in his eyes as his fingers bit into my arms and he shook me violently, trying to make some sense out of my pleas.

"Oh, Phillip. Thank God..." The words came in between great gasping gulps for air. "Help her help them fire." I pleaded my voice a raspy whisper. "Telephone......" The room leaped and plunged before my eyes as I hovered on the edge of blackness.

I felt his arms slip under my body and I was being carried. Movement, corridor, stairs. My brain fought desperately to try and relay the urgency, the need for help but my voice dissolved feebly in futile gasps.

Only semi conscious, I became vaguely aware that I was being carried back up the steps I had tumbled down, and back along the corridor I had crawled along. He didn't understand! My God! He couldn't know...I struggled to loosen his grip, to try to make him stop but my strength was gone. Then I saw the door, and Jennifer's almost lifeless body beside it. The same door I had crawled to, and forced our way through and then closed it after us to contain the fire.

Phillip opened the door and the flames reached forward with the draft in a renewed vengeance.

It was an inferno.

My mind recoiled in disbelief. This couldn't be true.

Someone was shouting, voices were getting louder. The flames roared now so close, the heat was searing, the noise terrifying. I struggled desperately but uselessly. My strength was gone. Suddenly, I was hurled through the doorway to the floor, my head coming down hard, cruel lights flashing across my brain.

The heat tore at my flesh, my lungs. Even above the roar of the flames, I heard the sound of the door pulled closed.

It was like an epitaph.

The last ounce of strength, the last shred of hope dissolved into a black empty void of unconsciousness.

MONDAY DECEMBER 25th.

I wanted to say to Paul that I thought this whole thing was getting monotonous, but I couldn't. My throat was dry and it hurt to breathe, even to move. Besides, it didn't matter. Nothing mattered. At least not to me.

Maybe to the others. They kept coming and going, talking in low voices, prodding and poking me. They were visions mostly in white, but occasionally in pale green and pink, like sugar plum fairies. Then, when I crawled out of my partially conscious cocoon, they'd gone and Paul had returned.

"Don't try to talk. Your throat and lungs are going to take time to recover from the amount of smoke they were exposed to."

He was right. My voice came like a stranger's, a painfully low, hoarse whisper. I sipped water through the straw he held to my lips and it eased a bit.

"How ... how ... long?"

"Since last night. You're at Centennial Hospital and by some miracle - apart from the scorching of your throat and lungs and some burns on your arms and legs, you're not in bad shape. But, compared to you, you'll be pleased to know, Jennifer's is alive and well. She's here at Centennial too - just down the hall."

"Here?" I croaked.

"Yep. Resting quite comfortably and recovering quite nicely. You saved her life. I don't think she'll be able to thank you yet - not for a while - but maybe in time."

"Oh thank God! Paul," I whispered, "she nearly died."

If there was a rule against smoking, he dismissed it. I watched the ritual of the pipe and tobacco but it remained unlit.

"You deserve to know some of the background, so I'll do the talking. All you have to do is listen, Okay?"

I nodded in reply.

"You weren't the only one who had Jennifer's her records checked. Over and above the psychiatric evaluation we had done, we took her history and had it dissected, verified and Cross-checked."

"Why?"

"Because all the other patients were a matter of record. Mostly police records - and rather prominent ones at that. Even Samuel Johnson's. But then he'd practically become medical history. As for Julia Fairchild, there was enough publicity about her fate to make it common knowledge. The Drysdale girl was the only one whose records were unsubstantiated. So we had them investigated.

"One of our men located an older son of the Millard woman, the woman who, as you recall, smuggled Jennifer away from the Bokarites. He was able to give us some of the missing details - rather important details as it turns out. But we're usually involved in rather orthodox investigations. We hire experts for the more unusual fields."

I didn't understand the implication of his last statement. But he saved me from saying it, or trying to.

"In fact - you may just have the opportunity of meeting him." He glanced at his watch and then headed for the door. "Be back in a minute."

It was seventeen minutes and twenty seconds to be exact. The luminous hands of the clock on the wall said so.

Then a small, gray-haired man in his middle sixties appeared, glasses perched halfway down his nose, his bow tie slightly askew. He hesitated for a moment and then beamed a smile.

"Miss Daniels? So very good to meet you." It was a strong English accent, a warm and sincere voice. Paul appeared behind him and pulled a chair up beside the bed for him, which he accepted and then Paul introduced him to me.

"This is Dr. Peter Berrisford, Head of the Department of Parapsychology, University of B.C."

The introduction began to confirm what I had come to suspect.

"Dr. Beresford is going to be examining Jennifer and I thought he could take a moment to explain what he believes accounts for her circumstances. Doctor?"

"You see, Miss Daniels," he began, "though I've often been consulted by the police on matters of criminal investigation, my field is rather ... difficult for the medical profession to acknowledge. Therefore I was honored when asked by these chaps to give my opinion of a patient hospitalized on such a long-term basis." He paused as if to somehow prepare me for what he was about to say.

"I think, doctor," I croaked, "I know…what you're about to say…."

His response was one of both surprise and pleasure.

"That's very perceptive of you, I must say."

"Not really." I faltered. "To think that I was …almost too late..." For a moment the horror swept back over me. I swallowed hard and continued. "It was there all the time…staring at us in the face. The dates ... each time something happened... her condition worsened. Abernathy's death - my visit - the fire. God knows what other horrors took place out there." My voice sounded like sandpaper I knew, but I persisted. "She wasn't guilty of those things that happened... when she was a child. She was there because she sensed ...not that they had happened but that they were going to happen. Am I right?"

"I believe you're quite right. I know how difficult that is for some people to accept, in fact for most people to accept, but I can assure you Miss - ah - Daniels - that there are valid, documented cases, hundreds in fact, of instances where people gifted with powers of preconception have been able to predict, to actually foresee events before they happen."

If I had been inclined to skepticism, I would have had to reconsider. The man's eyes radiated intelligence and conviction. "Perhaps you've heard of the Aberfan disaster?"

I shook my head.

"A mud slide destroyed a school. Seven children are believed to have had premonitions of the disaster that took one hundred and forty-four of their classmates.

"The Titanic?"

I nodded but remained mute.

"Nineteen authenticated cases of people, many of them children, who had premonitions of an impending disaster at sea, were reported before April 14, 1912 - the night the Titanic sank. One child broke into nearly uncontrollable hysteria upon seeing the ship as they were preparing to board. The parents were so distraught they rushed the child to the hospital. Needless to say, they missed their sailing.

"You see, children are for some reason often more gifted than adults at foretelling the future. Perhaps their young minds are still receptive to the transmission of energy waves. We don't really know why, yet the medical records of the Drysdale girl indicate - if you'll forgive me - a textbook case of clairvoyance. The headaches, dizziness, vomiting often precede visions and often are acute enough to cause severe emotional and physical distress - one of the reasons why that medieval act of witch hunting came into prominence. It was believed that this apparent sudden deviation in behavior was caused by the demons - that people had been possessed by the devil. Of course, that was utter nonsense." He smiled a rather sad cherub-like smile. "But then I'm afraid that these people, these Bokarites, are still rather medieval in their ways. I don't believe the Drysdale girl was responsible for causing any loss of life. I believe as you do, she foresaw what was to happen and was implicated, unjustly and unfairly, and punished for it. For a child of seven, it must have been dreadfully traumatic. We know that it was enough to push her mind into a catatonic state, at least as diagnosed when she was first institutionalized. That may have become her form of survival camouflage. Certainly it would have been easy to maintain in a place like Island View where she was given little, if any attention.

"How long she remained that way we have no way of knowing, but I believe that not long ago she began to again experience psychic visions. I daresay she must have considered herself really quite insane, poor child.

"I believe that's what led you to that place - as I understand, just in time. The dates of her disturbances in her medical records, as you no doubt discovered, preceded some rather unfortunate events. One I believe," he fumbled for a moment in his jacket pocket, extracted a piece of paper and peered intently at it. "Yes, yes...had something to do with an infant and not long after was the death of a certain Mr. Abernathy. The third date was, as I've been informed, the night you yourself were involved in - ah - a rather unpleasant experience out there and finally, her greatly agitated condition.

was, of course, what preceded this most unfortunate conclusion."

He took a long, deep sigh, then rose to his feet.

He turned to Paul.

"However, as tragic as it was, with competent care and treatment, I think Jennifer Drysdale has every hope of recovery."

Paul nodded and thanked him.

"Then I'll say good day, Miss Daniels. I do hope I've been of some help." He gave me another one of his little cherub-like smiles and was gone.

The pipe rested in his hand. He studied it for a moment, then spoke. "We'd been over those records - so had a team of psychiatrists. All the entries in all medical records carry dates. But it took a man like Beresford, one of the most prominent and well- respected men in his field to pull it all together. I don't doubt in the least that Jennifer was blessed - or cursed - with these so-called psychic abilities ... but you too?"

He raised his eyebrows in a skeptical gesture that was an oblique request for information.

After all the weeks of questions that had plagued me, and all the lack of information concerning Paul - who he was, and what he was involved with - at last I had reached an answer

even he had not known. Small consolation as it was, I had realized the connection that had led me to the horrifying truth.

Hoarsely, and with the help of paper and pencil when my voice threatened to disappear altogether, I managed to scribble words - my last visit to Jennifer – the charm – the Goddess of fire - her very fate that was only hours away, her fear at seeing the Panda Bear, a symbol of that poor Johnson creature, as it turned out, and my guilt at thinking I had reminded her of the nightmare fire years ago.

My head ached and it hurt even more when I tried to get my voice above a whisper.

"I went to her file to check the date of the fire that she had been accused of setting." I whispered. "I thought maybe it was an anniversary of that terrible tragedy. But I was wrong. That had been during the summer and it was now winter. Then I decided to check the date of Mr. Abernathy's death. That was the first hint of a possible connection. The night I went up to the fifth floor was the second. And the very day, yesterday, when I visited her, she was apparently worse than she ever had been. It meant that somehow she was seeing, sensing, and predicting something terrible that was to happen. I didn't - couldn't believe it was actually happening till I got there. The charm - the goddess of fire I wore around my neck - Jennifer saw as herself. The fact that there was no water in the taps ... if only I had known then ..." One of life's greatest clichés, I thought bitterly. The thought came as a dark shadow on my conscience and I left the sentence unfinished. "They told me that you arrived there minutes later. How did you know? Paul?"

"It was Michaelson. Gilbert Michaelson. I think you remember him? Our "temporary" night watchman?

"He'd seen you in your dressing gown earlier - standing on the deck, then, later, he caught a glimpse of you dressed and running to your car. He radioed me and for a man to follow. When it became evident that you were heading toward Island View, and by the way you were driving, that some crisis was pending, we moved in, a lot sooner than we had intended.

"It wasn't only you that tipped the scale. We tracked down the ambulance driver yesterday outside Dawson Creek. He told us he had been met by the supervisor of the fifth floor and delivered the infant to her. There was no record of the baby ever having been admitted.

"It was Mannering that gave us more than suspicions, in the end. When we questioned him later in the day about the infant, he denied any knowledge of how or why the absence of an admission record for the infant could have occurred. And he probably was telling the truth. But in questioning him about quite routine matters, such as staff security, administrative procedures and the like, he came across as being evasive and nervous. So we put a tail on him - and sure enough, we got what we were looking for."

Mannering?" I started to croak my disbelief.

"As soon as we left, he headed straight out to Island View. Obviously he was running scared. And there had to be link with that place that was somehow going to implicate him.

We didn't have to do much digging to come up with what was a simple case of blackmail.

"He was a homosexual - bisexual if you like. He had maintained a pretense for his profession, his marriage and his social position for a good many years. Homosexuality may have come out of the closet, but not for Mrs. Mannering. Not when he was married to a righteous, Bible-thumping Baptist like her - and a wealthy one at that! He paid for the position he held by overlooking everything and anything he was told to.

That's exactly what he did. That's why deaths were never followed up, why the place was kept in its obsolescence and anonymity. A place that nevertheless legitimately, routinely, maintained access to all pharmaceutical supplies, where treatment in that institution dispensed as many medications as most hospitals. But Mannering was only a pawn." He paused for a moment and then continued. "It was Caine who didn't fit. He was there – every day - with access, with authority. He had to be either very naïve which by your description didn't seem to fit, or he had to be very much a part of the operation. We did a little cross-checking of his alleged whereabouts and found that the Thursday night you were attacked by dogs he wasn't at Whistler. Your key snitching may have tipped him off - since obviously you or someone at least had gained access to places kept locked, but more than likely your just being there in the first place may have made him nervous and suspicious. The fact that he wasn't where he said he was gave us good reason to get suspicious. I'm guessing that he was there the night you went up to photograph Jennifer's records. Rutherford probably reported your presence to him and he released the dogs. Fortunately, the fact that you hid for those hours probably saved your life. Towards morning he must have been forced to recall them and have them leashed.

"It didn't take long to find a Jaguar car, a $500,000 condominium at Whistler and a large chunk of cash he'd stashed to figure that even a psychiatrist with his salary was pulling in another healthy income from somewhere. We already had had Island View under surveillance when you first made your appearance out there. Then our tail reported last night that instead of going on up to Whistler, he was headed back to the hospital. You were already there and he was about to arrive. We closed in.

"We found the chemicals for the production of Narcon-62. All being produced in a laboratory in a mental institution run by the provincial government. Old, established and taken for granted. Who would ever have suspected? All they were waiting for was a single package that was dropped over the side of a freighter but never recovered."

He glanced at me with a compassionate look. "I know you made references to the diver who you thought was dead. He was injured all right but we had a police boat pick him up and rush him to the hospital. He survived. And he's given us the connection we needed. Maybe that, in some small way will help ease the nightmare you experienced that night with me. Anyway, Caine is in custody. Woodcroft is being questioned but it will likely be Mannering who, to save his own neck in plea bargaining will implicate Caine."

For a moment there was silence. Then, as if he needed something to ease the tragic conclusion that was imminent, he returned his pipe to his pocket.

"The one bizarre aspect was Rutherford…I whispered."

"Apparently even bizarre to Caine." He replied.

"I don't think he thought twice about her. He must have decided she was just a bitter, miserable old woman and let it go at that. But we did an investigation of her, as well.

"Psychopathic, according to Beresford. But whatever they tag it, she was a killer. A cold, cunning, remorseless killer. It seems even the London police had some suspicions but no proof as to the death of one of her former patients. That evil mind of hers must have festered in her all those years under the self-imposed exile on the fifth floor.

"It was cancer that precipitated her actions. We traced certain medications back to her physician, a Dr. Ian McTaggart. According to him, she had undergone chemotherapy for lung cancer but had refused surgery. The cancer had begun to invade her liver and her spinal column and when she had asked him how long she had to live, he had given her three months. It was almost three months to the day when she ended it all, for her patients, for herself.

"My guess is that she was responsible for the infant's death. Even though the baby was going to die, she wasn't going to take the chance and have the fifth floor disrupted by additional nursing staff having to take care of a baby. She disposed of it in quite an efficient, though inhumane, manner. After she had smothered it.

"As for your Mr. Abernathy, I'm afraid without a body to autopsy, we'll never know for sure. But, there's a strong possibility he was murdered. Since he had unlimited access to the building and grounds, it's likely he uncovered things he wasn't meant to know about. Even if half of what he may have known was his imagination, he still posed a risk, particularly if he was seen talking to you, an outsider. I wouldn't be surprised if arsenic hadn't been administered to him in increasing dosages till it reached a critical level. It would be the natural poison to use for someone habitually using pesticides. "Your murderer here, though, would be Caine. There had to be a lot of subterfuge in operating that lab and getting supplies in and out. He's denied having anything to do with Abernathy's death but only because premeditated murder would likely commit him to life imprisonment. He's going up for a lot of time as it is. Murder and drug trafficking aren't misdemeanors. As for severing Abernathy's head for medical study, I'm sure that in Caine's case, aside from any research purposes that might have legitimized it, there was a perverse form of pleasure in obtaining that specimen.

He continued.

"But as for Rutherford, I suppose to take the lives of all those she had been responsible for when she knew she was going to die seemed to her in her own deranged mind, a just and fitting end." He looked at me very solemnly. "She succeeded too, I'm afraid, except for Jennifer and you.

"She probably sedated them all first and then administered an injection that would put them to sleep forever. At least they received a degree of humanity in their deaths.

Samuel Johnson wasn't so lucky. He was burned to death."

I closed my eyes and tried to blot from my memory the poor man's tragic ending.

"The fire was intended to then destroy all traces of the crimes. She turned off the water to that floor at its main valve head so that by the time the fire was discovered, they had even less chance of fighting it. I suppose the only consolation is that the fire was a salvation for others. The hospital's being closed. Patients on the other floors are being transferred out to the Burnaby Psychiatric Unit, Vancouver General, or in some cases, group homes like Victory House, where maybe they'll get the treatment they deserve.

"And by the way," his jaw muscles tightened. "I can tell you now about Rob's death. I'd rather not. But you had wanted to know. It was acid - very likely intended for you.

Caine had "contacts" to do a lot of the dirty work for him. We can only guess that when you knocked out the power, Rob went to investigate the problem, went to your house and encountered someone waiting for you." He saw my look of horror. "Acid can be very intimidating. But Mia, I don't want you to feel responsible for his death. Of that, you're entirely innocent. It was a matter of circumstances. He was in the wrong place at the wrong time. You couldn't possibly have known, nor did we, at the time, that events would lead to what happened."

He talked on and I listened, threads woven in and through the long and tragic story until there was nothing else to say. Then quiet filled the room.

Each moment seemed to mark a final farewell, the silence our unspoken hope for a lasting peace to those who had lived and died in a world more tragic than one conceived in hell.

"Paul." My voice was barely a whisper. "Isn't this Christmas Day?"

Almost apologetically, he replied, "Yes and in a few hours you would have been enjoying a tropical sunset with a Mai Tai." Then I croaked, "We haven't much time."

CHRISTMAS DAY

It cost me dearly. Mostly because of the effort I had to spend arguing with Paul. It's tough to argue when you can't talk. But by then I really needed him. He had a voice and I didn't. It got us through nurses and nursing aides, head nurses and doctors, and finally to the admitting desk where I was reluctantly released. Sitting in the mandatory wheelchair in the main waiting room Paul made the calls as I listed names for directory assistance. Then we were in the car, out onto the freeway and finally down the shady lane that led us to the little cottage with the lean-to greenhouse in back.

The phone call to Pedersen had been brief but he was expecting us. He shuffled through the ritual of tea making while I lay back on the couch and teased an innocent looking flower into stalking a pencil poised above its head, much to Paul's confusion.

The tea helped. It helped me croak in a coarse, dry whisper after Paul had laid out the facts. Between my whisper and some hand movements, I got across the information.

Pedersen at least understood it. He nodded his understanding. He nodded his consent. His eyes seemed suddenly bright and wet and his aged and weathered face shone with a long forgotten glow. It was one of the happier moments of my life, and no doubt of his.

Paul drove me back to the houseboat in silence. But then I didn't have a choice. My croak had croaked. I was reduced to a whisper. He stopped briefly at a market while I waited in the car. Then at his insistence, I climbed into bed apparently just in time for Jell-O and tea.

Paul sat on the edge of the bed and looked down at me. He looked tired and somehow older. But there was peace in his eyes and gentleness now in his voice that hadn't been there before.

"I took the liberty of calling your travel agent. The first booking he could get you was January 10th. I don't know if you still want to go but you have a reservation if you decide to use it."

It was raspberry Jell-O. Having missed lunch, I was starving. I'd always thought Jell-O was given only to kids who'd just had their tonsils out. That and ice cream. I wasn't being given any ice cream. Just Jell-O. There should be a law against serving raspberry Jell-O to sick people. But then there should be a law against Jell-O.

"The Snow Goose will be put up for sale next month. And I never did get any fishing done. It's a hell of a substitute for sun and sand but you really have a knack with pork and beans." The hint of a smile I hadn't seen in a long time began to play at the corners of his mouth. "I don't suppose you'd care to recuperate up along the coast? I hear that the Skeena Lodge is still accepting reservations. It has a big stone fireplace in the lounge and they make excellent martinis. The Seafarers' dining lounge doesn't even have pork and beans on their menu."

I squeaked now. That was all that was left.
"And no Jell-O?"
"No Jell-O."
I smiled up at him.
"Okay."

Two hours later, assured by Paul that he had done all the packing and made all the last minute arrangements, we left the houseboat. We were once more back out on the freeway, down the shady lane, and he was there and waiting impatiently this time, his assortment of boxes, packages and a shopping bag long ready and waiting on the porch. Pedersen sat in the front seat while I sat amidst his boxes in the back seat, content to have him direct Paul first back along the lane, then round and through a whole suburban network till we arrived at the long, low, ranch style house.

Jack met us at the door and I attempted introductions that were, in reality, only a formality. Janet arrived on his heels and we huddled in hugs and embraces avoiding my still bandaged hands, while the men shook hands through the tangle.

I peeked into the living room to be sure that all the arrangements had worked out. I couldn't have been more delighted.

She sat on the sofa, smothered in a soft pink dressing gown under a downy quilt, her long blonde hair brushed back and tied with a pink satin ribbon. I approached her slowly and calmly.

"Jennifer, do you remember me?" I watched as she turned her head and looked up at me, her eyes clear and focusing without fear and mistrust. For a long time she just looked at me and then, very slowly, almost imperceptibly, her head nodded slowly in acknowledgment.

"Jennifer," I began very slowly, "once you gave me a present, a very special present. Now I have one for you. One that you can keep and cherish for as long as you wish. Jennifer, look your very own."

I put the box on her lap and anxiously watched. She very slowly lifted the lid.

I don't know which came first the surprise or the meow, but the most beautiful childlike smile I think I'd ever seen crossed her face. Very slowly her hand moved to the kitten and ever so gently she stroked it. Janet knelt beside Jennifer and together they stroked and played with the kitten among the folds of the quilt.

I saw Pedersen quickly wipe a tear that had rolled down his cheek before he spoke.

"Got lots more where he came from."

Then he lowered his voice and added, "I'm not so old I can't do a little child mindin' while Janet's at work. And it won't be just for Christmas either. I'll see to that. Best thing for her home, love, care and attention. She's had enough of institutions and doctorin'. Best thing for Janet too. Always said she was a fine mother. Funny. If Katie had lived she would have been the same age as this one."

We slipped away shortly after leaving Pedersen sitting by Jennifer talking to her about kittens and Christmas trees, plum pudding and presents. Jennifer sat contentedly petting the now sleeping kitten in her lap, apparently captivated by the joy of this kind old man, a look of peace and tranquility that had finally come home in her innocent blue eyes.

Nearly an hour later, laden with Christmas packages of cakes and cookies and bottles of good cheer Jack and Janet had pressed upon us, we boarded the Snow Goose.

The tree was real all eighteen inches of it, positioned in the center of the wheelhouse table and trimmed with tiny colored Christmas lights and decked with tinsel. Beneath it was one very small gift wrapped package, with an equally tiny envelope attached.

Humphrey lay majestically sprawled over the table, beside the package, a paw strategically within range.

I heard the engines start, then a moment later the distinct pop of a champagne cork. I turned as Paul handed me a glass of icy cold bubbling champagne with one hand and slipped the other around my waist.

He kissed me lightly on the lips and turned to survey the tree.

"In keeping with tradition. One catnip mouse. Gift wrapped. With a card."

THE END

Thank you for downloading my book. I hope you've enjoyed reading it as much as I've enjoyed writing it.

If you like what you have read, check out my latest novel "Until the Last Friday" available on Kindle as well.

I would be interested in hearing your thoughts about my books, writing, or general interest in writing.

You can contact me at misskittyca@cox.net

Again, thank you for reading my book.

Happy reading.

###

Made in the USA
Lexington, KY
02 April 2013